BRUTAL DADDY

CHICAGO MAFIA DONS

BIANCA COLE

CONTENTS

BLURB

I'll die before I call him daddy...

Within hours of reaching Chicago, I'm taken. Strung up in front of the most dangerous man in Chicago. Spartak Volkov expects me to cower to him and give up my family.

He wants my submission. He wants me to betray the people I love. He wants to use me to end the war.

None of that scares me, though. It's the sick desire in his eyes when he looks at me. The way he calls me baby girl. The scariest part of all, the way my body reacts to his touch.

The man is not right in the head. He's dark, depraved, and everything I shouldn't want. And yet, in his capture I feel protected and wanted. His brutal ways are addictive and I fear I'll never want to leave.

I vowed to never call him daddy, but he's peeling

back my layers and laying bare my deepest and darkest desires. Perhaps we're not so different after all…

AUTHOR'S NOTE

*H*ello reader,
         This is a warning to let you know that this is a dark mafia romance much like many of my other books, which means there are some sensitive subject matters addressed. If you have any triggers, it would be important to proceed with caution.

As well as a brutal and crazy anti-hero who doesn't take no for an answer and who becomes ott possessive of the heroine, this book addresses some sensitive subjects, a full list of these can be found here. As always, this book has a **HEA** and there's no cheating.

If you have any triggers, then it's best to read the warnings and not proceed if any could be triggering for you. However, if none of these are an issue for you, read on and enjoy!

IMALIA

"*F*or fuck's sake," I mutter under my breath, watching as another load of bags crawl past me on the conveyor belt. None of them are mine.

Everyone on my flight has had their bags and left, and now there's a load of fuckers I don't recognize getting theirs. I glance at my watch, realizing it's been forty-five minutes since I got off the plane. Clearly, the airline has lost my bag on the way here from San Diego.

I draw in a deep breath and turn away from the baggage reclaim, searching for my airline's helpdesk. When I finally find it, my cell phone rings and I pull it out, groaning when I see it's Uncle Remy.

"Hey," I say.

"Where are you?" he growls, sounding irritated.

"I've been waiting for my bag for forty-five minutes and it still hasn't turned up." I meander toward the desk to put in a claim for the lost baggage. "I think they lost it."

"Fuck's sake. I haven't got time to sit out here all day waiting for you, Imalia."

I roll my eyes, as it's not my fault they lost my bags. "Right, because I made sure they lost my bag on the way here solely to piss you off." I sigh heavily. "Go home and I'll catch a cab when I'm done. I don't know how long it'll take to file a claim." I'm surprised he actually came himself to pick me up rather than send one of his men, anyway.

There's a few moments of silence. "No, I have a meeting to attend in twenty minutes. I'll send my driver back to pick you up."

I nod, even though I know he can't see me. "Sounds good. I'll see you later." I cancel the call, not waiting for his response, and stuff my cell phone back in my pocket as I reach the desk.

A woman with long blonde hair either doesn't notice me approach or is ignoring me as she types frantically on the keyboard.

I clear my throat and she glances up, eyes narrowing. "How can I help?"

"I think your airline has lost my bag, as I've been waiting forty-five minutes and it still hasn't come out of baggage reclaim." I shrug. "Everyone on my flight has left."

She rolls her eyes as she types on her computer again. "Name."

"Imalia Allegro," I say, clenching my fists, as this woman is beyond rude.

Her brow furrows as she glances up at me. "Can I see your boarding pass, please?"

I open my bag and rummage through it, searching for the boarding pass. My stomach dips when I can't find it. "Shit, I think I lost it."

She tilts her head. "And how do you expect me to check on this for you without your boarding pass?"

I grind my teeth. "Surely, you'll have a record of my boarding pass on your computer." I dig out my passport and place it on the desk. "Here is my ID."

She shakes her head. "I'm sorry, without your boarding pass, I can't make a claim. It's company policy."

"Are you fucking joking?" I ask, shaking my head. "Your airline has lost my bag and I want to see your manager right now."

She blows out an irritated breath. "The manager isn't on duty right now."

Seriously, this is the worst customer service I've ever experienced. "There must be someone on duty who is more superior to you. I want to see them now."

She glares at me before giving in and heading into the back. When she returns, a young dark-haired man follows her. "The best I can give you is the airport baggage manager. He'll take you to the other terminal to check the bag hasn't gotten mixed up and sent to the wrong place."

My brow furrows as I stare at the guy, finding it a little odd. "And if the bag isn't there?"

She rolls her eyes. "We'll deal with that if we come to it."

I grind my teeth and nod.

The man smiles at me, but it isn't friendly. "Follow me."

I follow him the opposite way to the exit, unsure where exactly he's taking me. "Isn't the other terminal in the opposite direction?"

He shakes his head. "We're cutting through the staff area."

I nod in response, allowing him to lead me through into an off limits section of the airport. It's odd that he's allowed to bring me through here, considering airports are always so hot on security. I ignore my unease and follow him down the long, dark corridor.

"What flight did you arrive on?" he asks, attempting to make small talk.

"Flight from San Diego. I've been waiting for my bag for over forty-five minutes." I sigh heavily, glancing at my watch.

Perhaps I should have ditched on my best friends' wedding three days ago and traveled with my mom and Fabio and Gio a week ago, as I hate traveling alone, especially when it doesn't go smoothly. I couldn't do that to Gabriella. We've been best friends since we were toddlers and I was her maid of honor, even though I'm not too keen on her choice of husband. "How far is the terminal?"

It's oddly quiet down in this staff area as we continue and we don't pass another person. "Not too far. It is quicker than taking the long way around."

I clench my jaw as we turn a corner, only to be met by a darker corridor. Dread creeps in, as I'm unsure where the fuck this guy is taking me. I fiddle with the hem of my shirt, becoming increasingly nervous. "It's dark down here."

He shrugs. "I guess the airport doesn't like to light it when few people come down here."

I swallow hard, my steps faltering until we round another corner into a lighter corridor. My brow furrows as I notice a light ahead coming through a large door. "Is that the terminal ahead?"

He glances over his shoulder and nods. "Yeah, almost there."

I relax, feeling a little less on edge as I hasten my pace, eager to get the fuck out of this creepy part of the airport. As he comes to the door, he glances at me. "Out here." He pushes open the door and I step through, only to be met by three other men standing in my path, all of them looking menacing.

"What the fuck—"

"Here you are lads, Imalia Allegro as promised," the so called *baggage manager* announces.

I glance at him questioningly.

"Sorry, sweetheart. It's not personal." And then he walks away, leaving me alone with the three men.

I spin around and try the door he disappeared back through, but it's locked. "Fuck."

One of the guy's smirks widens. "Yes, you're fucked."

I swallow hard, noticing he has a distinctively Eastern European accent. "What do you want?"

The same guy laughs, glancing at the two men flanking him. "What do we want, boys?"

"You," one of the men answers.

He smirks. "Yes, the perfect piece of leverage delivered right to us, tied with a pretty little bow." His eyes scan the length of my dress, which does indeed have a bow stitched to the front.

The other guy remains silent, but the look in his eyes is one of pure malice.

"Snatch her," the guy seemingly in charge says.

The other two men step forward and my heart pounds so hard it feels like I'm going to throw up. I duck once they're close and get under one of their arms, trying to run past the middle guy, but he snatches me around the waist.

"Tchyo za ga`lima?" he growls something in a foreign language, shaking his head. "You idiots can't do anything right. Open the back of the van."

I fight against this guy, trying to kick him as he drags me toward the back of a white truck, which is open. "Get the fuck off of me!"

After a ridiculous amount of writhing, I slip my leg into a perfect position and kick him in the gut.

"Blyad!" he shouts, as I take off in the opposite direction of the door I came through, pounding so fast away from them. My heart thuds faster than my feet on the concrete and the men shout behind me as they pursue me.

I can't believe I trusted that airline receptionist or the fucking bastard who claimed to be the baggage manager. Both may well work for this place, but someone paid them to bring me out here. I don't have a clue where I'm going as I come to a deadend behind a locked gate, trying to search for an escape.

Shit.

My only option is to slip into another building to my right, but they'll know I've gone in there since there's nowhere else to go.

Their footsteps get closer and I run through the door, hoping beyond hope there's an exit. The building is derelict and not used as I rush through the hallway toward the back, realizing it's some kind of warehouse. The echo of the door opening behind me makes my stomach dip, and then their murmuring voices follow.

I slip through a small crack behind an enormous machine to the right and crouch down, knowing that I'm out of options. They'll probably find me, but I am out of options.

I can't believe that attending my best friends' wedding has landed me in this kind of shit. If I had to guess, they're Russian and members of the Volkov Bratva, who my uncle has always had a tenuous relationship with.

My pursuers' footsteps grow closer as I place my hand over my mouth, trying to deaden the sound of my heavy breathing. I shut my eyes, praying that by some miracle they don't find me behind here.

The guy I kicked comes into view through a small gap in the machinery hiding me. I duck lower, struggling to contain my fear. My entire body shakes as I know what it means for me if I get caught by the bratva.

"She's not over here," the guy nearby calls, making hope rise to the surface.

There's a thud of footsteps. "She has to be here somewhere."

"The pakhan will kill us for failing." The man who had remained silent up to now says.

"Check every fucking inch of this place again," the leader says.

The two other guys head off, but the man who appears to be in charge lingers nearby. He starts moving stuff around, muttering to himself in Russian. I keep my hand over my mouth, knowing that one sound could give me away.

He gets closer, and then he peers around the back of the machine. His ugly smirk splitting his face in two. "There you are, princess."

I shudder. "Stay the fuck away from me."

He reaches through the gap and grabs hold of the front of my dress, dragging me out. My arms scrape against the metal and it cuts through my skin, blood trickling down my skin. "Got her," He shouts.

"Let go of me!" I try to break away, but he holds me firmer than before.

"No chance. Our boss wants you badly, Imalia."

I bite the inside of my cheek, knowing I don't really want the answer to my next question. "And who is your boss?"

He smirks. "You'll have to wait and find out." He nods, and that's when I realize that the guy who had hardly spoken is behind me. He grabs my shoulder and jabs a needle into a vein in my neck, pushing drugs into my system.

"What the hell?" I try to break away again, but my vision blurs almost instantly. Whatever shit he just pumped into me is strong as my captor's face blurs. "W-What d'ya gime?" I can't even speak properly, as I slump against him, struggling to keep myself upright. And that's when the leader hauls me over his shoulder and my entire world turns black.

2

SPARTAK

"You shouldn't have crossed us, Liam." I walk around his bloodied, beaten body.

Liam was our informer on the inside of the Callaghan Clan, but this idiot ran the moment the war broke out. He's been in hiding ever since. Until Timur tracked him down this afternoon at a dive bar.

It's been too long since my last torture session, and it feels like my skin is crawling over my flesh. After all, Maxim denied me the satisfaction of taking my violence out on Daniel, deciding to involve his wife.

His green eyes are dilated with fear as he stares at me, shaking his head. "I didn't betray—"

I slam my fist into his face, shutting him up before he can finish his sentence. "I don't want to hear it." Blood trickles down his chin from his mouth and I delight in the sight, smirking. "All I want to hear is you dying as I torture you slowly and painfully." I walk toward the table, where I keep several torture implements, and pick up a pair of pliers. I'm in the mood for inflicting serious pain with minimum damage, as I'm unsure how long it'll be until I get my next victim down here.

Hopefully, if my men can be competent, they'll be bringing me a little slice of deliciousness later today. A new toy to play with, but it's always a different brutality when I deal with a woman. Imalia Allegro should arrive at Chicago International airport at any moment now. She arrived later than her mother and Fabio and Gio, her two brothers, who turned up a week ago. Imalia Allegro's father died before she was born, but her mother took over control of their criminal enterprise, which is a strange feat in this day and age. Most men don't want to take orders from women. I think it helps that she's the coveted baby sister of my enemy, Remy Morrone.

When I learned of Imalia flying into the international airport today, I recognized our chance to take something precious from the Morrone family.

After all, I couldn't sit back and do nothing. Morrone has always been our biggest enemy, but someone killed Ronan Callaghan in Podolka and pinned the death on our family, throwing the city into chaos. The Irish were our allies in a city where chaos reigns, as everyone wants a piece of the action.

I needed to take drastic measures to counter the Morrone Family's growth. Ten years ago, we were the most powerful family in Chicago and now we're struggling to keep our heads above water as the organizations of the city come to blows.

The Italians and the Irish aren't the only vultures looking to swoop in and make gains. The Estrada Cartel remains neutral, but they aren't to be underestimated and the bikers are hot heads that can't be trusted not to make a killing off the back of this war.

I circle Liam again, delighting in the way his entire body shakes with fear. Once I'm standing in front of him, I move forward and grab a finger, gripping the end of his nail with the pliers and tearing it off of him.

The scream he emits is beyond satisfying. A sound that helps ease the chaos, but nothing beats taking a man's life. I work on all ten of his fingernails, ripping them off slowly as to inflict maximum pain. Blood drips from his fingers as his eyes lull back in his head, the pain almost becoming too much for him to bear.

I grab hold of his chin and dig my fingernails into it hard. "Now, now, Liam, no fainting on me. I've barely even warmed up yet."

His eyes are so dilated they're almost entirely black, and I relish the image. "Please, Spartak. I didn't give anyone any information. I—"

I slam the pliers into his mouth and grab his tongue, pulling hard. "Don't make me tear your tongue out, Liam."

My cell phone rings, making me growl as I release his tongue and step away. "What is it?" I snarl.

"Sir, it's done," Vitaly says. "I tied Imalia Allegro up and she's unconscious at the docks, as promised."

Some of my rage eases, hearing that my men actually pulled it off. We have Remy Morrone's niece in our hands. "Great. How long will she be out?"

"About four to five hours, as she put up a bit of a fight and I had to dose her up pretty good."

I smirk at that. "Good. Make sure you keep the docks guarded until I get there." I cancel the call and glance at the pathetic piece of shit I've been torturing.

I'm going to have to speed this up and get Maxim over to the docks to explain my plan to him. Maxim won't like it, but then he hasn't liked any of my plans lately. No one except my brother knows about our new venture, but I don't trust that snake not to say something to my son to stir up trouble.

I know Maxim is hung up on me shooting Viktoria, but I won't apologize for protecting our brotherhood from a traitor. Her betrayal stung me like nothing ever has. Marrying a man who outright declared war on our family is a disgrace to the Volkov name, even if Maxim insists they love each other. It makes me sick to my stomach.

"It looks like you have got off easier than expected, Liam."

His shoulders slump in relief, but little does he know that this news only cut our fun short. He'll be dead faster than I'd intended, as I don't have the patience to have two torture victims on the go at the same time.

I turn my attention back to my cell phone and call my son.

"Hey, what's up?" Maxim answers, sounding agitated.

"Can you meet me down at the warehouse at the docks in one hour instead of the restaurant?" I ask.

He sighs heavily. "Sure, why?"

"I'll explain once we're there." I cancel the call, not allowing him the luxury of questioning me further. As I haven't got long to finish my victim. I could leave the fun until after I bring Imalia here, but I'd rather focus on one victim at a time.

I move back to the implement table and grab the curved sickle knife, smirking as I glance back at my prey. A flash of a memory enters my mind as I stare at the knife. The same knife my father made me use the first time he brought me into this same chamber. I was seven years old when he introduced me to the delights of torture.

My mother begged him not to start so early, but he insisted I was getting off lightly, as his parents did not shield him from the brutality of war or torture in Russia. What she never knew was what my uncle did to me when we were alone. That's what truly scarred me in irreparable ways. I know his actions are in part to blame for my sickness, but there's no fixing it, not now. This is who I am.

Many have feared the Volkov name for years because of our brutality. It's a signature of our family which can't be lost, even though I went easy on Maxim compared to my father. The scars are like a birthright that you need to endure in order to claim the throne.

I guess when I first carved a man up at only seven years old; I was scared, but I soon learned to enjoy it. It became a pastime I couldn't escape, even if it earns me the rather well earned title of psycho.

I test the sharpness of the sickle pricking my skin and watching blood pool on the surface. "Perfect."

Liam's eyes widen when he sees the knife, as it's my signature weapon. Although, I've been getting quite fond of frying men to death lately, with a high voltage device. "Come on, Spartak, seriously. We can talk about this."

I march over to him and force his jaw open, yanking his tongue forward and slicing it off and tossing it aside. "That's better," I say, as blood spurts unrelentingly from his mouth, splattering my face. "I was fed up with hearing you speak." I hook the end of the blade into his chin and force him to look me in the eye as blood trickles down the knife. "I want to watch your eyes while I bleed you dry. Because you crossed us and ran, rather than facing your duties like a man. No one lives after fucking with us."

He tries to speak, his jaw working, but without a tongue it comes out like a gargled humming sound.

I slam the hooked knife into his gut and tear through his abdomen, forcing his eyes wide open. "I'm going to gut you like a fucking pig and then feed you to the dogs. No one will ever find your body." I rip the knife right through him, pulling out his guts.

The pure anguish in his eyes as I watch him bleed out in front of me spurs me on, as I wait to see that light in his them dim because of me. Once his body turns cold and pale and his eyes glaze over, I finally drop the knife on the floor and turn toward the sink in the corner. I run the faucet and wash the blood off my hands and face, glancing at myself in the mirror.

I stained my shirt with blood, but I don't have time to change. Instead, I grab my suit jacket off the hanger and head out of the room, leaving the chaos behind me.

Power flows through my veins as I shred another part of myself. I watched and enjoyed that man's death as much as I do anything on this planet. It's a sickness and one I revel in.

Happy Birthday to me.

"I DON'T LIKE IT."

I clench my jaw. "Don't be a fucking sissy, Maxim. I taught you to have thicker skin than to piss yourself over a few women being sold." I notice the flash in his eyes when I mention my *teachings*. He resents me because I was tough on him.

He crosses his arms over his chest. "This isn't the

Volkov way. Since when do we go around copying our enemies?"

I rub the back of my neck. "Since their power has increased, unchecked, while war wasn't on the cards. The Irish may have started this war, but we both know they're not the true threat to us. There are only two real players in the war and it's us and the Italians."

Maxim raises a brow, observing me for a few beats. "I've got to go," he says, turning his back on me.

Rage coils through me as I grab him by the shoulder and yank him back to face me, hard. "Remember your place, boy." I clench my fists, trying to stop myself from hitting him. "You don't turn your back on me unless I dismiss you."

Maxim's jaw clenches. "I apologize, but I'm late for a meeting with Timur to discuss Andrei's reaction to us cutting him off."

It kills him to apologize to me, as he wants to hurt me. I've seen it in his eyes ever since the incident with Viki. "What reaction?"

He pulls a piece of paper out of his pocket, passing it to me. "He's not happy."

Reconsider your position or experience the full terror of the New York Bratva. I will not hold back because of past alliances.
Andrei Petrov.

"That fucking piece of shit," I growl, thrusting the letter into Maxim's chest. "Why didn't you tell me about this?"

"Because I don't tell you every little thing that

happens, Father." He slides the letter back into his pocket.

I have half a mind to shoot my son any minute if he doesn't stop acting like a fucking idiot. "I'm the pakhan of this Bratva, and if something as significant as a threat from the Petrov Bratva lands on your desk, you come to me first, do you understand?" I shove my finger into his chest.

Maxim nods. "Yes, I merely thought Timur was best at dealing with this. After all, it's only words. He wouldn't dare attack us here in Chicago unless he has a death wish."

This is why I don't trust my son. He underestimates what our enemies or allies are capable of. "You don't know Andrei and what he's capable of." I spin my back to him. "Report to Timur and get his opinion on how to handle it. I want a meeting setup for tomorrow morning to discuss this."

"Sure. I'm going to be late—"

"Go." I wave my hand. "I'll see you tonight at the party."

"Of course, S dnyom rozhdeniya."

I wince at the half-hearted, happy birthday greeting from my son, knowing that he'd forgotten. It does not matter, as right now the only thing I'm interested in is unwrapping my birthday present.

I turn back around once Maxim is gone and fix my eyes on the pretty little niece of Remy Morrone. She's a beauty to behold and I think I'm going to delight in tormenting her. I grab the black fabric hood off of an old rusty bench and walk toward her, as I want her to be blind when she wakes. I have a drug that should bring her around in the next half an hour.

I can't wait to play with my new toy.

3

IMALIA

I groan as my head pounds and my eyes flicker open, only to be met with pitch-black darkness. That's when I realize my arms are killing me as they're tied above my head and I'm hanging from a fucking ceiling.

Panic kicks in as the reason it's so dark is that some son of a bitch put a cloth hood over my head. I kick around, thrashing out in terror as my memories resurface. The airport and the so-called 'baggage manager' who was helping me find my bag. It was a fucking trap and I should have seen it coming a mile off.

"I wouldn't waste all your energy if I were you," a deep, Russian voice cuts through the silence, stealing my breath away and forcing me to turn rigid.

"Who are you?" I ask, hating the way my voice breaks.

There's a soft chuckle as his heavy footsteps move

closer and closer. "It doesn't matter who I am, it matters what you can do for me. Imalia."

I swallow hard, realizing that I've flown right into a war zone and walked straight into one of my uncle's enemy's traps like a fucking idiot. "What do you want?" I ask, trying to steady my voice.

"I want an end to this war, just like your uncle."

A shiver travels down my spine as I sense he's close to me, as the rasp of his heavy breaths gets closer, making my heart race unevenly in my chest. "I'm not sure how I can help with that."

"You're my leverage, little girl," he murmurs. "I wonder if you're as beautiful as they say you are." He yanks the hood off of me and I groan, squinting to see my tormentor. Even though it's only dimly lit wherever we are, my eyes are too fucking sore and I have to blink multiple times before everything becomes clearer.

My heart leaps in my chest when I stare into the pale gray-blue eyes of a man so beautiful it looks like he dropped from heaven. He's older, perhaps late thirties, early forties, with dark curling hair and a neatly trimmed beard. His features are so perfect and rugged, and there's a hint of ink peaking out from beneath the collar of his tightly fitted white dress shirt. A dress shirt which is splattered with blood.

The man is tall, but it's hard to estimate how tall, considering I'm hanging from the ceiling. If I were to guess, about six foot three. He strokes a hand across his beard, drawing my attention to the ink covering the back of them. The corner of his mouth turns up into a rather unpleasant smirk. "Hey there, baby girl."

My stomach flips at that nickname and I shuffle uncomfortably, wincing at the pain radiating through my shoulder blades. "It's Imalia," I say.

He tilts his head slightly, watching me with the most unnerving look in his eyes. "I know your name."

"Who are you?" I ask.

He raises a brow. "So, you don't recognize me?"

I swallow hard. "Should I recognize you?" I ask, squinting harder and trying to rack my brain. I'm pretty certain I'd remember if I'd seen this stunningly beautiful man before.

He crosses his arms over his broad chest and narrows his eyes. "I'm Spartak Volkov."

The blood drains from my face as I stare at the man before me. A man rumored to be so fucking unhinged that even my uncle fears him deep down. He'd never admit it to his face, but Remy is terrified of what Spartak is capable of.

"I see," I squeak out, sounding more like a mouse than a girl. This situation couldn't be any fucking worse.

"Fear, it's strange how my name can draw it out of people so easily," he says, walking in a circle slowly around me, setting my already frayed nerves on edge. "When I first looked in to your eyes, Imalia, I saw desire."

"That's not—"

"Silence," he says. The tone of his voice is calm and

yet more fear inspiring than if he shouted. "You liked what you saw. I noticed the way your chest heaved more violently and your eyes dilated, and then the moment I told you my name, sheer intoxicating fear replaced the desire." He chuckles, but it's not a pleasant sound. "I find both arousing, although fear is my favorite." He returns to stand in front of me. "It really gets me hard when a girl fears me."

My throat bobs as I swallow hard, staring at the monster in front of me. "That's because you're depraved."

A wide smirk splits his face in two. "Indeed, if that was intended as an insult, then you clearly don't know the kind of man I am, baby girl."

A shudder races through me, hearing him call me that again. I can't understand why anything this man says affects me, but every time he says 'baby girl' in that Russian accent, my panties get damper between my thighs. It's fucking weird, as this man would probably laugh as he carved me into pieces and shipped me to my uncle. Another shudder races through me, but this time out of fear. "Stop calling me that."

His eyes darken. "Do you really think you're in any position right now to make demands of me?"

I don't answer him, glancing around at my surroundings, only now noticing we're in some rundown old warehouse.

"Answer me," he roars, making me recoil in response.

I swallow hard, narrowing my eyes at him. "I forgot what the question was."

His fists clench by his side and muscles bunch as he looks ready to unleash his rage on me in full force. Perhaps I'm going to die here, beaten and bloodied under Spartak Volkov's fist.

I screw my eyes closed as he advances toward me, but instead of being punched in the face, he unties that painful restraint from my arms and I drop to the floor in a heap. "Cazzo," I growl, glaring at the man who just bruised my ass. "What the fuck was that for?"

"You have a dirty mouth on you for such a pretty little thing," He breathes, kneeling down in front of me so those pale blue-gray eyes are level with mine. The scent of him invades me, and it's the most masculine scent I've ever encountered. It's musky and woody with a hint of alcohol, which I detect on his breath. "I've got some rules for you."

"What rules?" I ask.

He grabs hold of my chin forcefully, angling it up to him as he studies me. "No talking back and no questions from here on in. When you address me, I want you to call me daddy. Do you understand?"

A flash of heat spreads through me like a wildfire through a drought ridden forest. "No chance. Why would I call you daddy?"

"Because I make the rules and you can't deny me, baby girl."

I shake my head. "I don't know what sick game

you're playing, but you'll have to kill me before I call you that."

He growls, letting go of my chin and holding my gaze. "You'll learn the hard way, then. Every person, man or woman can be forced to submit." He brushes a hair from my face and I swat his hand away, which results in him grabbing my wrist hard and yanking me toward him. "I will break you, and once I do, you'll fucking call me daddy whenever I want you to. Do you understand?"

I glare into his eyes. "You'll never break me."

He chuckles and releases my wrist, standing and towering over me. "Every person has a breaking point, little lamb. Even I do, but no one has got close to finding out what it is." He grabs a handful of my hair and yanks me to my feet with it, practically tearing it from my scalp.

"Fuck you," I say, finding courage from somewhere, somehow. I won't lie down while this piece of shit bull-dozers over me. My mom taught me better than that. "I don't have a breaking point."

"What a naughty little liar you are. I can't wait to spank the denial right out of you." He grabs hold of my wrists and binds them together with rope roughly, making sure it's tied so tightly it feels like it's cutting the circulation off. "Time for me to take you somewhere more private, malishka."

I shudder as he grabs my hips, an involuntary reac-tion to his rough handling. The scent of him is overwhelming as he hauls me over his shoulder. I beat my tied fists against his back of solid muscle, but all it does is give me rope burn as he walks right out of the warehouse toward a parking lot.

A vehicle is waiting with the engine running and someone speaks in Russian to Spartak as I hear the door open. That's when I'm bundled in the back roughly like a doll, my head hitting the side of the door as I fall headfirst into it. "Damn it."

I swallow hard as I struggle to sit up straight with the restraints binding my wrists. And then I sense him slide close to me, his arm pressed against mine as he gives me no space at all, infecting the air with that harsh yet intoxicating scent of him. Every aspect of this man is a warning as I glance over at my captor, wondering what insane plans he has for me.

"Where are you taking me?" I ask.

His pale blue-gray eyes meet mine, stealing the breath from my lungs. "I'm taking you home to my torture chambers," he deadpans, as if it's obvious.

"Torture Chambers?" I ask, my voice sounding squeaky suddenly.

The smirk on his face makes dread spread through my veins like liquid ice. "Yes, baby girl, because you need punishing for not obeying me."

I swallow hard and tear my eyes away from the depravity sparking in his irises. This man isn't sane. I know that much from the things I've heard about him, but being in his presence hammers that home. He delights in my fear, so somehow I have to hide it from him. "What do you want from me?"

He chuckles, a deep and rich sound that sends goosebumps over every inch of my flesh. "I want information about your family, and I think I'll have some fun with you along the way."

I swallow hard. "I'll never betray my family." I glare at him. "No matter what you do to me."

"Never say never," he murmurs, sliding a rough, large hand onto my thigh and squeezing. "I wonder what makes you tick, little girl." his voice is almost seductive as he speaks. "I can't wait to open you up and learn all your deepest, darkest secrets." He inches his hand up the skirt of my dress, forcing me to writhe away from him, even though there's nowhere to go.

"Get your hand off of me," I spit, but I hate how feeble my plea sounds. I've got no power here, and he knows it.

Spartak chuckles, his hand still inching ever closer to my panties, which are shamefully wet. As he's right, when I first saw this god of a man, I wanted him. Stockholm Syndrome finally made sense when I looked into those pale blue-gray eyes, and I wanted to feel his hands on me, even though he'd taken me captive. Until I learned who he was.

I hold my breath as his fingers tease the edge of my lace panties, wishing I could die. Heat prickles over my skin like razor blades as he finally slides a finger right through my lace clad pussy, groaning as he does.

"You're soaking wet," he breathes, pushing the fabric aside and shoving a thick finger inside of me.

I gasp, shocked by the sudden invasion. "What the fuck?"

He smirks, lazily sliding his finger in and out of me. The wet sounds it makes as he does are beyond embarrassing, as I force myself to look anywhere but at him. "I knew I'd seen desire in those eyes when you first saw me." He licks his bottom lip, eyes flickering shut. "This is going to be so much fun, Imalia."

I swallow hard, hating that my body reacts to this monster's touch. He's just told me he intends to take me to his torture chamber and I'm dripping wet with desire. My eyes snap shut as I try to ignore him, try to ignore everything.

I've known for a long while that there's something wrong with me and my desire for pain and punishment. Normal, vanilla sex doesn't do it for me and never has, and so with this dark, beautiful and twisted man binding me and sliding his finger inside of me like he has the right, I fucking melt.

"Such a dirty girl you are, getting wet in the hands of a man who will utterly ruin you."

I glare at him, swallowing hard. "Fuck you," I spit, but even in my voice there's desire.

He chuckles and pulls his finger from my pussy, sliding it into his mouth and sucking it clean. "You wish, baby girl."

The sight of him doing such a dirty fucking thing

and calling me baby girl at the same time drives me wild as I clench my thighs together and force my attention out of the window.

I'm going to hell, but I'll be damned if I don't drag him down with me.

4

SPARTAK

*I*malia's chest heaves frantically as I drag her out of the car and head toward the chambers in the basement. Her fear is intoxicating, but the most intoxicating aspect is the fact she's excited by me. Her wet cunt was enough proof of that.

I swing open the door to the third room to the right, which is the nicer of the torture chambers, if you can call it nice. There's a plush bed at the back with restraints affixed and a cage at the bottom. All my torture implements and some more sexual ones are on display on the wall.

Imalia gasps, eyes widening. "What the…" she trails off, her face turning pale. "Kill me now," she mutters.

I smirk. "Why would I do that when I have every intention of enjoying you?" I push her inside and slam the door shut, turning the key and locking us inside together. "After all, it's my birthday and I want to

33

unwrap my present." I spin around and fix my eyes on her.

Imalia is trembling, backing away from me. "Don't touch me, my uncle—"

"I don't want to hear shit about your uncle," I growl.

Her face pales as she moves further away, cowering like a startled animal.

I can't help the twisted excitement flooding me when a woman shies away from me, as I stalk toward her, towering over her like a lion cornering a lamb. "Don't be scared, little lamb," I breathe, walking her toward the wall. "I'm going to blow your fucking mind."

Her lip quivers as her back hits the wall and her eyes widen. "Please, don't—"

I grab her throat, squeezing. "Begging already, baby girl?" I ask, smirking at her. "But the fun hasn't even started yet." I move my lips to within an inch of hers, allowing my breath to hit her face. "By the time I'm through with you, you'll be begging daddy to fuck you."

"Never," she spits, her beautiful brown eyes turning furious. "I've told you I'd rather die than call you daddy."

I growl softly and lick a path up the side of her cheek, making her tremble. "You don't know what you're talking about, because you've never stared death in the face. Once you do, you'll choose your words more carefully."

Her eyes dilate, whether it's from fear or lust or a mix of the two. I don't know and I don't care.

"Now, then. What shall I do with my pretty little present?" I move my hand lower and cup her firm, large breasts through the fabric of her dress, groaning at how good they feel beneath my hand. "So fucking pretty," I muse.

Imalia shudders, her entire body trembling. "Get your hands off of me," she says, trying to sound tough.

I chuckle, shaking my head. "Or what, little lamb?" I inhale her sweet scent, which is a mix of strawberries and jasmine. It's utterly intoxicating. I move my hand lower, gripping her wide, curvy hips with both of my hands roughly. "How are you going to stop me?" She's frozen like a rabbit caught in headlights, but then suddenly she thrashes out, bringing her knee up to my crotch, forcing me to let go of her as I double over. "Fuck," I growl, as she slips away from me and rushes toward the door, which is locked.

When she tries it, and it doesn't open, she turns to face me. The look of pure horror on her face is both amusing and arousing.

"Big mistake." I move toward her, and I see the cogs whirring in her brain as she tries to formulate a plan. "There's no escape."

She dashes across to the other side of the room and

grabs a knife off the wall, pointing it at me. "Don't come near me, or I'll stab you."

I tilt my head. "Have you ever stabbed anyone before, Imalia?" I ask, slowly moving toward her.

Her brown eyes dart between me and the door again, even though she knows it's locked. My cock thickens in my pants at the thought of her fighting me with that knife. She's delectable. A rare beauty in a sea of false goddesses. It's one of the first things I noticed about her, that's she's not caked in layers of makeup or wearing the latest designer clothes, despite her family's wealth.

Her lip trembles and so does her hand as she shakes the knife at me, stabbing it forward. "I said don't come near me!"

I smirk and move closer. "I don't mind if you want to cut me, baby girl." I slide my tongue over the bottom of my lip. "As long as I get to cut you, too."

Her nostrils flare as she takes a step back, eyes widening. "You're a psycho."

"I've been told that many times." I shrug. "What's your point?" I continue moving toward her, backing her against the table.

"I will stab you," she says, but it's as if she's trying to convince herself more than me.

Once I'm a few feet away from her, I tear open the front of my shirt. "Come on, little lamb. Let's see how well I bleed." I walk closer until the tip of the knife is pressing into my scarred, tattooed skin. "I bet you bleed so good," I breathe.

There's a flash of both shock and desire in her eyes as she takes in my muscled body, eyes dipping down shamelessly to my abs. "Are you insane?"

"Most probably," I say, applying more pressure as the tip of the knife sinks into my flesh and a trickle of blood drips down my abs. My eyes flicker shut at the sharp yet exquisite pain. "Do you enjoy making me bleed? Perhaps you'd enjoying licking it off my skin," I murmur.

Imalia shakes, withdrawing the knife from my chest. "I just want to go home." Her voice is fragile and I open my eyes to see her beautiful brown eyes wet with unshed tears.

I move closer, grabbing the knife out of her hand gently. "Once I'm through with you, you'll never want to go home," I breathe, letting my lips brush hers softly.

Her chest rises and falls frantically as I move my lips to her eyes, kissing away the salty tears.

"Do I scare you, or is it what you'll learn about yourself that you fear the most?" I ask, lacing my fingers in her soft, caramel brown hair and yanking her head back. "Are you scared what truths I'll reveal about your deepest and darkest desires?"

Her throat bobs as she swallows, and it's beautiful to watch. I'm insane and it's something I've been aware of for a very long time, but it doesn't bother me. My late wife hated the depraved side of my personality and so I hid it from her until it became almost impossible to hide it.

I loved her, but she didn't love me, not the real me. It's why after her death I vowed never to hide the darkness and to embrace who I am. It's what gives me power, anyway. It's why I have such a feared reputation.

"Perhaps you'll realize how good it is to tumble into the darkness and give in to your most primal desires, malishka," I murmur, lifting her up and tossing her over my shoulder. "It's time for me to test my theory on you." I chuck her onto the bed so she's sitting up against the headboard and quickly grab her right wrist, affixing it to the bed with the restraint.

Imalia watches me, no longer fighting. "Why are you doing this?"

I tilt my head. "To be honest, I'd intended to string you up and leave you in one of the usual rooms until Remy answered my demands. Maybe question you a bit and find out if you had any useful information on my enemy." I grab her left wrist and fix the restraint around it. "Until I set my eyes on your beautiful face and body, and that's when I decided to have some fun with you instead."

Her eyes flicker shut and more tears escape, wetting her long eyelashes.

"How old are you?" I ask, wondering if my estimation of twenty-six is correct. I rarely get a person's age wrong.

Her eyes narrow. "Too fucking young for you," she spits, glaring at me.

I smirk. "Don't be silly, baby. I think you're probably twenty-six years old."

Her eyes widen a little, giving me the answer I wanted.

"Exactly twenty years younger than me as of today, which is a perfect age-gap." I clap her two ankles in the restraints, forcing her thighs open for me.

Her nose wrinkles. "You look younger than forty-six."

My smirk widens. "Don't worry, older men do everything better." I kneel between her thighs and yank the hem of her dress up. "Which you're about to learn."

She tries to writhe away as I slide my fingers into the waistband of her black lace panties. "Please, don't do this."

I pause, looking into her alluring eyes. "You're begging a man who has no fucking morals, malishka." I yank her panties down and groan at the sight of her sweet little cunt glistening wet. "Not to mention you're so fucking wet." I lean down and press my nose to her center, inhaling her arousal. "It would be a shame not to taste you."

I drag the flat of my tongue through her center, making her jolt. Her breathing becomes deeper, more raspy, and it makes me harder than a rock. She tastes like pure innocence and sin all wrapped up together.

"You taste like heaven," I breathe, glancing up at her beautiful, doll-like face, which is now flushed red. "I can't wait to make this pretty little cunt come."

Her lip trembles and she shakes her head. "That's not going to happen."

Even as she tries to tell herself that, I see the doubt in her eyes. The desire that I've lit a match beneath, ready for the bonfire to take off. "It is, little lamb. Wait and see." I suck her clit into my mouth, watching as her face twists with pleasure. She bites her bottom lip hard, trying not to make a sound.

I slip my tongue inside of her, tasting her more deeply.

Her hips buck toward my mouth, making me smirk.

"Someone is impatient," I murmur, holding her gaze. "Hold still, baby girl." I place the flat of my palm on her stomach and push her hard against the bed, continuing to lick her into a frenzy.

Finally, a luscious moan escapes her lips.

I smirk, loving the way her eyes widen in shock that she actually made that sound.

"That's it, baby girl. Moan for daddy."

Her eyes dilate further at that comment as her pussy gushes, driving me wild. "Never," she spits.

I shake my head. "So stubborn." I slide two fingers into her soaking wet heat and draw them toward the inner wall, stroking that spot inside of her. "I can't wait to break you."

Her entire body shudders and she moans louder,

eyes rolling back in her head. My cock leaks into my boxer briefs as I watch her dangle on the edge, sinking her teeth into her thick bottom lip. I'd love to bite it and make her bleed.

I drag the tips of my teeth back and forth over her sensitive clit as I continue to finger fuck her, wishing it was my cock buried deep inside of her.

Imalia groans. Her nipples are so hard against the cotton of her cute little dress, it makes my cock strain against my pants.

I reach down and unzip them, pulling my cock out of my suit pants and tugging on it.

Her eyes shoot open at the sound of the zipper and widen when they land on my cock, hard and heavy in my hand. The desire in her eyes is unmissable as she pulls her bottom lip into her mouth and sucks, making me long to feel those pouty, pretty lips wrapped around it.

"Do you like what you see?" I ask, smirking at her.

My question snaps her back to reality as her brow furrows. "No."

"Why do you like lying so much, malishka?" I ask, searching her eyes. "I can tell you're practically gagging to be split apart with my cock." My fingers move faster and harder as I drive her toward the edge, even as fury takes over her expression.

"You're an arrogant asshole," she says, but there's no masking the lust in her voice.

I suck her clit and then nip it with hardly any pressure, but enough to make it impossible for my little lamb to resist the cliff edge. Her body shakes uncontrollably as she comes apart, her arousal flooding her pussy as I lick up every single drop.

No matter how hard she tries to deny it, I know she's like me. A dark and dirty soul who needs freeing from the bounds of society.

5

IMALIA

*S*hame hits me like a freight train as my orgasm fades away, and Spartak emerges from between my thighs, wiping my arousal from his mouth.

The look in his eyes is wicked as he smirks at me. "Fucking delicious."

I shudder, partially from shameful arousal and partially from terror. There's no reasoning with a man who's not right in the head, but I know that's not the only thing that scares me. It's how deep he can pull me into his insanity with him, as a part of me enjoyed what he did. A part of me delighted in being forced into submission by a man as dominant and depraved as he is.

Spartak stands, fisting his hard cock in his hands. "Since it's my birthday, Imalia. Will you wrap those pretty lips around my cock?" he asks, tilting his head.

"When hell freezes over."

He smirks. "You're already in hell, baby girl." He moves forward, drawing my eyes to the huge length between his thighs. "Might as well enjoy it while you're here."

"I can't promise you won't lose it if you come near me with that thing."

He tilts his head, eyes sparking with excitement as he flexes his chest muscles. "I'm pretty sure you don't have the guts to bite my dick off, Imalia." He shrugs. "Unfortunately for you, I'm crazy enough to test that theory."

Shit.

Of course, he's crazy enough to find out if I'll bite his cock off. It's so thick I'm not entirely sure I could. My mind recoils at the idea of sucking his cock and yet a part of me longs to obey him. A man who only half an hour ago told me he intends to spank me into submission. "Your funeral," I say, testing the restraints on my wrists. They're strong enough to hold a man double my weight, which means I'll never break out of them.

He gets onto the bed with his knees on either side of me, eyes flashing with desire. "Perhaps I'll just stroke myself to climax and come all over your pretty little lips instead." The head of his cock rests on my lips and I grimace, trying to get away from him even though there's nowhere for me to go. "Open up," he demands.

I glare at him, but there's a part of me that wants to.

A part of me that wants to obey this psycho holding me captive in a dungeon.

"You know you want to." He reaches down between my thighs and strokes his finger lightly through my soaking wet entrance. "Be a good girl and open your mouth," he murmurs.

I swallow hard, knowing that the moment I give in to his demands, I hand him all the power. Even as my mind screams at me to resist, I let my lips open a little and he pushes forward, forcing my jaw open with the thick head of his cock. The taste of him is pure masculinity and salty as precum leaks onto my tongue.

I shut my eyes, enjoying the helplessness and being at the mercy of a man like him.

"Such a good girl," he praises, thrusting his cock deeper, so he's hitting the back of my throat. "Take every inch."

I gag, tears prickling my eyes as he moves in and out, fucking my throat. The lack of control is both intoxicating and fear inspiring as I hold his gaze, trying not to choke.

"Breathe through your nose, baby girl. You're doing so fucking well," he groans, eyes rolling back in his head.

I follow his instruction, my pussy getting so wet as he continues to fuck my throat like an animal. The guttural deep sounds coming from him are such a turn on as he leaks more precum into my mouth. None of this should arouse me, since he's taken me against my will and is forcing his dick down my throat.

I relax, almost enjoying his assault as I pleasure him the way he pleasured me. The guilt of enjoying such a dirty act with my captor slowly melts into the background as redhot arousal takes over. I moan around his shaft, knowing that I've never been so turned on in all my life.

I've not exactly had much experience, even at twenty-six years old. One boyfriend who was a lousy partner sexually, and that's all. He never wanted to experiment with sex or do anything kinky, even when our sex life became non-existent.

My mom was upset when I broke up with Jamie, as she expected me to marry him. The son of a crime boss in Los Angeles who our family had been friends with for years. But thankfully, she didn't push the matter. It was a mutual decision to part ways.

As I choke on this God of a man's cock, I realize just how dark and depraved my desires are. I can't get aroused by normal sex, but have a psychopath kidnap me, chain me up and shove his cock down my throat, and I'm practically ready to come with no stimulation. My nipples are so hard they ache and my pussy is dripping wet. I moan again around his cock, writhing against the restraints as the need inside of me heightens.

"Baby girl, you're so fucking good at this," he breathes, blue-gray eyes holding mine. "You're going to make me come right down that pretty little throat, and when I do, I want you to swallow every drop. Do you understand?" His hips continue to move rhythmically, thrusting in and out of the back of my throat.

I try to nod my head, but it's difficult.

He seems to register it. "Good girl." His thrusts become more powerful and my body reacts in kind. "Such a good girl."

I choke all over him, saliva spilling down my chin and coating his balls. Tears stream down my face and I must look fucking disgusting right now, but I don't care. My body is on fire, ready to explode. Every nerve ending on fire as he takes what he wants from me.

"Fuck, yes," he grunts, eyes shuttering as he pumps one last time.

A flood of hot cum hits the back of my throat and that's when I come apart, too. My entire body shaking as my second shameful orgasm hits me.

"Fuck, baby girl. You just came because I shot my load down your throat." He sounds in awe, and I open my eyes to see him looking down at me like a hungry animal. "Such a dirty little lamb, coming with my cock down your throat," he breathes, continuing to thrust into my throat, draining every drop of cum from his balls.

Finally, he stops and his semi-hard cock slips from my lips. The shame I'd felt before increases tenfold as I stare up at his cocky smirk, realizing I gave him so much power over me way too fast.

He leans down and grabs my chin, angling my face up unnaturally. "So perfect," he says, his breath hitting my face. "Such a good little girl." He licks a path up the side of my face, sending goosebumps through me. "I can't wait to hear that dirty little mouth call me daddy."

I grit my teeth. "You'll never hear it."

He chuckles, the smirk on his face bordering on manic. "Such a naughty liar, you are." He unfastens the restraints on my wrists and ankles, but doesn't allow me to move, grabbing my ankles. "Get under the sheets."

I narrow my eyes at him, but do as he says, as I'd glady cover myself up from his predatory gaze. "What now?" I ask.

"Now, you sleep. I have a party to get to." He turns away and walks toward the door, unlocking it and pushing it open. He pauses, glancing over his shoulder. "Sweet dreams, baby girl." He walks away and slams the door behind him, leaving me confused.

A mix of shame, lust and guilt coil through me over what I let that man do to me. The worst thing is, I enjoyed every second. Spartak is right. I don't fear him as much as I fear what sick truths he'll uncover about me.

THE SLAM of the door wakes me as I squint through the darkness, observing the tall figure in front of it.

"Hey, little lamb," Spartak's deep voice cuts through the silence, reminding me where I am.

I sit up suddenly, rubbing my eyes. "What time is it?" I ask, glancing around the dark room.

"It's just after midday." He moves forward, allowing me to see his face through the darkness. "I brought you something to eat." He holds up a takeout bag.

I swallow hard, my stomach rumbling. "I'm starving," I admit.

He smirks, coming to sit on the edge of the bed and opening the bag. "I hope you like hamburger and fries."

I nod. "I'd eat anything right now." I eagerly grab the hamburger out of his hand and eat. It's a fast food burger, but it tastes so good considering how hungry I am.

"Slow down," he urges.

I narrow my eyes but listen to what he says, as I was close to swallowing the entire thing whole. It tastes so good as he passes me the fries and I grab them, setting the box down against my knee. Once I've finished eating, he passes me a coke and I drink it, enjoying the way the cool liquid soothes my too parched throat.

"You should be well and truly recharged now," he murmurs, eyes sparking with dangerous intent. "Are you ready to call me daddy, yet?"

I narrow my eyes. "Never."

The smirk on his face widens. "I'd hoped you'd say that. As I've been looking forward to punishing you."

A shiver travels down my spine as he grabs the trash from my food and chucks it to one side. His eyes fix on me with such intensity it's enough to make anyone quake from fear.

"Don't fucking touch me," I say.

The smirk on his face widens as he grabs hold of my hips roughly and tosses me over like a doll, positioning me on all fours.

I shudder as he slides the flat of his palm over my bare ass.

"Such a lovely ass, malishka. Perfect for spanking red."

I freeze, fear and desire morphing into one odd sensation that both twists my guts and drives me wild. "Please, don't."

He spanks me then, hard and firm. I recoil, the stinging pain both intense and intoxicating. "Scared you're going to enjoy the pain too much, baby girl?"

I don't answer him. I can't. As that's exactly what I fear. Instead, I clench my jaw and wait for him to continue. His hand caresses my skin almost tenderly and then he spanks me again with more power, making me jolt in shock. I bite my bottom lip, forcing myself not to react to his assault.

There's no reality in which this should arouse me, and yet the desire heightens as he rubs his rough palms across my skin. "I think I need something firmer to give you a real good spanking."

A shudder races down my spine as he walks toward

the wall, where I grabbed the knife the last time we were together. I swallow hard, waiting to see which implement he chooses. Spartak assesses the option before reaching for a rather painful looking paddle that makes my heart skip a beat. "This is perfect." He holds it up so I can see the word etched into it.

Daddy.

My stomach dips as I realize he intends to brand me with it and leave the mark on my skin. "No, don't."

The smirk on his lips it utterly evil. "Sorry, but I don't play nice." He moves toward me, and I consider running, but there's nowhere to go. I'm trapped at the mercy of this monster.

He grabs my hip with one hand and then slams the paddle hard into my left ass cheek with no mercy.

I scream at the top of my lungs, the pain so intense it burns long after he removes the paddle. Softly, he kneads the stinging skin, sending a hot inferno blazing right between my thighs. I groan, realizing that the pain is only intensifying my desire.

"That's it, accept the pain and pleasure," he breathes, his hand sliding between the soaking wet lips of my pussy. "So wet for me, malishka."

I moan, unable to contain it any longer. The wrongness of it hits me and yet I still can't help it.

Spartak uses the paddle on my right cheek so hard it makes me scream again, but the pain quickly morphs into exquisite pleasure as he massages the skin and slides his finger through my entrance, bumping my clit.

He does it five more times on each cheek, making me sure I can't stand the pain any longer. Although, with each impact of the paddle, my desire heightens. If he doesn't stop soon, I'm sure I'll come apart from the pain alone.

"I want you to see my brand on your ass, baby girl." He yanks me off the bed and pulls me toward a floor to ceiling mirror on the wall, turning me around. "Look at your ass."

I bite my lip and glance over my shoulder into the mirror, shuddering when I see the word Daddy etched into each cheek in angry red marks.

"You're mine, malishka. Do you understand?"

I swallow hard, unable to speak. The welts on my ass should inspire fear, but they turn me on like nothing ever has. I feel my nipples harden and the need for friction increase as I rub my thighs together, trying to ease the need between them. My clit is practically throbbing.

"Good girl," he breathes, grabbing my hand and yanking me toward the bed. "Such a good girl getting turned on by seeing my brand on your ass. I knew you were as dirty as me."

His praise only elevates my desire as he forces me onto the bed on my back. I watch him as he claps the restraints around my arms and legs. "It's time for me to give you a reward."

My entire body shakes in anticipation as he licks his lips and then delves between my thighs. I moan loudly, unashamedly, desperate for him to turn me into a puddle of desire on the bed.

He moves away from my pussy, staring at me. "Are you going to be a good girl and call me daddy?"

I can't understand his insistence that I call him that word, but I won't give in. No matter how badly I need my release, or how badly I want to call him it. It's such an intimate word—a word I've never used in my entire life. The intimacy wouldn't make sense and yet there's that sick part of me that wants to submit to his demands and scream it while he drives me over the edge.

I shake my head. "No."

He sighs. "Shame."

I whimper as he pushes off the bed, leaving me needy.

The door to the basement room opens, flushing me with heat. Spartak growls, spinning to face the intruder. "What the fuck do you want?"

The man bows his head, averting his gaze from me. "I'm sorry to interrupt, sir, but Maxim is here, and he says it's urgent."

Spartak waves him off. "I'll be up in a moment." He spins to face me, eyes darting between my pussy and my face. "I have to deal with something, but I'll be back quickly." He moves toward me and leans down, his lips an inch from mine.

My heart skips a beat as he kisses me for the first time, his lips forceful as he thrusts his tongue into my mouth, caressing my own as he deepens the need inside of me. I moan, shamefully, which makes him smirk.

"Don't miss me too much." He walks away, leaving me aching and panting for more.

I swallow hard, wishing he'd at least released me from the restraints before leaving me here. God knows how long he'll leave me like this. I can't even rub my thighs together as my clit throbs with need.

This man is a bastard for torturing me like this. I swallow hard and shut my eyes, trying to ignore the demanding pulse between my thighs as I grind my teeth and wait for my kidnapper to return.

6

SPARTAK

*T*he darkness is breathing around me like a living thing, clouding my vision and driving me insane. They shot my son, my heir. If the Morrone family thinks I'll let this go, they'll have to think again. Rage unlike anything I've experienced is overpowering all my senses, driving me crazier than normal. I pace up and down in front of the floor to ceiling glass windows of my office in the Datatech Corporation building. I almost forget Timur is in the room until he speaks.

"What's the plan, boss?" He asks, running a hand through his dark hair.

I narrow my eyes. "Distribute the guns to our men. They shot Maxim during a peaceful sitdown, which means we can't let this lie."

Timur's jaw works. "They had a viable reason."

"Are you questioning me?" I snap, my resolve waning. My son was in surgery last night after being shot as we fled Remy's casino. It's been one problem after another. First, Luca Morrone tries to kidnap my daughter-in-law and now this shit. I can't let it go, no matter what consequences it might have for the city and the bratva. They've gone too fucking far.

I know a good father would be at the hospital, checking in on his son, but I haven't had the time. I'm a crappy father and it was inevitable considering the example my father gave me. Ever since the shit hit the fan last night, I've been in meeting after meeting with my men, planning our strategy for the escalation of the war—an escalation I intend to start.

He shakes his head, crossing his arms over his broad chest. "Of course not. I'm merely suggesting caution about escalating things further."

"Caution?" I scoff, pacing up and down the office of the warehouse. "Do you think they'd grant me the same courtesy if I'd shot Massimo?" I ask, shaking my head. "No, I'm fed up with lying low. We hit them where it fucking hurts."

Timur's eyes widen. "Do you mean—"

"Yes, hit their club, Le Stelle, in the center of their territory. I want the entire building blown to the ground."

Timur's Adam's apple bobs as he swallows, as I know how insane it is to enter Morrone territory and blow apart their nightclub, which is secretly their auction house. The lifeblood of their operation, but it's exactly what my father would do if he were here. You can't let people like Remy get away with harming your own flesh and blood and not retaliate hard.

He bows his head. "Which team do you want on this?"

I consider the question, wondering who is reliable enough to carry out such a dangerous operation. "There's only one man capable, and that's Vitaly. Ask him to assemble a small team of his best men, but I'll go with them."

Timur's eyes widen. "Sir, it's far too dangerous."

I straighten, glaring at my sovietnik, who has been increasingly more vocal in the past few weeks. "Too dangerous for Spartak Volkov?" I ask, narrowing my eyes. "Do you forget what I'm capable of, Timur?"

He bows his head. "I mean no disrespect, it's not a job I'd expect my pakhan to undertake."

"It's too important for me not to." I run a hand through my messy hair. "We're at war, and I'm not a pathetic leader who hides behind my men. I will be on the front lines."

Timur clearly senses there's no way he's talking me out of this. "Very well. I'll arrange it."

I clap my hands. "Good, I want the plan in place no later than this time tomorrow."

"I'll text you the details as soon as it's arranged." He places his hands in his pocket. "Is there anything else?"

I shake my head. "No, go." I wave my hand toward the door, needing to be alone right now. I slump into the chair behind my desk, finally able to breathe. I've been on the go for twelve hours solid since last night. Someone knocks on my door, setting my frayed nerves on edge. "Who is it?" I snap.

"It's me brother," Artyom says.

I draw in a deep breath, knowing that he's the last person I want to see right now. A part of me blames him for this shit, as snatching Imalia was his idea. I was a fool to go ahead with it, but I guess I've been getting sloppy lately. Artyom's plan sounded viable, but now I realize it was probably a ploy to cause chaos for me. "What do you want?"

"Can I come in?" he asks, irritation clear in his voice.

"Fine."

He opens the door and enters, a false look of concern on his face. "How is Maxim?"

"He's stable, but they're holding him for a few days." My relationship with my brother is tenuous, and it doesn't help that he reminds me so much of our uncle. Somehow, he took after him in looks, whereas I always resembled our father.

Artyom nods and sits opposite me, crossing one leg over the other. "What's the plan now, brother?" he asks, a hint of amusement in his tone.

I tilt my head. "You'll find out at the meeting later."

His brow rises. "Come on, you've got to clue me in to what the plan is."

I clench my fists beneath the table, rage clawing at my insides. "I don't have to do shit."

His face hardens, eyes narrowing. "What the fuck is your problem?"

"My problem is that Remy Morrone's men shot my son." I clench my jaw, glaring at him. "I'm not in the mood for this shit."

He nods. "Fine, but I have an important matter to discuss with you."

"What matter?"

"The bikers approached us, wanting a supply of cocaine since the Callaghans keep letting them down."

I run a hand across the back of my neck, knowing that despite their constant pushing, we don't want to deal with those hillbillies. "I've told them I'm not interested."

"It could be a lucrative deal."

I clear my throat. "Lucrative and more trouble than it's worth. The bikers are trash and we don't deal outside our territory."

He taps his fingers on his knee, mind kicking into overdrive. "I told him I'd at least get a meeting."

"Told who?"

He sighs. "Axel wanted a meeting, and I agreed."

Rage coils through me as I glare at him. "What right do you have to agree to a meeting on my behalf?" I should have taught my younger brother a lesson years ago, but that stupid, familial need to protect him has ruled me since we were young.

After all, I ensured our uncle's attention was always directed at me, protecting him from the worst trauma I experienced in my childhood, worse even than the abuse my father subjected us both to.

To this day, no one knows the truth. It died with my father and I keep it locked away, deep inside of me. A dark, disgusting secret that'll never see the light of day. No one knows the reason my father lost his shit and murdered his own brother in cold blood, but it was for a good fucking reason. It fueled those rumors of how unhinged he was, making everyone fear him, even his enemies.

"You can attend the meeting. I won't meet with him." I clench my jaw and glare at him.

He looks irritated, shaking his head. "On another note, what do you intend to do with the Allegro girl?" Artyom asks, his gaze assessing me.

Imalia.

Panic strikes me right to the core as I forgot entirely about her, overwhelmed by the war heating up. I left her chained up naked in the basement two freaking days ago when Maxim interrupted us and dropped the bomb on me that the Morrone family had tried to kidnap Livia. My heart pounds unevenly in my chest. As with all the shit going on, I have barely had a moment to stop, let alone remember what I was doing before it all.

"Don't worry about her. I know what I'm doing."

His eyes narrow. "Are you certain, brother? I heard everything at the casino."

Shit.

I forgot he was listening to us, which means he heard my caveman like declaration that Imalia Allegro is mine. "What's your point?" I snap.

He runs a hand across the back of his neck, sighing. "Remy won't forgive you if you never let her go. The war will escalate in ways we can hardly comprehend."

"I know," I mutter, but even as I say it, there's no chance in hell I'm letting her go. There's something about the beautiful Italian girl that calls to me, turns me into an obsessed, possessive monster that wants to own her in every single way.

Artyom stands and walks toward the door. "I'll speak with the bikers alone, but Axel won't be pleased." He rubs a hand across the back of his neck. "If I can agree to a deal, will you at least consider it?"

I nod in response, even though I won't. Right now my mind is solely focused on Imalia, who I abandoned in a rather uncomfortable position. He needs to leave so I can go to her.

"I'll see you in three hours at the meeting," he says.

I clench my jaw, glancing at my watch. Three hours doesn't give me long to get back to the house and make amends with Imalia, but I have to. I can't leave her any longer. Whatever this sick and twisted thing is between us, I can't risk it over a mistake.

Otherwise Remy succeeds at destroying that as well,

and ever since I looked into her beautiful dark eyes, I've known that there's no way in hell I'll ever let go of her.

She's mine and I'll be damned if anyone takes her away from me. I don't care if she doesn't accept what this is between us. I'm not a man who plays by the rules and I can live with her fighting me for the rest of our lives. In fact, I think I'll enjoy it.

7

IMALIA

$\mathcal{I}$ shudder as I awaken, realizing I'm so frozen cold I can't move my toes. It's been like this for God knows how long, as I lay here naked and alone. I can hardly feel my hands, as Spartak hasn't returned quickly as he promised to, leaving me naked and chained in the basement like an animal. I've had to piss on the bed, which is beyond embarrassing, unable to get to the makeshift toilet in the corner since he kept the restraints on.

I don't know how long I've been lying here, but it feels like weeks. Unlikely though, considering I haven't had a drink since the coca cola Spartak bought me, and would probably have died of dehydration by now. I sigh heavily and groan at the ache in my shoulders. My calves are killing me as they've been cramping while I sleep, waking me.

The sound of a key turning in the lock both relieves

and scares me. Suddenly, the door swings open and Spartak walks inside.

His brow furrows as he turns on the light, forcing me to wince at the intensity hitting my retinas. "Shit. You've gone almost blue." He paces toward me and unfastens the restraints on my wrists and ankles. "I'm sorry, baby girl. I expected to get back to you right away, but then everything went crazy and…" he trails off, his brow furrowing as if he can't understand why he's explaining himself to me. "All I'm saying is I didn't intend to leave you like this for two days."

Two days.

"Is that all it's been?" I ask, my voice croaky.

"Quiet, don't talk." He cups the back of my head almost tenderly and brings a water bottle to my mouth.

I swallow the water slowly, only now realizing how desperately thirsty I was.

He brings the bottle away, making me whimper. "We need to get you out of here and warmed up." He maneuvers me like a doll and lifts me out of the soiled sheets, still naked. He shrugs off his jacket. "Put this on."

I shudder as I try to put it on, but I'm shaking too much.

He helps me, steadying my arm and sliding it into the jacket before doing the same for the next arm. Once I'm in it, he wraps it around me and lifts me, carrying me toward the exit of the torture chamber. I'm so cold as he carries me up a set of stairs, not entirely aware of my surroundings.

I shut my eyes, drifting in and out of consciousness until I'm flung onto my back in a huge bed. Spartak tucks me in and then strips himself.

"W-what are you doing?" I ask.

"You are cold, and the fastest way to heat you up is skin to skin contact."

I shake my head. "No freaking way. Stay away from me."

He sighs. "Don't be silly, little lamb." He drops his shirt to the floor and I hate the way my body heats at the sight of him topless. He's so utterly flawless and yet flawed in every way. Those deep scars marring his skin only make him more appealing, along with the ink all over his body. "You might catch pneumonia if I don't warm you up." He drops his pants to the floor, leaving his boxer briefs on, and then slides under the covers with me.

I shudder at the warmth of his skin against mine as he wraps an arm around my waists, pulling my back against him. Instead of shying away, I lean into his warmth, craving it. "Why's it so cold down there?"

He shrugs. "It's an underground torture chamber, and I don't need to keep dead people warm."

Dead people.

I sense that most people he locks up here end up dead pretty swiftly. Although, the room he had me in appeared more like a sex dungeon than a torture chamber, given the odd implements hanging from the wall and the cage beneath the bed.

"Are you going to kill me?" I ask.

There's a moment of hesitation before he says, "Never."

It seems an odd thing to say, since I sense all the prisoners of the torture dungeon end up dead in the end at this man's hands. "Why not?"

"Because you're mine." He presses his lips to my shoulder and draws me even closer. "You belong to me and I'm never letting you go."

Never.

Any blood I still have in my face drains away as I shiver, fear and cold penetrating my limbs. If this crazy guy thinks he can have me forever, then that's what he'll do. He'll keep me locked away in a cage no better than an animal, wasting away in his dungeon or in a pretty room like this. It's all the same. "What about leverage against my uncle?" I shake my head. "I thought you wanted to trade me."

"I offered your uncle a deal for you last night. He declined." He flattens the palm of his hand on my stomach and pulls me even closer to him, forcing his hard cock against my ass. "And then, the bastard had his men shoot my son."

I swallow hard, knowing that doesn't bode well for the war or me.

"Which means he's going to pay and one way is never seeing you again, Imalia."

Tears flood my eyes as I continue to steal his warmth, but hate him at the same time. "I want to see him and my mom."

"Hush now," he murmurs, pressing his lips to the back of my neck. "All will be okay. You'll realize how good it is to be free of people like them." He rocks me gently back and forth, as if soothing a crying baby.

"I don't understand. I love my mom and my uncle. Why would I be happy to be free of them?" I ask, trying to work out how this man's brain works.

"Because deep down under all your sweet, innocent facade is a beautiful, dirty phoenix waiting to arise from the ashes," he breathes, grabbing my shoulder and forcing me to turn over to face him. Tears stream down my face, and much like the first day he brought me here, he kisses them away. "They bind you by society's rules, telling you to live a certain way even though deep down you long to be free."

A twinge pulls at my chest, as he's right. For a long time, I've realized I'm not like my mom. She's always been sweet and kind, even though she became ruthless to rule our empire. Under it all, there's a purity. But I have some sort of sickness in me.

The moment I saw my environment at the ware-house and set eyes on my captor, it aroused me. Add that to the way he looked at me and I was practically dripping with need, desperate to be taken against my will. A fantasy to be tied up, hurt and fucked while I scream at him to stop, all the while enjoying every second.

I swallow hard, wondering if I'm delirious from the cold. As my lips move toward his, desperate to kiss him.

"That's it, little lamb. Come to daddy," he breathes.

I stop moving, my heart pounding frantically. Another thing that makes me wetter than I've ever been is his weird insistence that I call him daddy.

"You've never had a man to take care of you. Never had a daddy, have you, Imalia?"

I shudder, realizing that he's talking about the fact my father died before I was born. Guilt coils through me as I wonder if that's why I'm so fucked up. "Let go of me," I say, but it's half-hearted.

He tilts his head. "Kiss me like you want to, baby girl. Let's see how good it can be to drown in each other."

I bite my bottom lip, hating that I want to take him up on that offer. This man who is clearly insane.

"Fuck it," he breathes, grabbing a fistful of my hair and yanking my lips against his. "I'm not a patient man," he says, before sliding his tongue through them and tangling it with my own.

I moan, clawing at his warm, muscular body as he deepens the kiss. It's sick and twisted that I still want this monster, even after he left me naked and freezing in this basement, chained up for two freaking days in my own piss.

He bites my lip hard enough to break the skin and

pulls away, licking the blood from it. "You taste like heaven."

"You're insane."

He nips at the skin on my neck, sending a prickling awareness through me. "I am insane, and I'm sorry I left you like that, baby girl. How can I make it up to you?"

"Let me go home," I say.

He shakes his head. "Anything but that, Imalia. You are home." His hands move up and down my arms in soft, soothing caresses. "I told you I'm never letting you go."

This man is fucking crazy. "So you'll keep me trapped like a caged animal for the rest of my life, or until you get bored?"

"I have no intention of getting bored." He kisses my neck softly. "But for now, until you accept the inevitable, yes, I'll keep you caged." His teeth sink into the juncture between my neck and shoulders, sending a shot of pleasure through me. "I quite like having you caged and at my mercy, malishka."

A shiver races through me as I recall him spanking me with that paddle and seeing the word Daddy imprinted on my skin. It made me so needy. The need still hasn't gone, even as he left me desperate and throbbing for two freaking days. It took ages for the arousal to wear off, but once it finally did, the cold took over. "I should hate you," I breathe as he continues to lick and suck at my skin.

"You should," he agrees, meeting my gaze. "But you don't hate me, do you, baby girl?" He grazes the edge of his teeth right down the center of my naked body, heating me.

I'm certainly no longer cold as he turns me into liquid fire. "No," I mutter, admitting the deep, dark truth I try to hide from.

He tilts his head. "And why is that?"

My lips are too dry as I wet them with my tongue. "Because I'm sick," I say.

He shakes his head. "No," he says harshly. "You're perfect." He kisses a path right to my center and then stops, shaking his head as he glances at his watch. "Shit."

"What is it?" I ask.

He gives me a sad smile. "I've got to get going. There's a meeting I'm going to be late for." He pushes off the bed, leaving me needy for the second fucking time. "I'll be back soon, I promise, and this time I will be." He runs a hand across the back of his neck as he grabs his pants and pulls them on. "Olga, my house-keeper, will bring you some food and drink. You need to eat."

I swallow hard and pull the comforter up around me, covering myself.

He moves to the side of the bed and grabs a fistful of my hair, angling my face up to him. "See you soon, malishka," he breathes, kissing me as if we were a couple and he's saying goodbye before work.

I sit, dumbfounded, as I watch him walk out of the room, locking the door behind him.

Why am I disappointed that the psycho who kidnapped me just left?

I should be thankful, and yet I know that within a few days of captivity I've grown to desire my captor. A man so utterly depraved I know I've not seen anything yet. The paddle was probably child's play for him.

I get out of the bed and walk toward the door on the left, finding a bathroom and enter. The need to shower after four days since I got captured is strong, as I head toward it and turn on the faucet.

I glance at myself in the mirror, shocked at what a mess I look.

How the hell can Spartak want me looking like this?

I turn around and glance at my ass in the mirror, unsurprised to find it bruised. It has been hurting like hell, lying on that bed without being able to move.

Tearing my eyes away from the image, I get under the warm spray of water and sigh heavily, thankful I can wash the dirt and grime away, but I know I can't wash away my sick desire for the man who kidnapped me. No matter how badly I want to.

8

SPARTAK

*A*ll eyes are on me as I pace the boardroom floor, wondering if telling the entire bratva the plan is the right idea. If something gets in the way, then there's a rat amongst us, but that's a risk I have to take.

"Vitaly, you and your group will be in charge of our attack on the Morrone family," I say, meeting my most ruthless and trusted brigadier's gaze.

He gives me an unwavering nod, but he hasn't yet heard the insane plan I've cooked up.

"They attacked my son, which means they declared an escalation of war first." I cross my arms over my chest. "This evening we will blow apart their most lucrative aspect of their business, Le Stelle."

A few whispers break out and most of the men stare at me like I'm insane, which I am. If they didn't know that by now, then they're fucking stupid.

Timur stands, drawing my attention to him. "Everything is in place, sir. It would be a good idea for me to brief Vitaly's group after this meeting."

Artyom hasn't turned up for the meeting, probably pissed at my refusal to meet with Axel, the leader of the bikers. I'm thankful, as he would have a bad opinion about this plan. "Good. Also, the other three groups need to distribute the guns we stole amongst yourselves, as I'm expecting a fallout like none Chicago has ever fucking seen."

I notice the concern etched on some of the less courageous members' faces, but most of the men look ready for a fight. The Italians may have a certain power in this city, but their men don't follow as loyally as mine. "Does anyone have questions about the plan?"

Kirill puts his hand up, and I nod.

His jaw clenches. "An associate of ours says that they're expecting a shipment of more arms tonight at midnight."

"What associate?" I ask, as I wouldn't take all of our associates information as gospel.

"James Kerry," he says, shrugging. "I don't think he's bullshitting me."

James Kerry is the head of customs clearance at the docks, who is as crooked as all the mafia organizations put together. He takes bribes to clear illegal goods into the city, and yet at times he tips us off, which only concerns me.

What if he tips off the Morrone family about our shipments?

"Did you pay him for the information?" I ask.

Kirill nods. "Yes, he wanted money, but if he's right, then this could be a serious win for us. As this one is two times the size of the shipment that we seized the other day."

I run a hand across the back of my neck, as we have to be careful who we trust going forward. "Fine, you take your group and seize it, but make sure you're careful. The Morrone family will be on high alert once we hit Le Stelle."

"Sir," Kirill says, bowing his head.

"If that's all, you're dismissed."

The men get up, but I give Vitaly a look that tells him to stay behind. He sits back down, waiting as the men disperse from the boardroom.

"I'm coming with you tonight," I say, once we're alone.

His eyes widen. "Isn't it too dangerous, sir?"

"I'm the pakhan of this bratva, and I won't sit by while men like Remy Morrone make a mockery of my family. He shot Maxim, and he'll feel the full force of my rage. I need to be there."

He bows his head. "Of course, you'll be a valuable asset." His brow furrows. "Do we intend to hit it while people are inside?"

I shake my head. "Thursday night they're shut, so as far as I'm aware. No, there won't be anyone inside. At least not civilians." I may be ruthless, but organizations that bring civilians into the mix come under heavy scrutiny. We pay off hundreds of officials to keep hush about our operations and bury it, but when you kill civilians everything becomes more complicated.

Vitaly looks relieved at my answer. "Fair enough, but I doubt it'll be unguarded."

"No, it won't be. We will need to be heavily armed and ready for a fight." I pace the width of the board-room. "As long as no one slips the information to the Morrone family, we'll have the element of surprise."

"Do you believe we have a rat in the ranks?" Vitaly asks.

I shrug. "We still don't know who slipped the infor-mation about Maxim and Livia's wedding." I scrub a hand over my jaw. "Maxim is convinced it was Artyom."

Vitaly nods. "I wouldn't put it past him, sir."

"No, neither would I." I slide my fingers through my messy hair. "He wasn't in attendance today, even though he said he would be."

His brow pulls together. "Why wasn't he here?"

I shake my head. "No, idea. I intend to drag him along with me tonight, to ensure he can't fuck this up."

There's one thing I know for sure, and that is that I can't trust my brother. Ever since this war broke out, he's been more opposed to my ideas than ever before. I sense he's up to something, and that's why Timur has him on twenty-four seven surveillance. If he puts one foot wrong, I won't hesitate to end him. I don't care if he's my brother.

Anyone who crosses me dies. There are no exceptions.

THE CITY IS QUIET TONIGHT, unusually so.

Perhaps it's the calm before the storm. Le Stelle is shut, as it is every Thursday. We can't be sure whether there's anyone inside, but I don't care. War means collateral damage.

"Vitaly, what's the plan?" I ask, glancing at my brigadier.

He clears his throat. "I'll enter through the back entrance and ensure there are no alarms set. Once it's clear, I'll give the signal for everyone else to follow through the same door." He pulls out a map and places it on the floor in the back of the van. "There are four key points to the building we need to hit if we're going to do maximum damage." He points at the four points. "In teams of two, we'll split up and set the charges in those four places before returning to the door and leaving as a group." He shrugs. "Once we're all out, then we hit the detonator."

Excitement pulses through my veins at the thought of the utter chaos we're going to leave in our wake. "It's likely some men will be inside, so keep your wits about you. Shoot first and make sure they can't alert their boss."

Artyom shuffles uncomfortably next to me. "Are you sure this is a good idea?"

I give my brother a pointed look. "Are you questioning my decision on the cusp of pulling it off?"

His brow pulls together. "No, I'm merely saying this is fucking insane."

"Pull yourself together and get suited up," I say, grabbing my bulletproof vest and putting it on over my shirt. None of us are taking any risks tonight. If we pull this off, it'll be the greatest fucking move of this war. While the Irish have been our focus, and we're still hitting their supply chain, we need to bring the Morrone family down a peg.

Once I'm kitted up with enough weapons, I turn to my men. "Ready?"

"Yes, sir," they all respond, except for Artyom, who shakes his head in disapproval.

"Come on," I say, opening the back of the van and jumping out into the dark alleyway behind Le Stelle. Artyom sticks near me, since we've been tasked with setting the charges on the west-side of the building. Vitaly and one of his more junior soldiers, Ilya, are setting them on the upper levels. Jakov is his second in command and along with Ilari, they're going to set charges in the basement and lastly Matvey and Pyotr are going to set the charges on the east.

Vitaly nods toward the back of the alleyway, cloaked in shadow. "Wait there until I give you the signal."

We move fluidly into the shadows, watching from

afar as Vitaly works his magic. Within a couple of minutes, he has picked the lock into the place and disappears inside. There's a tension amongst the men, but I'm hyped up. It's been too long since I felt the rush of being in the field like this.

After another minute, Vitaly returns and gives us the nod.

I charge in first, followed by my brother. The rest of the men follow close behind.

"Any signs of guards?" I whisper.

Vitaly shakes his head. "Not yet."

"Okay, keep alert and get your charges set as fast as possible and meet back here." I glance at Stas, a soldier on Vitaly's team. "You keep guard and radio us if there's any movement."

"Sir," he says, nodding.

I glance at Artyom and nod in the direction we've got to go, keeping my gun out in front of me as I move. "Stay close," I breathe.

"This is insane."

"Quit your whining and get your head in the game."

He falls silent, keeping his gun outstretched and scanning the vicinity as we move through the dark, deserted club. My brother's too loud breathing fills the air as we reach the west wing of the building.

"Do you have the charges?" I ask.

Artyom lifts the bag housing them and I snatch them from him, opening it and quickly getting to work at setting them up. As always, my lazy brother stands guard, but he wouldn't know the first thing about setting up a bomb.

I guess he resents me because my father taught me everything and left Artyom to navigate this world alone, since he would not inherit the throne. Little does he know the blessing that was, as it meant he didn't have to endure the brunt of my father's abusive behavior.

However, I know it's what made me the man I am today. A feared ruler, rather than a weak one.

Once all the charges are in place, I turn to him and nod. "Let's get the fuck out of here."

"I won't argue with that," he says, pacing ahead of me.

"Where were you this afternoon?" I ask, as it's been bugging me ever since he didn't show up.

"Axel wanted the meeting this afternoon, and I thought it more important to attend that."

I growl. "You think some redneck hillbilly biker is more important than a Bratva meeting?"

He sighs heavily. "The deal I brokered with him could increase our revenue by millions." He shrugs. "I'll give you the details tomorrow so you can consider it."

I narrow my eyes, as I'm not a man who backs down. Axel is a piece of shit and so are his men. They're bottom feeders who leech off of the scum of the city, plowing the poorest people full of product with no care in the world. Too many people OD on Axel's shit and I won't shoulder than responsibility. It will bring the police down on us hard.

We may have a lot of crooked cops in our pockets, but there's a reason for that. Our trade is discreet and high-end. We make more money selling our shit to rich buyers who pay a premium for how good our product is. The bikers cut it, which is dangerous and reckless.

"I wouldn't get your hopes up," I say, as we make it back to the door. My shoulders sag in relief as Stas, Vitaly, Ilya, Jakov and Ilari come into view, already back and waiting by the door. "Where's Matvey and Pytor?"

Vitaly shrugs. "Not back yet. I'm sure they'll be here shortly."

"No signs of anyone in the building?" I ask.

All four men shake their heads, which only fills me with dread. I expected a few guards at least, and I don't like it when things are too easy. It's unnerving.

As if on cue with my thoughts, a gunshot has all of us freezing to the spot as we simultaneously grab our guns. It came from the East of the building. "Fuck," I say, shaking my head. "They must have encountered trouble." I give Vitaly a look. "You come with me to check it out. If we don't return in five minutes." I glance at my brother. "You leave."

Jakov clears his throat. "Sir, isn't it—"

"No questions, Jakov. Five minutes and then leave." I nod to Vitaly, who follows me toward the east wing of the club as another gunshot sounds, sending adrenaline pulsing through my veins. It's been too fucking long since I felt a rush like this. The build up to a fight can be so intoxicating.

Vitaly is close by my side, scanning the dark club. "How many do you think are here?" He whispers.

I shrug. "Not many, or we would have heard more gunshots."

"Fuck," I hear someone mutter from my left.

I give Vitaly the signal to be quiet and to keep watch while I investigate.

The concern etched into his features is clear. As Pakhan, my men believe they should keep me out of harm's way. I creep toward the source of the noise to find Matvey lying on his back, a gunshot through his side. His eyes widen when he sees me.

I crouch down. "Where is Pytor?" I whisper.

"Dealing with Morrone's men," he replies, wincing as he tries to sit up.

"How many?" I ask.

He shrugs. "Three, I think." He nods up ahead. "They're up there."

I nod and return to Vitaly. "Matvey is injured. Pytor is taking on three men ahead."

Another gunshot sounds, and a thud as a body hits the floor. I swallow hard and push on, knowing that we're at risk of losing good men. We come to the body and thankfully it's not Pytor. It's a young Italian who Pytor obviously shot through the head, which means he's still alive.

"Over there," Vitaly whispers, signaling to movement ahead.

I move slowly and quietly toward the movement, finding Pytor and another guy wrestling on the ground, trying to kill each other.

I cock my gun, which draws both of their attention to me. "Get off my man before I blow your brains out," I say, my voice calm yet deadly.

The man's eyes widen when he sees me and he rolls off him, holding his hands in the air. He opens his mouth to speak, but I don't hesitate. I shoot him through the head and blood splatters my face and shirt as he drops to the floor. We can't have any witnesses. Even if Remy will suspect me, I won't have it confirmed by his men.

I walk to Pytor and offer him my hand, dragging him to his feet.

"Thanks for the assist, sir." His brow furrows. "Thankfully, no one got word out as far as I'm aware. I dealt with them as fast as I could."

I nod. "Are the charges set?"

"Yes, but Matvey is shot." He nods to where I found the young brigadier.

"We need to get out of here." I rush back toward Vitaly and Matvey.

"Help me get him to his feet," I say to Vitaly, who gets on his left and I get on his right, supporting him. Matvey has gone almost white from the blood loss as we hobble back to the exit.

Artyom is the only one waiting. "Where are the others?" I ask.

"In the van with the engine running." He glances at his watch. "You cut it fine. It's been six minutes, but I didn't want to give up yet." He eyes Matvey's injury, and the blood splattered over my face and shirt.

He leads the way out of the club and we bundle Matvey into the back of the van. Artyom jumps in with him to see if he can stem the bleeding, but I get in the passenger's side.

Quickly, Vitaly reverses out of the alleyway and then hits the road slowly. He comes to a stop once we're a safe distance away and meets my gaze. "Ready, sir?"

I nod. "Light it up."

He smirks as he grabs the detonator and presses the button, followed by a boom that shakes the ground beneath us as the building shatters apart. I watch as bricks and mortar crumble and a cloud of ash rises into the sky, knowing it's the start of havoc like we've never seen before. I live for havoc and chaos.

The question is, do my enemies?

9

IMALIA

A sharp knock echoes through my dreams, pulling me out of the light slumber I'd fallen into. I sit up, realizing I fell asleep still wrapped in a towel. The exhaustion I feel is beyond anything I've experienced before, but I claw myself off the bed and approach the door, hugging the towel tightly around me.

An older woman is standing in the doorway, holding a tray of food. She smiles kindly. "I brought you some food on request of the pakhan."

I swallow hard, my stomach giving an embarrassing growl as the delicious scent hits my nostrils. "Thank you, I'm rather hungry."

She comes past me into the bedroom and sets the tray down on the coffee table in the corner. I was so out of it when Spartak brought me in here, I hardly looked around. There's a coffee table set in the corner and two chesterfield leather sofas positioned on either side, along with a large flatscreen television on the wall. "There you go. I'll let you eat in peace," she says, walking toward the door.

"Thank you. What's your name?" I ask, wondering if this kind woman realizes I'm a prisoner or not.

"Olga. Enjoy your food." She turns to leave again.

"Wait." I stop her, clutching onto a small strand of hope that she might help me. "Can you help me?" I ask.

Her eyes narrow as she turns to look at me, and that friendly aurora around her disappears. "Help you?" She asks, her tone colder.

"Yes, I've been kidnapped and I—"

"I'll stop you right there." She holds up her hand, face turning furious. "Out of all the people Spartak tortures and holds prisoner, never once has he asked me to bring food to one of them in his own room." Her nostrils flare and she shakes her head. "You don't need help, but clearly you're stupid enough not to realize it."

"I miss my family," I say, pain clawing at my throat. It's hard to believe that she can be so cold toward a woman who has been taken against her will.

"It's not my problem," she says, turning her back on me. "Eat your food and be thankful you aren't still in that basement." With that, she walks out of the room, firmly locking the door behind her.

My shoulders dip and any ounce of hope I had fades away. As I glance at the food, my stomach rumbles again. I scrunch my nose, hating that I have to accept anything from these people, but knowing that I haven't eaten in two days and will probably go mad if I don't eat. I sit down and pick at the food.

It's a spread of flatbreads, dried meat, pickles and cheese. As well as a rather delicious looking slab of chocolate cake, that makes my mouth water. I arrange the cheese and meat on the flatbread and nibbling at it. It's good, but that might be because I'm so darn hungry.

Once I've finished most of the food, I wash it down with a pint of orange juice and then turn my attention to the television. The remote is on the coffee table, so I pick it up and turn it on.

My heart skips a beat when I do as it's set on security cameras over the entire property. I spot Olga in what I assume must be the kitchen, washing up. There're screens set up all over the mansion I've yet to see properly, even screens in the torture chambers.

My stomach churns as the bed I'd been lying on is in clear view, making me wonder if Spartak watched me while I was down there. He says he got caught up, but I wonder if it was part of his fun witnessing me in distress, chained up and powerless. A shiver courses down my spine as another screen shows a similar room, but there's no bed, just a hard wooden chair in the center stained with blood.

I guess I got off lightly being offered a bed. As I glance around the room—Spartak's room—my stomach flutters with nerves. Now he has me in his room as his personal plaything and it scares me not solely because the man isn't right in the head, but because every time he touches me, I love it. The desire to submit to a man like him has been on my mind for a long time. I never had the guts to explore my kinks.

Now, I don't have a choice, and that makes this even more exciting. I shake my head and try to force the fucked-up thoughts out of my mind. And switch over the source on the television, shocked when I see my uncle's club in the headlines on the news. It's late, just past eleven o'clock. And the headline is 'an explosion at Le Stelle'.

I turn up the sound as the newscaster says. "It's rumored that out-of-control gang wars are responsible for the explosion, but the police are questioning any witnesses or people in connection to the club."

I swallow hard, wondering if Spartak is responsible. After all, Uncle Remy's men shot his son. The only viable retaliation to that is a hit on his most lucrative operation. It's never sat well with my mom that her brother is so deeply involved in trafficking of women. I think it's harder to accept as a woman, whereas men just see it as business.

I bite my bottom lip, hating that since Spartak left I've been beyond horny, desperate for him to return. Any sane person wouldn't be thinking about their kidnapper in that way, but perhaps Spartak and I have something in common. We're fucked in the head.

As that thought enters my mind, the lock to the bedroom turns over and the door swings open. My stomach dips when I see Spartak walk in with a wild look in his gray-blue eyes. And then my eyes drop down to the blood splattered all over his shirt. It's a haunting image to behold as he storms right past me as if I'm not even here, walking straight into the adjoining bathroom.

I turn off the television, certain now that he was indeed responsible. After all, why else has he charged in here so late with blood all over him? My mind runs wild as I wonder who the blood belongs to. Concern coils through me as I wonder if it's the blood of a family member, as he doesn't care who he hurts to get what he wants.

The rush of water from the shower echoes from the bathroom as Spartak left the door ajar. I tap my feet on the floor, curious about my kidnapper.

Did he forget I'm even in here?

I glance at the door, wanting to steal a peek at him despite the danger. If he were to catch me, God knows what he'd do. My nipples peak and I stand, driven by the idea of him punishing me for spying on him.

It's insane, but for a while I've wondered if I'm not quite right in the head. Perhaps we can be insane together. I creep toward the door and glance through the crack, drawing in a sharp intake of breath when I see him.

Spartak has his eyes shut and his back against the

shower wall, facing me. His hard and huge cock is in his hand as he strokes it up and down slowly, making my mouth water at the sight. I groan at how big he is, even though I had him in my mouth. A soft groan escapes his lips, echoing through the room and toward the doorway as he increases the pace.

I squeeze my thighs together. The need is so intense it's as if I'll burst into flames any moment if I don't get some relief. After all, Spartak has left me on the edge more than once now.

I slide my fingers under the towel and rub my clit, watching the man who kidnapped me. The shame of watching him quickly melts away as I thrust my fingers inside of myself. The mere fantasy of Spartak thrusting his cock inside of me drives me wild as he fists himself harder and faster.

His body is beyond perfect as his muscles tense. I let my eyes move further up his body, taking in every single inch of him and memorizing it. When I get to his face, I freeze. Spartak's eyes are open and glued to me. Once our eyes meet, a smirk twists onto his lips and I squeal, rushing away from the door.

Shit.

He just caught me fingering myself and watching him in the shower. I fling myself into the bed and under the covers, trying to forget what had just happened. The rush of water continues, but suddenly I hear soft footsteps padding across the hardwood floor.

He yanks the covers off of me and stands over me,

dripping wet and naked. His hard cock dangling inches from me. "Out of the bed and in the shower now," he barks.

I shake my head, backing away from him. "I'm sorry, I won't do it—"

He grabs a fistful of my hair and yanks me with it out of the bed, pulling me against him. Only my towel separates his nakedness and mine. "I don't want to hear excuses, baby girl. We both know what you were doing. In the shower, I won't ask again."

I shudder, staring into those cold gray eyes. "Fine." I yank myself free and rush toward the bathroom. Fear overwhelms the desire, and I shut the door and lock it behind me, which results in a lionlike growl from Spartak.

"Don't play games, Imalia. I'll break the fucking door down and be far more angry by the time I get to you." He knocks harshly on the door. "Open it, or endure my wrath."

I stare at the door, shuddering.

Why the hell did I have to spy on him?

"Or perhaps that's what you want," he continues, knocking the door harder now. "Maybe you want me angry and vicious, ready to tear you apart."

I shake my head and force my shaking limbs forward, unlocking the door and swiftly moving away from it.

Spartak enters slowly, eyes trained on me like a lion

ready to pounce on its prey. "Wise choice," he says, walking toward me.

I step backward, moving away from him. "Please, don't—"

"Don't what, baby girl?" He asks, cutting me off before I can finish my sentence. "Are you begging me not to give you what you want?" He stops once he's a foot away from me, tilting his head slightly as his eyes dip down my towel clad body.

"And what do you believe that is?" I ask.

His smirk widens. "This," he says, fisting the huge length between his thighs.

The movement draws my attention to his cock again, which I'd been desperately trying not to look at. "I don't know what you're talking about."

He steps the last step toward me, backing me against the wall. "You're such a naughty liar, little lamb." He tilts his head. "How shall I punish you?"

My knees shake as I press my back hard against the wall. The word punish arouses me more, which I hate. I need to control myself around this man, but it's hard when he's standing in all his naked glory, staring at me as if he wants to consume me.

"Perhaps I'll get that paddle back out and paint your ass with the word, daddy. After all, someone rudely interrupted us the last time." He grasps my throat firmly, nostrils flaring. "I can't stop thinking about your pretty little ass, Malishka."

My nipples are so hard they ache against the rough

fabric of the towel. "Please, don't do that," I say, but my plea is feeble and pathetic. "Did you leave me for two days on purpose?"

A flash of rage enters those otherwise cold and calculating eyes of his. "Don't be so ridiculous."

"Why do you have cameras, then? Was it fun to watch me in distress?" I push, knowing I need the answer to this question.

His jaw works as he tightens his grip on my throat so hard I'm sure he's about to strangle me. "Careful, baby girl. I may be crazy, but I'm anything but a liar." He moves his lips to within an inch of mine, staring me right in the eyes. "If I'd been taking pleasure out of watching you on that camera, then I'd fucking well tell you." His lips skirt over mine, barely touching. "I was otherwise indisposed with a war."

As I stare into his manic, yet beautiful eyes, I know he's telling the truth. Why would he lie to me? He doesn't care about my opinion of him, which he's made abundantly clear from the start. "Please let go of me," I rasp, struggling to breathe.

He releases my throat and grabs the towel I'm wearing instead, yanking it off.

I swallow hard as it falls away and his eyes drag slowly over every exposed inch of my skin. This is the most naked I've been in front of him, the most vulnerable.

"So fucking beautiful," he muses, gripping the heavy

length of his cock and tugging at it. "It's time we got better acquainted, Imalia."

Dread and arousal morph into the most confusing sensation I've ever experienced as I stare at my kidnapper, realizing how fucked up this situation is. If I ever make it out of here, I'm not sure I'll be the same again.

10

SPARTAK

*I*malia cowers away from me, her fear only driving me on.

She can't deny the truth. My little lamb wants me as badly as I want her. After all, I caught her with her fingers in her cunt as she fingered herself, watching me stroke my cock. There's no going back from being caught in such a compromising position.

"Stop fighting it and embrace the darkness," I murmur, reaching for her. I grab her hips in my hands and drag her against me, groaning when her large, firm breasts press against my ribcage. "It's time for you to accept your predeliction."

Her slender throat bobs as she swallows. "What predeliction?"

I smirk at her feigned innocence. "The desire to be taken against your will, malishka." I press my lips to her neck and sink my teeth into it, making her whimper.

"The desire to be dominated in every possible way," I breathe.

Imalia shudders against me, her knees wobbling so much I'm sure she'd collapse if I didn't support her. "I-I don't know what you're—"

I spank her firm ass hard with my hand, forcing her to stop mid-sentence. "And the desire for pain and punishment. Lying is the best way to get punished, baby girl."

Her lip quivers as she tries to pull away from me, but I keep my body pressed to hers. "Please don't do this," she murmurs, beautiful brown eyes blazing with a desire that drives me insane.

I groan, as I love hearing her beg me. "Is that what you want?" I move my lips to her collarbone, pressing soft kisses along it. "Or do you want me to continue, despite you begging me to stop?" I sink my teeth into her collarbone, which results in a sharp hiss of pleasure as her body jolts toward me. "I think that's exactly what you want," I murmur, before pushing away from her. "Get in the shower, now."

Imalia holds my gaze for a few beats before finally admitting defeat and walking toward the shower.

My cock twitches when I see the dark bruises visible on her beautiful, firm ass. I follow her, knowing that there's no holding back anymore. Remy Morrone wouldn't agree to my terms, so Imalia is mine in every sense of the word. I intend to stake my claim on her body, mind, and fucking soul.

She gets under the spray of the water, keeping her back to me as I enter the cubicle.

"Look at me, little lamb," I say.

Her shoulders heave as she breathes heavily before turning around to face me. Those beautiful brown eyes are filled with unshed tears as she struggles to hold my gaze. "What are you going to do to me?"

I move closer to her, grabbing her hips in a firm and possessive grasp. "Claim you," I breathe, unaffected by her fear. I've never had any morals.

Her body trembles. "Why?"

The ultimate question. Why this pretty little lamb? After all this time, I've kept every sexual encounter purely detached. Most of the women I've been with since my wife were hookers, and I'd never see them again afterward.

And then, I looked into those dark brown eyes and saw myself in this girl. A beautiful butterfly being held back by her cocoon, unable to free herself from a society that expects her to fit into a box. We're all bound by society's expectations, but there are few people like her and I that are truly suffocated by them.

"Because you are smothered by all the bullshit your family, your friends, and everyone around you expect you to conform to." I slide my fingers higher and trace the womanly curves of her form. "I can spot a caged lamb from a mile off, malishka. Now stop fighting your-self and accept the truth." I press my lips to hers, kissing her deeply. My tongue thrusts in and out of her mouth, making her moan as I caress her breasts with my calloused hands. "You've been longing for a man to dominate you for as long as you can remember, haven't you?"

Imalia swallows, eyes dilated with longing as she nods her head only a fraction, still too scared to admit it.

"Good girl," I breathe, sliding my fingers between her legs and feeling the wetness pooling between them. "Do you want to please daddy?"

Her nostrils flare as she instinctively clenches her thighs the moment I say that word, proving how much she longs to call me it. "I told you, I'd rather—"

I bite her lip hard, making her yelp. "Don't lie to me, Imalia. You don't mean it." I run the flat of my tongue across her lip. "Death is something you should never speak of so lightly." I thrust two fingers inside of her, making her moan. "I want you to just feel, stop thinking with that pretty little head of yours."

"Fuck," she breathes, as I finger fuck her roughly.

Her body shudders as I hook my fingers forward, stroking the spot that's guaranteed to force her to come undone.

"Good girl, let go for me, baby girl," I murmur, adding another finger and stretching her tight cunt more.

She bites her bottom lip, eyes dilating. "Okay."

I can sense she's close to breaking point as I still my

fingers inside of her and move my lips to an inch of hers. "Okay what?"

Her eyes flash. "I'm not saying it."

"Why not?" I bite her bottom lip hard enough to break the skin, groaning when I taste her blood. "What are you afraid of?"

"You," she breathes.

"Now that's not true, is it, little lamb?" I move my mouth to her neck and bite her there, sucking on the flesh to leave a bruise. "You're not scared of me. You're scared that if you fall into the madness with me, that you'll love it too much to claw yourself back out."

I move my fingers inside of her again, making her whimper. "Tell me I'm wrong, Imalia."

She holds my gaze, but doesn't say a word, because we both know that I'm right. I rarely read people incorrectly. Instead, she tentatively moves toward me and grabs a fistful of my hair, dragging me toward her. "You win," she breathes into my ear.

My cock swells hearing her say that, as I kiss her lips, enjoying the victory. "Tell me what you want me to do, baby girl."

"I want you to let me go home." There's an odd spark in her eyes, as if she's reluctant to tell me she wants me, because it will shatter the fantasy she longs to live.

"I'll never let you go," I say, grabbing hold of her legs and lifting her against the wall. My cock nudges against her soaking wet entrance. All it would take was a firm thrust, and I'd be buried inside of her.

"What are you—"

I thrust forward only an inch, allowing the head of my cock to slide through her soaking wet lips. "Fight me, baby girl," I murmur.

She digs her nails into my skin, dragging them down my chest. "Please, stop,"

I bite her earlobe and thrust forward more. "I don't care what those pretty little lips say. I knew the moment I saw you that you were a dirty little girl who longed to be dominated by a real man."

She whimpers, sinking her teeth into her bottom lip. "Spartak, please," she begs, but it's not clear if she's begging me for my cock or to stop. Either way, nothing could stop me now, short of a fucking gunshot to the head.

I thrust my hips forward and bury myself balls deep inside of her. The release of finally being inside her is exquisite and exactly what I need right now. "Fuck, you're tight," I growl.

Imalia's mouth falls open, but nothing comes out as she stares into my eyes. Her body tense and yet her pussy dripping wet and coating my cock. "Don't do this," she grinds out behind closed teeth.

I grab her bruised ass cheeks and part them further, allowing my cock to sink a little deeper. "You are mine," I murmur against her skin. "I don't care if you beg me to stop, because deep down I know you don't fucking want that." My teeth graze her neck before I sink them hard into her skin, breaking it. "You want my cock more than anything, but you're too stubborn to admit it. Either that or you fucking love telling me to stop while I continue on, anyway."

I pull back and look into her haunted brown eyes. "Which is it?"

She sucks on her thick bottom lip. "I'm sick."

I shake my head. "No, society is sick for making you think there's anything fucking wrong with you."

She moves her hands from my shoulders into my hair, tugging at it. "I like being taken against my will," she admits, wincing as it finally leaves her lips.

"Good girl," I breathe, kissing her deeply. "Such a good girl for telling daddy the truth."

She moans, eyes rolling back in her head as I praise her the way she desires. "Fuck me," she murmurs.

"What's the magic word?" I ask, teasing her. She knows what I want to hear, what I know she longs to call the man in her life, which is what I intend to be from here on in.

She can fight it all she likes, but we're meant for each other. I knew it the moment we met. Imalia is a girl who can accept who I am. The real Spartak Volkov. She may even be a girl who can grow to love the monster behind the man.

"Fuck me, please."

I shake my head. "Don't play dumb with me. Or I'll tie you to my bed and leave you desperate for release."

I'm well aware that I've left her gagging for release twice, and this would be the third time. She's too desperate not to give me what I want.

"Fuck me, daddy," she says, her voice so quiet, but it's enough. By the time I'm through with her, she won't be able to stop screaming that word.

I lose control at that moment, thrusting my hips into her with hard, powerful strokes as her back slams against the shower wall. "Good girl," I murmur, dragging my teeth down her neck. "I know how badly you want daddy's cock, malishka, because your tight little cunt is soaking wet, gripping my cock like a vice." I dig my fingertips hard into her hips, knowing I'll leave bruises. "Moan for me, like a good little girl."

She moans, her walls slowly tumbling away as she accepts the inevitable. The moment our eyes met in that warehouse, she belonged to me. She was just too stubborn to admit it until now.

My muscles strain as I fuck her against the wall, trying to break her apart as I promised I would. I slip my cock out of her, which results in a whine of protest from her. "Turn around for me and put your hands on the wall, malishka."

She swallows hard, her delicate throat bobbing before she turns around, setting her hands on the wall and arching her back for me.

"Good girl," I breathe, grabbing her bruised ass cheeks and parting them. My cock twitches as I consider thrusting my dick in her tight little back hole.

"Have you ever had anything in here?" I ask, pressing my finger to her puckered ring of muscles.

Imalia shudders, hesitating about answering. "I have used toys, but my ex never wanted to try anal."

I growl, irritated by the mention of another man. "That's because he was a boy and not a man." I wrap my hand around her throat, forcing her back to arch further. "Would you like daddy to fuck that pretty little asshole?" I breathe.

Her entire body shakes. "I don't think it would fit."

I bite her shoulder hard, leaving my teeth marks on her skin. "Believe me, I'll make it fit." I grab a bottle of lotion off the caddy and lube up my finger, sliding it inside her tight little hole. "Fuck, it's tight, baby girl."

"Please don't, it's too much."

I groan as I slide my finger in and out of her, lining my cock up with her pussy. Thrusting forward, I bury myself to the hilt with my finger still lodged in her ass. "Don't worry, we'll work you up to my cock. By the time I'm finished with you, you'll be begging for a dildo in your tight little cunt and my cock in your ass, tearing you apart while you scream daddy for me."

She doesn't fight this time, moaning loudly. Her muscles flutter around my cock, warning me she's close to coming undone.

"And because you are such a good girl, you will love everything fucking second. Won't you?" I ask, slamming my cock in and out of her in slow, yet forceful thrusts.

"No," she breathes, shaking her head. "This is wrong."

"You haven't got close to seeing how wrong I can get," I murmur into her ear, nipping at the sensitive flesh of her earlobe. "When you do, you'll either embrace the darkness or fucking drown in it."

I slam into her with more speed, struggling to hold myself back as her cunt grips me so tightly. "I hope it's the former, little lamb. As you'll realize just how fun it can be to break societal norms. To revel in your deepest and darkest desires. And I'm going to be the man to coax them from you, no matter how hard you fight to bury them."

"Fuck," she moans, her thighs trembling as her release hits her. "Oh God," she screams.

I bite down hard on her shoulder as she comes apart, groaning when she squirts all over my cock, a flood of liquid gushing all over my balls. "You come so fucking well, baby girl. Such a good girl coming on daddy's cock like that," I breathe, knowing one more thrust will force me apart along with her.

I grab her hips hard and slam into her with all my force, making her yelp in pain as I bottom out as deep as fucking possible inside of her and spill my cum. The idea of making my little lamb pregnant drives me wild, even though she's fucking twenty years younger than me. It calls to a sick part of me that once she's growing big and round with my baby, there'll be no doubt who she belongs to.

"Good girl, take daddy's cum inside of you," I murmur, thrusting repeatedly until my balls are spent. "Are you on any birth control?" I ask.

She gasps, trying to pull away from me. "Shit, no!"

"Good," I say, holding still deep inside of her. "I want you pregnant with my child."

"Are you fucking insane?" She asks, still trying to wrestle away from me.

"I thought we'd already covered that. Yes, I am, and you love it." I wrap a hand around her stomach and pull my cock out, groaning when I see some of my cum escape. "You need to lie down, so my cum doesn't drip out of you."

"I can't get pregnant with your baby, you psycho!" She gets free of me and turns around, slapping me hard in the face.

I growl, and lift her over my shoulder, carrying her to the bed as she tries to beat against my back. "Stop fighting the inevitable, Imalia. You're mine in every sense of the word and if I want you pregnant with my baby, then that's what'll happen." I slam her down on her back, towering over her. "Accept it and stop fighting. You don't have a choice."

"So now I'm some prize breeding bitch?" She asks, her voice furious. "You're locking me in a cage and fucking breeding me like an animal."

"You're being irrational."

"Me?" she shrieks, shaking her head in disbelief. "I'm not the irrational one here."

I clench my jaw and chuck on a shirt and grab a pair of sweatpants, throwing them on. "I'll leave you to cool off." I turn around and head out of the room, leaving her to calm down. Clearly, she's not yet embracing her new reality, but once she does, it will be easier for both of us. I'm hers and she's mine. The sooner she accepts it, the better. There is no escape for her.

Imalia is never leaving me. I won't apologize for the darkness that rules me, and deep down she longs to be embraced by it. The pretty little Italian will be bound to me in unbreakable ways, ensuring she'll never escape. Soon enough, she won't want to. I guarantee it.

11

IMALIA

*a*fter attempting to force open the second-floor window for over two hours, I slump exhausted to the bathroom floor and sob like a baby. The tears come like a river as my chest heaves up and down. Never in my twenty-six years of life have I never been so helpless and pathetic.

I tried to pick the lock to the door, but it's not any old lock. It's sophisticated, and I'd imagine even the most skilled locksmith might not be able to break it open.

I may have wanted Spartak for a moment. While he was fucking me, I felt free for the first time in my life. The way he praises me and talks dirty to me drives me wild, but then the fantasy was shattered when he revealed how fucking insane he truly is. My mind can't stop replaying his words like a broken fucking record.

You're mine in every sense of the word and if I want you pregnant with my baby, then that's what will happen.

He's crazy if he intends to keep me locked up here forever and breed me. Uncle Remy won't stand for it and neither will my mom, which means we'll be in the middle of the most intense mafia war any of us have ever seen. I long to go home to San Diego so badly right now, but this place is a fucking fortress. There's no escape from the monster who holds me captive.

The worst part of all is that I gave him what he wanted. Despite vowing to never call him daddy, I did, and loved calling him that until he revealed his insane plan to make me pregnant with his child. There'd be no going back from that. It wouldn't matter if he forced it upon me. I'd be carrying a Volkov baby, and he'd have a rightful claim over me.

Remy or my mom couldn't fight him if that became a reality. Regret charges through me as I stopped getting the contraceptive shot three months ago when I split with Liam, so it will be well and truly out of my system by now.

I hear the lock turning in the door, making dread seize hold of me. After all, it's early morning and Spartak hasn't returned to his own bedroom. It's likely to be him. Footsteps pad through the bedroom toward the bathroom door, which I locked. After all, I didn't want to be caught trying to escape.

"Imalia," Spartak says my name, making sickness coil through me. "Are you in there?"

I remain quiet, staring at the door. The man behind it is a monster, and I'd rather die in here than face him. As soon as he left the bedroom, I sat on the toilet and tried to drain every drop of his cum out of me. I'm not ready to be a mother, and especially not to a psychopath's child.

He bangs on the door loudly, making me jump. "Open the door."

I stand to my feet and grab the screwdriver I found, wielding it as my weapon. It's useless against the window, as I'd hoped removing some screws may have made it possible to open, but it's designed so that no one can open it without a key, which makes me wonder how many girls he's held captive in here.

"Open the door or I'll break it down," he growls, sounding angrier than I've ever heard him.

"Never," I shout back, clinging to the screwdriver as if it will protect me. If he breaks down the door, I'm not stupid enough to believe I could overpower him and do damage with a fucking screwdriver. "I'd rather die."

"That can be arranged, little lamb."

I shudder. "Don't call me that." I hate that he keeps calling me a lamb, as if I'm his prey. No doubt he sees himself as the lion, ready to devour me.

"What else should I call you?" He says, his voice oddly calm, considering.

I don't answer his question, keeping my back pressed against the furthest wall.

"Open the door, Imalia," he says again, voice dangerously low. "I won't ask you again."

"Fuck you!"

It goes silent on the other side of the door as I hold my breath, waiting for his next move. And then I hear a jangle of keys on the other side and one slipping into the lock, and I can't believe how stupid I've been. Of course, he has the keys to his own bathroom lock. "You'll wish you opened this door, Imalia." He pushes it open and I keep the screwdriver in front of me, thrusting it forward.

"Stay the fuck back."

He tilts his head. "What exactly have you been doing with that, baby girl?" His eyes move to the window, which is scratched up in my attempts to force it open. They narrow as they move back to me. "Trying to escape?" he asks, shaking his head. "There's no escape from me." He moves forward.

"I'll stab you with this screwdriver." My hand shakes, betraying the fact that I even have what it takes to stab a person. "I'm serious."

"Just like you were going to stab me with the knife?" he asks, amusement in his tone. "And I thought we'd made progress, especially after you called me daddy."

"That was before you told me you intend to get me pregnant." I glare at him. "I made sure I got as much of your cum out of me as physically possible after you left."

His eyes flash and he comes for me fast. I thrust the

screwdriver forward hard, embedding it in his chest. He doesn't cry out, glancing down at it as blood stains his shirt.

I shake, my hand still gripping the handle.

"Twist it, little lamb, see how much you can hurt me," he goads.

I stare at him, knowing I'm not cut out to stand up to his depravity. When I do nothing, he closes his hand around mine and twists, making more blood stain his shirt as he shuts his eyes and groans. "I love pain, baby girl, so stabbing me only made me horny." He uses his other hand to pull down his sweatpants and reveal his rock hard cock. "Do you see?" He meets my gaze and twists the screwdriver more, his cock twitching and leaking precum. "I fucking love it."

I shudder, realizing I never should have tried to stand up to a man like him. There's no winning against someone who has no morals or sense. He tightens his grasp on my hand and pulls the screwdriver out of his chest. "Do you enjoy making me bleed?" he asks, grabbing hold of my throat firmly and dragging me toward him. "Or would you prefer I make you bleed?"

The blood continues to ooze out of the wound, staining his shirt. He releases my throat as I stand there, frozen by fear and disgust at the way this man reacts to violence. Spartak pulls the shirt off and looks at the cut, which isn't deep but seems to bleed a lot. "Look what you did, little lamb." He grabs my throat again tightly. "Does it turn you on, hurting me?"

I shake my head, despite the desire pooling between my thighs. The sickness that tugs at my insides, daring me to fall into the darkness with him. I don't enjoy inflicting pain, but after he spanked me with that paddle, I sure as hell like being subjected to it. In fact, I crave it. Despite the fact I should crave nothing from this bastard after he revealed his true intentions.

"Come and patch me up," he orders, releasing my throat and pulling his sweatpants back up to hide his hard cock, but it still tents his tight sweatpants. "There's a medical kit under the sink." He turns and walks out of the bathroom and into the bedroom.

I swallow hard and grab the kit from under the sink, surprised he's not punishing me for stabbing him. It makes it even more scary that Spartak is so unpredictable. Tightening my grasp on the kit, I clutch it to my chest and enter the bedroom, where he is sitting on the edge of the bed, bleeding.

"There should be a needle and thread in the kit. It needs stitches."

I shake my head. "Isn't it best you see a doctor? I can't stitch you up."

"You can." He pats the space next to him. "Come here."

I slowly make my way over to the bed and sit as far as I can away from him. "I can't stitch you."

"Have you ever sewn anything before?" He asks, those cold gray eyes burning into me.

I shrug. "Sure, but that's different."

He shakes his head. "It's not. Get out the needle and thread," he instructs.

I open the medical kit and pull out the items as instructed, wishing in that moment that I hadn't stabbed him.

"Give them to me," he orders.

I place them in his hand, and he threads the needle before stitching his own wound. Blood trickles down his tattooed skin as he works.

"What are you doing?" I ask.

He narrows his eyes. "Fixing your mess, since you don't want to."

I reach for the needle. "I'll do it."

He lets go and I slowly stitch the skin together, surprised I don't feel more sickened as I watch his flesh pull back together.

"How do I tie it off?" I ask, glancing up to find him watching me intently. Those gray-blue eyes are so intense that they steal the air from my lungs.

"Just tie a knot," he says.

I swallow hard and try my best to do a neat knot, but it looks a mess. As I step back, I swallow hard. "Is that going to heal okay? As it's a pretty shitty job."

He nods and doesn't even look down at it, grabbing a dressing from the medical kit and placing it over the wound, using surgical tape to hold it. Once done, he packs up the kit and places it on the floor. "Get into bed," he orders.

I don't have the energy right now to disobey, so I get

into my side of the bed and turn my back on him. Soon enough, his arm wraps around me and he pulls me against him. "Sweet dreams, baby girl," he breathes into my ear, making me shudder.

I shut my eyes, wanting nothing more than to wake up from this nightmare.

THE LOCK CLICKS OPEN, and Olga enters, carrying a tray of food. "I bought you lunch."

I glare at the housekeeper, knowing that there's no way in hell I'm playing nice anymore. These fuckers are holding me against my will and acting as if I should be grateful that Spartak hasn't gutted me in his torture chambers instead.

Death would probably be a mercy compared to what that sick son of a bitch has planned for me.

She places it down on the coffee table. "Spartak asked me to ensure you eat it all."

I don't move from the bed, shaking my head. "I'm not hungry."

Her jaw works as she glances at the door. "I'm under instruction to get the men to force you if you don't comply. Wouldn't it be easier for you to just eat?"

I appreciate she's trying to help me avoid being manhandled, but I can't understand why a woman can happily watch while another woman is caged like an animal for a man's pleasure. "Why do you do what he says?" I ask.

Her brow furrows. "He's my pakhan."

I shake my head. "And you're alright with caging women up like breeding animals?"

Her eyes widen slightly. "You're the first woman Spartak has ever kept locked in his room." She shrugs. "Clearly you mean something to him."

My stomach flips, wondering if that's true. Am I really the first woman he's locked up in here like this, and if so, why? "He's insane, mentally ill," I say, tears prickling my eyes. "I don't want to be here."

"Come and eat," she says sternly. "I won't ask again."

I grind my teeth, but not wanting her to call the guards, I begrudgingly get out of bed and walk over in my pajamas, sitting down and picking at the food slowly.

Olga stands with her arms crossed over her chest, watching me.

"It will not help if you stand there and watch me," I say, setting down the flatbread in my hand. "Why don't you come back in an hour and I promise I'll have eaten it all."

Her eyes narrow. "Because my pakhan gave me strict instructions."

I huff and continue to eat despite having no appetite at all. As if forcing a pregnancy I don't want onto me isn't bad enough, now he's force feeding me too. "This is bullshit."

Olga glares at me. "You really don't understand how lucky you are, Imalia."

I shake my head. "Are you insane? A man who has a sick obsession has kidnapped me and is trying to force me to call him daddy. If that isn't bad enough, he's also forcefully trying to get me pregnant. How the hell am I lucky?"

Her face twists with disgust at my claims. "I don't know about all that. All I know is the Volkov Bratva captures hundreds of people and we give none of them food or a bed to sleep in. That has to be lucky, or would you rather be bleeding to death in his torture chambers?"

"Honestly, that would be kinder."

She scoffs. "Foolish, naive girl. Life is the most precious thing in this world and you want to be dead." She shakes her head. "I thought a Morrone would have more guts."

"I'm an Allegro, not a Morrone."

She waves her hand dismissively. "I don't care. Stop wallowing in self-pity."

I fall silent and finish my food in a hurry so that Olga will leave. As I hate the woman almost as much as I hate Spartak. There's no justification for his actions, even if she believes I'm lucky. Clearly, she's almost as unhinged as he is. No one would call me lucky for being locked in a cage for Spartak to use when he wants.

Once I'm done, she clears away the tray and leaves without a word, locking me inside my cage again. I slump back into the chair and turn on the television, knowing if I don't have some background noise, my thoughts will drive me insane.

SPARTAK

I crack my neck and stretch my arms out, wincing as the stitched wound Imalia inflicted on me is still hurting. It's amusing that I came away from the most dangerous operation in years unscathed, only to be injured by a little girl.

My men's eyes are on me, waiting for guidance in the most turbulent time the Bratva has ever seen.

Remy hit back almost immediately, and he hit back hard. We lost five men at the docks last night, and we didn't manage to steal the shipment of half a million dollars from the Morrone family.

Using Imalia as a bargaining chip to the end of the war is no longer an option, not that I really ever liked that idea. However, she could still prove instrumental to the end of the war, if she would stop fighting me and accept that we're meant to be together. After all, she was on the inside of the operations, which means she knows how Remy works.

Once I win her loyalty, then victory will be within my grasp. The difficulty is she's not as easy to tame as I first believed. I didn't expect she'd actually stab me with that screwdriver, but then here I stand with a fucking badly stitched up hole in my chest.

"Today we grieve for our brothers, but we also have to plan our strategy." I glance between the faces in the room, feeling Maxim's absence more than ever. He's still in hospital, which means I'm sure once he gets back I won't hear the last of this. Maxim never would have hit first the way I did yesterday. He's too strategic for that, but strategy only gets you so far. "It's only a matter of time until Remy strikes again and when he does, we're going to be prepared."

Artyom clears his throat. "How are we going to do that?"

"Glad you asked," I say, knowing that ultimately he had hoped I didn't have an answer, but I'm always prepared. "There's one glaringly obvious weakness that the Italians have overlooked, which we can exploit."

A smirk spreads onto Timur's lips, as if he knows exactly what I'm thinking, and he probably does.

"San Diego," I say.

Most of the men appear confused, but Artyom shakes his head. "Are you insane?"

"I get fed up with hearing that question from you in particular," I growl, glaring at my brother. "Remy has brought his sister and a lot of her men here, leaving San Diego open. We hit them where they're least protected and make it fucking hurt."

"The Allegros aren't truly involved in this war," my brother points out.

"The moment Diana Allegro brought her men onto Chicago soil, she involved herself."

"I like it," Timur says, giving Artyom a sharp glance. "It's smart and they won't expect it at all. It would force the Allegro family to return to San Diego, weakening Remy's power here in Chicago."

Chatter breaks out amongst the men as they discuss the plan amongst themselves.

"Silence," I order.

Everyone falls quiet. "Two groups will head down to San Diego tomorrow with Timur." I turn my attention to my sovietnik. "You'll decide which two to take with you."

He nods. "Vitaly's group and Artur's group."

"Very well," I say, thankful his choices were the right ones. They're most suited to this kind of job, particularly since they're adaptable. I give Vitaly and Artur a meaningful glance. "You'll listen to Timur as if he were your pakhan in my absence, since I'll remain in Chicago to fight the war here."

Vitaly nods.

"Of course, sir," Artur replies.

"Good," I say, running a hand across the back of my neck. "That will leave Kirill's and Roman's group here to hold the fort, but Vito will need to come through for us. We'll need his men to back us up while our numbers are down."

"About time that piece of shit pulled his weight," Artyom quips.

I ignore his comment and turn my attention to my obshchak, Osip. "Get a meeting setup with Vito for this afternoon. You and I will attend."

He bows his head. "Sir."

"Roman and Kirill, I need you both to pull together and work as a team, as the city is going to be dangerous." I have been considering how we keep our supply running when we could be hit at any turn. "Any routine you normally follow, I want it changed. We can't make it easy for them to hit us."

Kirill nods. "Yes, sir."

I glance across the faces watching me. "Does anyone have questions?"

Roman clears his throat. "Is it possible that James Kerry betrayed us? You had your doubts about his information and then Kirill's group got hit." He glances at Kirill, who bows his head in shame.

"It's possible. We will investigate." I intend to pay the piece of shit a personal visit and look into his eyes to find the truth. Men like him are easier to read than a fucking book, and he won't live another day if I believe he betrayed us to the Morrone family to make a quick profit. He may think he's untouchable being the manager of the dock, but he's fucking wrong.

Every man is replaceable and I won't hesitate to remove him from his position. "If that is all, you can get to work."

Everyone stands, except my brother. "Can I have a word?"

"Sure," I say.

"Here is the proposal from the bikers." He hands me a folder. "It's lucrative, brother." He narrows his eyes. "If we want to ensure that we keep the money flowing during the war, it makes sense to consider supplying them."

I open the folder and check the proposed figures, not finding them as impressive as my brother claims it to be. "This isn't worth the hassle. I told you I didn't want to deal with the bikers, but you wouldn't listen."

His eyes turn furious. "Axel claims he'll have no choice if we don't agree, but to approach the Morrone family."

"Let him." I wave my hand dismissively. "They can get into bed with the bikers, and it'll be their downfall." I cross my arms over my chest, standing my ground as Artyom visibly becomes angrier. "I've watched the way the bikers operate over the years, and they will cut our product too fucking much. That's why the Irish are renowned for supplying shit, even though the product they supply is probably as pure as ours." I shake my head. "I won't risk our impeccable reputation for such a small reward."

His jaw clenches and his vibrant blue eyes narrow.

"If that was your opinion, why allow me to meet with Axel?"

I shrug. "You insisted. And I'm not in the business of telling my brother what to do." I turn away from him. "Can you get Adrik and Valeri to attend a dinner at my home tomorrow night?" I ask, not looking at him. "It's been too long since we got together as a family."

"Of course. I'll make sure they're there."

"Perfect. Eight o'clock tomorrow evening." I walk away from him, feeling a sense of unease. My brother's scheming and plotting is worsening and I fear that despite Timur unable to find any concrete evidence against him, he's working to bring the bratva down and ensure I fail.

I'll be damned if I ever let him dethrone me.

THE DOCKS ARE busy as workers rush around the warehouse, distracted by a huge shipment arriving on a cargo ship.

I scan the area, searching for my intended target. The office is my first bet, which has been fashioned from an old container. I walk toward it, the weight of violence coiling beneath my skin crushing me.

If this bastard is the reason five of my brothers died, he will wish he was never born. The loss of the five hundred million dollars of product is nothing compared to five well-trained and loyal soldiers.

I walk up the ramp and knock on the door.

There's a grumble on the other side and then the door opens. James Kerry is standing on the other side and his eyes widen when he sees me. "Spartak, to what do I owe this pleasure?"

"Can I come in?" I ask.

He nods and steps aside, opening the door wide. "Of course."

As I move, the hooked blade grazes against my skin. It was the only way to get a weapon in here, keeping it beneath my clothes.

"How can I help you?" he asks, sitting down on the other side of his desk.

I tap my foot on the linoleum floor, glaring at him. "Do you have any idea how the Morrone family found out about our shipment last night?"

There's a flash of fear in his eyes the moment I mention the Morrone's name. "No idea, Mr. Volkov." His jaw ticks. Another sign that he's lying to me. "I can check who was on last night. Perhaps one of our workers tipped them off."

I step closer to the desk and lean over it, setting my hands flat on top. "Are you telling me that your workers know the contents of each shipment?"

His nostrils flare as he breathes erratically, shaking his head. "No, but it's possible they may have found out," he says, his voice increasingly less confident.

"Cut the bullshit." I walk around the side of the

desk and grab his tie, yanking him out of his seat. "Did you sell us to the Morrone family last night?"

The fear increases and the truth flashes through his eyes as he stumbles over his words. I let go of his tie and he falls back into his chair, clawing at his tie, which is tight around his throat.

"I won't ask again. Did you or didn't you betray us?"

He shakes his head. "I'd never betray the Volkov Bratva," he says, but there's uncertainty in his tone.

"Where are the ledgers?" I ask.

His eyes dart to a filing cabinet on the right and I walk over to it and open the door. However, my eyes are drawn to something on top of the cabinet. A solid gold signet ring with the Morrone family crest imprinted on it. It has to be at least an ounce of gold worth a few thousand dollars. "Well, well." I pick it up and turn it over in my hand. "Where did you get this, then?" I ask, turning to show him the ring.

His face turns ghostly pale as he stands, shaking his head. "It was a gift."

"Hmm. A gift for what, exactly?" I walk toward him, not wanting to give this snake a chance to escape my clutches. "Information on my drug shipment that cost the lives of five of my men?" I ask, continuing to corner him in behind his desk. "Stand up," I bark.

He stands, shaking like a leaf. "Please, I don't want any trouble."

"Too bad," I say, reaching under my shirt to pull out

my knife. "As you've found it, James." I grab hold of him before he can scream and slam the hook of the knife into his chest, just beneath his ribs. Blood bubbles up his throat and spills out of his mouth as I slam it in harder, looking into his pale green eyes as they widen in shock.

"No one crosses a Volkov and gets away with it." I drag the knife to the left and hit his heart, pulling on it until he dies. The satisfaction isn't enough as I watch the life leave his eyes, but I wouldn't get out of this dock alive with James in tow.

I unhook the blade from his body and wipe it clean with a handkerchief, letting his body drop to the floor in a lifeless pool of blood. Stepping away, I walk up to the mirror on the wall and observe my appearance.

I wore an entirely black suit and black shirt to ensure any possible blood stains would be difficult to detect. The knife slides back into its hiding place and I take off the gloves I wore when I entered his office.

I'm unsatisfied by the swiftness of his death, as he deserved far worse punishment. After one more glance in his direction, I walk out of the office and casually make my way back to my car in the parking lot. With any luck, I'll be long gone before anyone finds him.

The workers here will learn a hard lesson today, never cross a Volkov.

IMALIA SITS on the edge of the bed with her head in her hands as I enter the room the next evening.

"Get dressed. You're going to have dinner with my family tonight."

Her brow furrows as she looks up and meets my gaze. "Dinner?"

I nod. "Yes, I have a dress for you to wear." I hold up the garment bag. "Put it on, malishka."

She glares at me for a few beats before standing and approaching me.

It's impossible not to let my eyes wonder down her beautiful body as she moves, knowing without a doubt I've never been so consumed by another human in all my life.

Imalia snatches the garment bag out of my hand and turns toward the bathroom, but I catch her hand and yank her back against me. "Dress where I can watch you," I breathe, making her shudder as my breath hits her earlobe.

"I'd rather have privacy."

I chuckle. "I don't care, baby girl."

She releases an irritated exhale of breath before walking toward the bed and placing the garment bag on it. Slowly, she unzips it, gasping softly when she sees the dress, which she'll be breathtakingly beautiful in. "Is this a Valentino?" she asks, glancing back at me.

I nod. "Yes, only the best for my little lamb."

Her eyes narrow. "It must have cost a fortune."

"Not exactly. Fifty thousand dollars isn't a fortune."

I walk toward her and set my hands on her shoulder. "It's not nearly as much as you're worth, malishka." I take a deep breath, inhaling her sweet jasmine scent that drives me wild. "Take off your clothes."

Imalia is tense before me, but she does as I say, pulling her sweater off and then her sweatpants, standing in nothing but her lacy underwear. "I should really shower."

I shake my head. "There's no time for that, and you smell divine." I inhale her scent again. "Better than divine. Now be a good girl and put the dress on."

She glares at me over her shoulder. "How do you know it will fit?"

"Because I know everything about you." I let my eyes dip to the perfect curve of her ass, groaning as my cock strains against the zipper of my pants. "Now put the dress on before I'm forced to fuck you first."

That gets her moving as she quickly pulls out the red Valentino dress and steps into it, pulling it up to her bust. "Can you do it up for me?"

I step closer and reach for the zipper, slowly sliding it up her back. Once it's fixed, I kiss her shoulder and then neck, making her moan softly. "Unfortunately, we need to go down to dinner right away. My brother and nephews are already here."

I turn her so she can check herself out in the mirror. "You are more beautiful than any work of art I've ever seen."

Her cheeks turn a deep pink as she looks at us in the

mirror, my hand firmly pressed to her stomach as I hold her against me. It's clear as I look at the two of us how perfect we are together, even if she's yet to embrace it.

"Don't we look good together, baby girl?"

Her eyes narrow as she stares at me in the mirror. "No, we don't." She tries to pull away from me, but I hold her firm.

"In time, you will come to realize how foolish all this fighting has been." I grab her hand and spin her to face me. "Now, I want you to be a good girl at dinner. Can you do that for me?"

Her brown eyes flash with irritation as she clenches her jaw. "Fine."

I pull her against me and kiss her lips, enjoying the softness of them. "Good girl," I purr.

And then I yank her out of the room and down the corridor toward the stairs. This is the first time I've allowed her in the main house as we descend the stairs where Artyom, Valeri and even Adrik are waiting for me. My brother's brow raises the moment he sets eyes on Imalia and then notices my hand wrapped tightly around hers.

"Thank you for coming, brother," I say, letting go of Imalia's hand and embracing him. My attention moves to Adrik and Valeri. "And for both of you, for indulging me. It's been too long since we had dinner together, hasn't it?"

Adrik doesn't respond, but Valeri nods in agreement. "Indeed, it has." He glances around. "Is Maxim not up to it today?"

"He only got released today, so he's resting." I clench my jaw, as I haven't had the guts to face him yet. Livia is looking after him, and I'm sure he'll be fine. "I'd like to introduce the three of you to Imalia." I grab her hand again and pull her against me. "Imalia, this is my brother Artyom, and my two nephews, Adrik and Valeri."

Her jaw works as she glares at the three men. "I see."

Artyom steps forward and takes her hand, kissing the back of it. "It's a pleasure to meet you."

"The pleasure is all yours," she spits, her nostrils flaring.

Artyom and my nephews laugh. "I see why you like this one, brother. She has fire." His eyes meet mine, dancing with amusement.

"Shall we?" I ask, gesturing toward the dining hall.

I'm reeling from seeing my brother touch Imalia. The bastard knows how possessive I can be and did it, anyway. Perhaps this was a mistake, but I wanted Imalia to see what life could be like if she'd accept the inevitable. Instead of being a caged animal, she could flourish by my side as my queen.

13

IMALIA

"So, Imalia. How are you enjoying life as Spartak's plaything?" Adrik asks.

This results in a deep growl from the man by my side, who glares at his nephew like he wants to stab him through the heart with his steak knife. "I'm not enjoying it," I say, clenching my jaw as I bow my head and continue to nibble small pieces of steak. My appetite is pretty non-existent right now.

"What exactly do you intend to do with her, brother?" Artyom asks, speaking as if I'm not sitting right in front of him.

Spartak straightens, giving his brother a glare that could stop most hearts. "That's none of your fucking business."

Valeri clears his throat. "Have you seen Maxim since he returned from hospital?" he asks, his attention fixed on his uncle.

Spartak's jaw works. "Not yet. He's not taking visitors at the moment."

I remember Spartak mentioned one of my uncle's men shot his son. It's a surprise to hear her hasn't even been to visit his son. Perhaps they aren't close to one another, unlike our family, which is inseparable. My chest aches as I miss my family so much, especially my mom.

"Oh, I'd hoped to call on him this evening," Valeri says, shoving a large piece of steak into his mouth.

"Another time, perhaps," Artyom suggests.

I can't say that Artyom and Spartak act like close brothers, instead they appear to be more like rivals on first impression. The look on Spartak's face when his brother kissed my hand was furious. I thought he was going to knock him out for it.

Artyom meets my gaze. "Tell me, Imalia. How close are you to your uncle's operations?"

My brow furrows. "What do you mean?"

He tilts his head. "Do you know how he operates? Can you provide our organization with vital information about your family's operations?"

I grip my knife hard, glaring at him. "No, and even if I could, there's no world in which I'd disclose any information to you."

He smirks and then looks at Spartak. "So, why exactly are you still alive, then?" The question isn't directed at me, but at his brother.

Spartak's hand slips onto my thigh and he squeezes

gently. "Because Imalia is mine," he says, his voice deadly as he glares at his brother. That's all the explanation he gives, as again his nephew Vitaly changes the subject.

"What of the plan to strike on two fronts?" He eyes me warily. "How is that going?"

"Timur and his team will arrive at his destination tomorrow and start gathering intel before we strike." Spartak glances at me briefly as his hand leaves my thigh. "I'll keep you informed."

Valeri nods as an uncomfortable silence falls over the table. I wonder what he's talking about, striking on two fronts. Clearly, they have a plan to hit my uncle hard after what happened to Maxim. It's only a matter of time until the City of Chicago erupts into a war like no one has ever witnessed before.

THE NEXT TWO weeks go by in a blur as Spartak repeats the same old cycle with me. I don't see him for a couple of days, and then he turns up and fucks me before falling asleep with me in his arms. By the time I wake, he's always gone.

I should be thankful that he's not around more, but he's the only company I have other than Olga. And our conversations are frosty to non-existent, especially if I appear ungrateful about the position I'm in. She continues to insist I'm lucky to be alive. Every day that passes, it's more difficult to accept that as my mind rots in front of daytime television.

The invitation to family dinner was a cruel torment, giving me a tiny taste of freedom and normalcy only to rip it all away again.

As I sit staring at the television mindlessly, a tug pulls at my chest as I miss my family so much. Fabio, Gio, and my mom are probably so worried about me, but I can't understand why Uncle Remy refused Spartak's offer to return me. No doubt I'm not hearing the full story, as it probably means Spartak's demands were ridiculous.

The click of the lock draws my attention to the door, expecting to see Olga with my lunch. Instead, it's Spartak holding the tray. My stomach dips as I shuffle under his electric gaze.

"Where's Olga?" I ask.

He tilts his head slightly as he walks in and slams the door shut before walking toward me. "I've bought you some food and then we can spend some time together." There's a flash of something sinister in his eyes.

"Why?" I ask.

He shrugs. "You've been stuck in this house for weeks. It's about time you stretched your legs. Don't you think?"

I can't work out if it's a trick question. All I want is to run as far away from here and never look back, so if he gives me a chance of escape, I'll take it. "Stretch my legs where?" I ask.

"We'll go to Millennium Park for a walk." He smirks. "Would you like that?"

I swallow hard and nod. "Sure, beats this shit." I nod to the TV.

He grabs the remote and turns it off. "It's settled then. Eat, little lamb. And then we'll go out together."

I watch as he walks into the adjoining bathroom and shuts the door, leaving me reeling. Millennium Park is huge and if I can give him the slip, there's every chance I'll escape. I grab the plate of food and eat it all, knowing I'll need my strength if I'm going to run from the man who kidnapped me.

After about fifteen minutes, he emerges from the bathroom with damp, messy hair and only a towel wrapped around his waist. I scorn myself as my eyes dip low to his crotch, which is hard and outlined in the fabric. Quickly, I focus anywhere but on the man who tilts my world upside fucking down. I know I should hate him, but it's so damn hard.

"I want you to watch me, baby girl," he murmurs, that voice as smooth as silk.

I clench my fists by my side. "Watch you what?" I ask, keeping my attention on the wall opposite.

"Look now before I force you onto your knees in front of me," he growls, his voice full of pent up rage.

I turn around in my seat and clench my thighs the moment I see him standing in the center of the room with his cock hard in his hand. His balls are heavy and full of cum as he jerks himself up and down. My mouth waters at the sight, and a sudden desperate need for him sweeps over me. Although I swore to myself I didn't want him, not anymore.

"Why don't you come and have a taste, malishka?" His eyes are dilated and lustful as he focuses on me.

I grind my teeth, knowing that deep down I want to, before I escape him forever. Instead of resisting, I stand and walk toward him. Once I'm within a foot of him, I drop to my knees and grab hold of his huge length. He pulses in my hand, precum spilling from the tip. "Such a good girl, you didn't even need any persuading," he purrs, lacing his fingers through my hair.

I lick my lips and he groans, looking feral as he stares down at me. Opening my jaw as wide as I can, I slide forward and allow him to take control, as I know he wants to. My eyes remain fixed on his as he thrusts in and out of my throat, his breathing becoming labored.

"That's it," he breathes, tightening his grasp on my hair. "Take every fucking inch."

I moan around his length, tasting him for the last time. There's no guarantee that I'll escape him at Millenium Park, but I'm going to try my damned hardest.

"You're so fucking good at sucking daddy's cock," he murmurs.

My nipples harden at the word as I meet his ravenous gaze, breathing through my nose as saliva spills all over him.

"Fuck." He yanks my head back, pulling out of my

throat suddenly. "You almost made me shoot my load down your throat, baby girl."

I tilt my head, brow furrowing. "Isn't that what you want?"

He smirks, and it's a wicked one that quickens my heart rate. "No, I want to breed that pretty little cunt of yours."

I shake my head. "You can't."

He narrows his eyes. "I will do what I want, Imalia. I've made that perfectly clear."

I swallow hard. "No, I mean I'm on my period."

His smirk widens, which only makes dread root deeper in my gut. "What's your point, little lamb?" He yanks me to my feet and brings my lips to within an inch of his. "Do you really believe a little blood will put me off?" And then his lips are on mine, stealing the air from my lungs at the prospect of being intimate with him while bleeding. It's too much as I attempt to wrestle away from him.

"No, it's not right," I say, pushing him away.

He shakes his head. "And here I was thinking you were finally coming around to the idea of us."

"Us? There is no us." I step back, putting distance between me and him. "You kidnapped me and locked me away. There's no chance there will ever be an *us.*"

His smirk doesn't waver as he advances towards me. "Stop fighting the inevitable." He grabs my hips and yanks me against his hard, naked body. "I'm having you, whether you tell me you want it or not." He wrenches open my blouse, breaking the buttons off. And then, he lifts up my skirt and tears my panties in two, making heat pulse through me.

"What are you—"

He pulls out my tampon and chucks it into a paper waste bin, and then before I can gather my thoughts, he's inside me. "Fuck, I've needed this for all damn day, malishka." He lifts me in his arms, blue-gray eyes dilated as he carries me to the bed. "The war has kept me from your tight little cunt too much, but I will make more time for it, I promise."

I groan as his huge length fills me, quenching a deep ache he'd ignited inside of me. "Spartak, please don't—"

He bites my nipple hard, making me scream. "Don't what, little lamb?" He then licks it softly, tenderly. The swift change between pleasure and pain is even more enjoyable. "Are you begging me to stop fucking you?" His hips move hard and fast, thrusting into me without mercy. "Because there's no fucking chance of that happening."

I bite my bottom lip, shutting my eyes as the pleasure is undeniable, even if the man above me is certifiably insane.

"Tell me the truth," he breathes into my ear, stilling inside of me. "Tell me how much you want it, baby girl."

I shudder, shaking my head. "You're crazy."

"That's not the correct answer."

He bites my other nipple as hard and then licks it with such gentleness. "Be a good girl and tell me what I want to hear."

My resolve crumbles as my eyelids flutter open and I gaze into those blue-gray eyes of his that seem to haunt my every waking thought. "I want you to fuck me, daddy," I breathe, my body trembling the moment I say those words to him.

I can't understand why calling him that gets me going as much as it does.

His nostrils flare, and he growls like an animal, moving his hips in sharp, brutal thrusts. "Good girl, Imalia," he murmurs, lips brushing against my cheek. "Aren't you such a good girl, telling daddy to fuck you?"

My body trembles, my climax so close, even though he's only just started. "Please," I moan. Hearing him call me a good girl does something to me. I shouldn't crave this psychopath's validation and praise, but there's this dark, hidden part of me that wants to give in and embrace the madness.

My nipples ache as he plows into me ruthlessly, as if he's trying to tear my body apart.

"Look at my cock disappearing inside your slick, bloody cunt," he growls, reminding me I'm on my period.

I do as he says, looking down at where we join and the mess we're making. His cock coated in blood should be an off-putting sight as he pulls almost all the way out of me before slamming back inside. Instead, it turns me on more than anything ever has. The raw, primal desire he holds for me, unaffected by the fact I'm bleeding all over him.

"Don't you find it disgusting?" I ask, intrigued by his opinion of it.

"No fucking chance, baby girl. I think it's the sexiest fucking thing ever, sliding into that cunt while you bleed." He lowers his mouth to my ear and murmurs, "I wouldn't mind making you bleed with a knife while I fuck you." His tongue slides down the length of my cheek, sending shivers right through me. "The only shame is that I can't get you pregnant tonight, but there's plenty of time for that."

I moan, hating how turned on I am right now. So turned on that even the mention of his sick fantasy to get me pregnant can't douse the fire blazing deep within my soul. Instead, it makes it roar with more intensity as I grip his hair and drag his lips to mine, kissing him deeply.

His tongue thrusts into my mouth, dominating the kiss as he ruts into me with even more force than I believed possible. Every single muscle in my body tightens as I know I'm going to fall over the edge any second. "Fuck, I'm going to come," I warn him, knowing that I can't hold out any longer.

He groans, "Such a good girl, make that pretty pussy come for daddy," he breathes, his voice so gravelly and deep it's enough to pull me over the edge.

"Fuck, daddy," I cry, forgetting every inhibition in that moment.

He growls, sinking his teeth into my shoulder like a feral animal. His thrusts becoming erratic as he comes right along with me, filling me with his cum. The mess we make as it spills out onto the bed doesn't seem to bother him as he continues to thrust into me long after he's come apart. His teeth still sinking painfully into my shoulder.

When he finally stops, he groans and then kisses my lips. "You're so fucking perfect, baby girl."

I swallow hard, unable to break the intense eye contact between us as he stares almost adoringly into mine. No one has ever looked at me the way he's looking at me right now, and it makes me feel more special, more desired than I've ever felt before. My chest aches as I come down from my high, realizing how wrong this is.

He kisses me quickly before pulling out. "We'd better get showered before we go to the park." He smiles at me and nods toward the bathroom door.

My stomach flips as I get out of the bed and join him, knowing that I have to escape today, otherwise I fear I'm going to lose myself. The longer he has me ensnared in his trap, the deeper I fall for his sadistic charms.

14

SPARTAK

*I*malia walks a little ahead of me, engrossed in the surrounding nature. It's unsurprising, considering I've locked her in a room for the best part of a month. My stomach is in knots as I watch her, knowing I haven't felt like this for anyone but my late wife.

It's a complication, but one I have every intention of embracing. Once Imalia drops her shields entirely, she'll realize we're meant for one another.

"Would you like an ice cream, malishka?" I ask, noticing the truck parked nearby.

She spins to face me, those beautiful deep brown eyes finding mine as she smiles softly. "Sure."

I walk toward her and set my hand on the small of her back, which makes her shudder. Slowly, I steer her toward the truck. "What would you like, little lamb?" I ask, gently moving my fingers in circles on her back.

She bites her lip in a way that drives me wild. "I'll have an ice cream sandwich."

I smile and order her choice, handing her it.

"Aren't you having one?" she asks, tilting her head.

I shake my head. "No, I'm good."

Her brow furrows, but she tucks into her ice cream sandwich, moaning as she does. "This is so good. You should get one."

I laugh. "Let me have a taste of yours." I drag her close, her breath stilling as she stares up at me. Leaning down, I take a bite of the ice cream sandwich in her hand as I hold her gaze.

"It's good," I say, nodding. "But not nearly as tasty as you."

Her cheeks flush a deep red at that and she clears her throat, stepping away from me. "You're crazy."

"You don't need to keep telling me that." I smile at her, keeping my hand on the small of her back. "I already know and I don't give a shit. Neither should you."

"What's that supposed to mean?" she asks.

"It means you shouldn't give a shit what society or anyone else thinks of you or your choices."

Her brow knits together in confusion and it's utterly adorable.

"If we were to be together, people wouldn't approve."

She steps away from me, crossing her arms over her chest. "I don't want to be with you."

I tilt my head, smirking. "That's what you keep telling yourself, but deep down under all your layers, there's a woman who wants to be dominated and owned by a man like me." I move closer to her, yanking her against me hard. "I see it in yours eyes. A kindred soul that desires for the same twisted darkness that my soul craves."

Imalia shudders, shaking her head. "You're wrong."

"Rarely." I kiss her lips softly. "The more you fight it, the harder it will try to surface."

"There's no world in which I could ever be happy with you." Her brown eyes turn furious as she shakes her head. "How could I be when it's not even my choice? You're trying to trap me by getting me pregnant, forcing me to stay with you."

"Because that's what you've always wanted. To be taken care of by a man who makes those choices for you." I bite her bottom lip and suck on it. "You can deny it all your like, but in the end, the truth always comes out."

Her eyes flicker shut as I move my lips to her neck, sucking her there until the flesh bruises.

"You're mine, Imalia. Once you accept it, you can have more freedom." I tease my lips softly over her skin. "Wouldn't that be nice?"

She shakes her head. "That's called blackmail."

I pull back and sigh. "No, it's called realism." I hold her gaze. "Fairytales don't exist. It's time you understand how the real world works. After all, your mom no doubt intends to sell you off to a man you don't know. Why not choose one who can awaken your deepest desires instead?"

She searches my eyes. Those beautiful brown gems glazed in a layer of unshed tears. Even though deep down she knows I'm right, she can't accept it. "Because at least if I'm sold off to some man, he won't be as much of a monster as you. No one is." She turns away and rushes toward a tree-lined section of the park.

I sigh and give my bodyguard Yuri a nod to go after her. "Be gentle."

His brow furrows, but he runs after her, chasing her across the park. I always knew coming here was a risk, since Imalia hasn't accepted her fate yet. I'd hoped giving her a bit a freedom may have helped her feelings toward me, but I fear it's had the opposite effect.

If she thinks I'm going to run after her, she's mistaken. Slowly, I follow in the direction of my body-guard, certain he'll catch her without trouble. A woman runs in the opposite direction, looking startled, and that's when doubt sets in. And then, a gunshot echoes through the trees and forces me into a sprint in that direction.

When I get there, Yuri is on the ground bleeding and Imalia is clutching onto her cousin's arm as he leads her away.

How the fuck did he know to find her here?

"Imalia," I shout her name and they both stop, turning to face me.

Imalia's face pales as I reach for my gun and aim it at Massimo, knowing that I have to stop him at all costs. As I'm about to pull the trigger, she steps in front of him, blocking him with her body.

The blood drains from my face as if I shot my baby girl by accident. I couldn't live with it. "Get out of the way, Imalia," I growl, taking a few steps toward them.

Massimo matches my movements, moving them back as one unit. "Never," she says, holding my gaze. "Accept that you've lost. Massimo found me and I'm going home."

My jaw works as I want to tell her home is with me, but I'm reluctant to show my true feelings in front of my enemy. Instead, I remain silent as she pushes Massimo toward the exit and they dash away, sending rage spiraling out of control inside of me. "Fuck," I growl, turning my attention back to Yuri, who has been badly injured.

I dial Osip's number, since Timur is down in San Diego.

"Boss?"

"Yuri has been shot in Millenium Park. Send help as quickly as possible." I cancel the call and return to my bodyguard's side to tend to his wound. The shot has gone through his abdomen and he's losing a lot of blood.

"I'm sorry, sir. He took me by surprise." He shakes his head. "I hardly had time to react."

"Quiet." I hold my hand firm against the wound, trying to stem the blood flow, but my hopes wain at the sight of the pool of blood beneath him. "Osip is sending help as we speak."

His eyes flutter shut as his breathing becomes labored and erratic. There's no doubt Yuri won't make it. He's in his sixties and even a young man would struggle to survive this injury. "I'm not going to make it, sir."

I increase my force on the wound, clutching at straws. "That's not the Volkov Bratva spirit, is it?" Yuri was a bodyguard for my father when I was a kid. The thought of him not being there is unbearable. The Morrone family will pay heavily for this. Once I get Imalia back, and I will, they'll wish they never tried to take her from me.

There's no way Imalia could have spoken to her cousin and told him, which means they have the house under surveillance and followed us here. My desire to give her some freedom lost me more than my little lamb.

Yuri takes his last breath as he stops breathing, lying unmoving in a pool of his own blood. There's blood all over my hands and suit, but I can't bring myself to move. All I can do is stare at the lifeless body of a man who has been there as long as I can remember, a twinge pulling at my chest. There are no tears. I haven't cried since I was a child, not even at my wife's funeral or when she died, despite loving her. I'm broken in that respect.

"Sir," Osip calls my name, rushing toward me with the doctor in tow.

I shake my head. "It's too late."

His jaw clenches as his eyes find Yuri's lifeless and bloodied body. "I'll have our men collect his body." Osip steps away to make the call as the doctor confirms my bodyguard is indeed dead.

Once he returns, he sets a hand on my shoulder. "What happened?"

I swallow hard, knowing that Yuri's death and losing Imalia are all my fault. "I decided it was time I got Imalia out of the house, but it appears we were followed by the Morrone family. Massimo shot Yuri and then took off with Imalia."

"Motherfuckers," he growls, shaking his head. "Is this in retaliation for the war waging in San Diego?"

I shake my head. "No, I believe they've had the house under surveillance, and it's the first time I took Imalia out of it."

His brow furrows. "Why did you bring her here?"

I clench my jaw as, although I hate being questioned, Osip is one of my most respected men. "That's not important," I say, pacing the floor. "What's important is stealing her back."

Osip looks at me like I've lost my mind. "Is that

important?" he asks. "Surely it's important to focus on the war rather than on some girl."

"She's not just some girl," I growl, knowing that if I don't get her back quickly, I'll lose my mind entirely. "She's mine."

Osip pales and then runs a hand across the back of his neck. "I see. That complicates things." His brow furrows. "Does she reciprocate?"

I shake my head. "She's denying her true feelings."

There's uncertainty in his eyes, but he nods. "Very well. How are you going to get her back?"

"I hear they're throwing an event in town at Remy's casino this weekend."

His brow raises. "Is it wise to return there after last time?"

Osip is always my voice of reason, but right now, reason doesn't factor into this decision.

I'm driven by a primal need to reclaim what belongs to me. "It may not be wise, but it's necessary." I crack my neck as the tension increases. A dark and dangerous rage bubbles beneath my skin. "Hopefully, Imalia will be in attendance and I'll snatch her back right under their noses."

"How do you propose entering without being seen?" Osip asks.

I clear my throat. "Don't worry about that. I have my ways." I pat him on the shoulder. "Clear up this mess for me and inform Yuri's family. We'll need to have the funeral swiftly at our private graveyard."

Osip nods. "Of course, sir."

I return to Yuri and pull the car keys from his jacket pocket, hating seeing such a great man reduced to nothing but flesh and bone with one pull of a trigger. The Morrone family will pay for this. Once I reclaim my little lamb, I'll ensure she'll never escape me again.

15

IMALIA

My mind is broken as I stare aimlessly out of the window as the concrete buildings rush past. I sit in silence next to my eldest cousin, Massimo, numbness spreading through my flesh.

All I can see in my mind is the expression on Spartak's face when I stepped in front of my cousin. It was one of pure anguish and heartbreak that I'd betray him, but what did he expect? The man gave me no choice, and yet here I sit, more dejected than relieved that I'm finally going home.

That's when Spartak's words echo in my mind.

You are home.

I can't help but wonder if he brainwashed me, as I felt sick when I left him in that park. Sick that I'd never be with him again, never hear him call me baby girl. I swallow hard as Massimo shifts next to me.

"Are you okay, Imalia?" he finally asks, breaking the silence.

Tears pool in my eyes, but I can't work out why. "Not exactly," I murmur, shaking my head. "I think I'm broken."

Massimo pulls me against him and holds me. "It's okay, piccola. You're safe now." He tightens his grasp on me. "And that bastard will pay for everything he did to you… I'm just sorry it took this long." He looks down at me and I glance into his dark, familiar eyes. "I'd hate to think of what you endured, but he gave us no possible chance to get you until today."

Massimo's chest heaves as he breathes in deeply. "I could hardly believe it when the car drove out with you in the back."

"You've been watching the house?" I ask.

He nods. "Yes, ever since we found out he took you, we've been trying everything we can to get you back."

My brow furrows. "Spartak claims uncle refused a deal to get me back. Is that true?"

Massimo shakes his head. "He was asking for the impossible, as if he never wanted us to consider it, anyway."

I nod, clasping my hands together in my lap. That makes perfect sense, as he's been pretty clear from the moment he set his eyes on me that he didn't want to let me go.

"Did he try to get information out of you?" Massimo asks.

"Not really. He made remarks I must have some insight into uncle's business practices but never truly tried to get any information from me." I meet Massimo's puzzled gaze. "Is that odd?"

"Very." He shuffles uncomfortably. "What exactly did he do with you, then?"

I break his gaze and turn my attention out of the window, heat flooding my cheeks. "I don't want to talk about it."

Massimo growls. "That slimy son of a bitch took advantage of you. Didn't he?"

I cross my arms over my chest and glare at my cousin. "I said, I don't want to talk about it. How is my mom?"

"Worried sick about you, but she's had to rush home to San Diego."

My brow furrows. "What? I thought we were staying here for a few months or more."

"That was the plan, until Spartak split the war and attacked the Allegro mafia in San Diego, taking us by surprise." He runs a hand across the back of his neck. "Fabio and Gio have returned too, so if you want to head home—"

"Not right now. I think I'll stay here for a bit," I say, knowing the idea of fleeing this city makes dread seize hold of me.

He nods. "Very well, you can stay as long as you like with us." He smiles, but it doesn't reach his eyes. "I'm so sorry we didn't protect you, Imalia."

I shake my head. "Don't be stupid. This isn't your fault. It's Spartak's." I turn away from my cousin as I say his name, fearful of what he might detect in my eyes. The mere thought of his name draws memories I'd rather forget to the forefront of my mind. Memories of his hands on me. Memories of him inside of me. I swallow hard, realizing mere hours ago he was fucking me like a sex-crazed animal in his bed and now I'm never going to see him again.

I should be relieved, but all I feel is regret for running away from him in the park. I got his man killed, as no one would survive that shot and now we're apart. I fear hiding the part of me he's being trying to coax to the surface is going to be more difficult than ever before.

After a silent twenty-minute journey, the car pulls in through the grand entrance gates onto the Morrone estate.

"Uncle is waiting to speak with you. He's probably going to ask you about what Spartak did with you all this time." Massimo's eyes blaze with sympathy. "I'm not sure you telling him you don't want to talk about it will fly with him."

He's right, as Uncle Remy can be intense at times. He's easily angered, but the idea of telling him anything that happened between me and Spartak during however long I've been captive makes fire flame through my veins. "I know," I mutter.

"Come on," Massimo says, giving my shoulder a quick squeeze before exiting the back of the car.

I get out of my side and walk hesitantly after him toward the entrance of the house. It's not that I fear telling them the truth. I fear what they might detect from me. The fact I enjoyed being touched by him. The fact that Spartak's touch plagues my every waking thought. It's almost impossible to get him out of my mind.

As I walk through the doors, I'm greeted by my numerous cousins and uncle all rushing toward me. Camilla and Mia pull me into a hug and Leo and Luca approach, standing back a bit as their father approaches me. "Welcome home, Imalia," he says, those dark brown eyes fixed on me. "I'm sorry we didn't save you sooner."

I swallow hard and nod. "At least Massimo got to me when he did," I say, smiling at my cousin. It's forced, as right now I'm not sure I'm happy about being home.

Remy moves his two daughters out of the way and sets a hand on my back. "Come, we need to talk. You can catch up with your cousins shortly." He gives his children a dismissive glare and then steers me toward his study.

"Have a seat, piccola mia," he says, nodding to the large sofa on the right.

He's called me his little one since I was a kid, and never stopped even though I'm twenty-six years old now. I sit down and shuffle my feet nervously, knowing I'm about to be interrogated.

"I meant what I said. It's my fault they kidnapped you from the airport, as I was too impatient to consider your missing bag was a trap set by the Russians." He rubs a hand across the scruff on his chin. "Your mother is furious with me."

"It's not your fault, uncle." I shake my head. "It's the Russians' fault." I purposely keep Spartak's name out of my mouth, knowing how perceptive my uncle can be.

"Does Mom know I'm back?" I ask.

He nods once. "I called her the moment Massimo told me the news. She's so thankful and wants to speak to you later."

I nod in response, looking down at my hands in my lap.

"Did he probe you for information on our family?" Uncle Remy asks, jumping straight into the interrogation.

I shake my head. "Not really. There were comments made at times that I must have information, but I was never forced to hand it over."

My uncle's brow furrows and I dread the question that's going to come next. "So, what did he do with you?" His jaw clenches as he waits for my answer.

I swallow hard, looking down at my lap. "He was obsessive over me." I shake my head. "First, he kept me in a basement and punished me, but then things escalated and he kept me locked in his bedroom." I make sure I don't look at my uncle, knowing that he might detect I'm not being entirely truthful. Most of the times, I was a willing partner in both the punishment and the sex.

"That fucking bastard," he growls, standing and pacing the study. "He molested you."

I take a brief glance at my uncle, whose muscles are bunched under his tight shirt and his fists are clenched. "When I get my hands on him, I swear to God I'll make him wish he was never fucking born."

Fear floods me as I consider what my uncle would do to him. The idea of him coming to harm because of me scares me, even though I should want him to hurt. Everyone would say I'm insane if they knew the thoughts in my head and my desire to be reunited with the man who held me against my will. "At least I'm alive."

He growls. "Indeed." He walks toward me and places a finger under my chin, forcing me to look at you. "But what damage did that monster do to you?"

I shrug. "I'm stronger than I look."

He smiles, but it's a sad smile. "I know you're strong, piccola mia. You inherit that from your mother, but he will pay. I promise you."

As I stare into my uncle's eyes, there's such determination in them that it worries me. "Don't do anything reckless on my account, uncle."

He releases my chin and walks away. "We're at war.

Every move is reckless, I'm afraid. Go and settle in and get some rest." His brow furrows. "If you want to return to San Diego—"

"No, I'd like to rest here for a while, if you don't mind."

He smiles, but it's a weak one. "Of course I don't mind. If you're up to it, my annual ball is on Saturday and it's Camilla's eighteenth birthday. Perhaps it'll do you some good to have fun with your cousins."

"Perhaps," I mutter, standing. "Thank you. I'll go and get some rest." I bow my head and then walk out of his study, knowing that Spartak broke me in ways people will never understand.

Deep down I was always broken, desperate for the dark desires to be coaxed out of me, but they lay dormant. Spartak awoken a darkness deep inside of me that I can't ignore forever. I walk into the hallways to find my cousins still there.

Mia rushes toward me. "Are you okay?"

I nod. "I'm fine, just really tired." I smile at Camilla, who keeps her distance this time, clearly sensing I'm not in the mood to be fawned over.

It's nearly the end of summer, which means she's only got a couple of weeks until she returns to the Syndicate Academy for her senior year. "If you guys don't mind, I'm going to rest and will catch up with you all soon."

"Of course," Camilla says, tugging at her sister. "Let Imalia get some much deserved rest."

Leo and Luca watch on with that same guilty glint in their eyes I detected in Massimo's. "Thank you." I force myself up the stairs and go into the spare room I always use, locking the door behind me and setting my back against it.

I sag to the floor, overcome with emotion as I sob uncontrollably. The question is, am I sobbing from relief of finally being free or from being torn away from a man I inexplicably care for? I fear the answer is the latter, which only raises a more important question.

What the hell is wrong with me?

16

SPARTAK

"Father, can we talk?" Maxim asks, leaning against the doorframe into my study.

It's been over two weeks since he got out of the hospital, but I still haven't seen him. My cowardice kept me away as I'm a shit Father.

"Of course," I say, gesturing to the seat in front of my desk. "Take a seat."

An awkward silence falls between us as he takes a seat. "How are you doing?"

His jaw clenches, and he glares at me. "Fine, you might have known that if you'd bothered to come upstairs to visit me in the last two weeks."

The real reason I couldn't face seeing him in that hospital or debilitated is he's the last family I've got and the thought of losing him scared me. Because of my anger, I alienated my daughter, but Maxim is still here. I may have my brother and nephews, but it's not the same. My brother has always wanted to undermine me.

"You've been busy in my absence," Maxim says, changing the subject.

I nod in response. "We had to retaliate for them shooting you."

Maxim shakes his head. "You blew up Le Stelle and killed God knows how many women inside."

I stand and walk toward the dresser, housing my decanters of alcohol, pouring myself a glass of vodka. "Collateral damage is always inevitable in war, Maxim. You know that." I bring the glass to my lips and knock back the fiery liquid, pouring myself more. "The war escalated because those bastards shot you. I couldn't sit back and do nothing."

"Bullshit," Maxim growls, forcing me to look at my son. "You can't resist pushing things further. After all, you're the one who escalated it by snatching that girl. The girl who escaped you in the park two days ago."

I lean against the edge of the dresser, observing the man my son has become. He's too compassionate for a pakhan, but I still hope he'll learn. Perhaps it's because despite him resenting me for my brutal treatment of him, his childhood was nowhere near as hellish as mine was.

"When you become pakhan, Maxim, you'll learn that you have to make hard decisions to protect your family and empire." I tilt my head and sip the vodka in my glass. "Otherwise you could lose everything. We have nothing if we don't live up to our ruthless reputation."

Maxim crosses his arms over his chest. "And what of the girl?"

"What of her?" I ask.

He sighs heavily. "The last time we spoke on the matter, you made it pretty clear you have your sights set on her. You told me clearly she is yours, like a possessed fucking caveman."

I clench my jaw, remembering the possessiveness I felt at the mere suggestion of letting her go, and yet I lost her, anyway. "I intend to get her back this weekend."

"This weekend?" Maxim asks.

I nod. "Yes, there's an event at Remy's casino, and—"

"For fuck's sake," Maxim interrupts me, shaking his head. "Haven't you learned your lesson from last time? Never walk into the lion's den, especially not when the war is more intense than ever."

I growl, standing taller as I approach my son. "Don't speak to me like that. I taught you better." I loom over him. "I will put no one in harm's way except for myself. I intend to go in alone, snatch what is rightfully mine without being seen." I narrow my eyes. "And then return home."

Maxim shakes his head and stands. "Right, because everything is always that simple in reality."

"It doesn't matter." I sigh heavily. "If it were Livia, what would you do?"

He growls softly. "Stop comparing our situation to yours. Livia is my wife, and I would fight tooth and nail to get her back. Imalia is a girl you snatched against her will and kept prisoner. No wonder she ran from you, and now you're trying to suggest that she means something to you." He shakes his head. "But how does she feel about you, Father?"

I clench my fists by my side as she hasn't accepted what this is between us yet. I'm confident in my ability to read people. Imalia cares for me and she wants me. "I'm not sure. I'm not prepared to let her go without a fight."

"Do you love her?" Maxim asks.

I meet my son's gaze. "Yes."

"So you're just forgetting about Mom?"

Rage coils through me at the suggestion as I lunge forward, grabbing him by his lapel. "Don't you dare," I growl, shaking my head. "You were the one who made it clear I'm living in the past. I loved your mother, but the fact is, our relationship wasn't always an easy one, Maxim." I narrow my eyes, letting him go as he slumps back into the chair. "She didn't love who I really was. She loved a part of me that wasn't really me." I swallow hard, running a hand through my hair. "I'm fucked up in the head and she struggled to accept the dark parts of me."

I meet my son's gaze, knowing this isn't what he

wants to hear. "You believe I screwed you up as a kid, and I accept I wasn't the best father, but Maxim, you don't understand what true suffering can be as a child." My jaw clenches as I realize how close I am to unveiling the truth I've told no one. "Let's just say your childhood was like a fucking picnic compared to mine."

Maxim stands, fists clenched. "If that's true, then why treat me the way you did?" He shakes his head. "If I ever have a child, which I'm not sure I will because of how damaged I am—"

"You must carry on the Volkov name," I interrupt.

"Shut up," he growls, looking at me in a way I've never seen before. "If I ever had a child, I sure as hell wouldn't repeat your mistakes." He thrusts a finger into my chest. "I'm broken, Father. There's no fixing what's wrong with me, but I'm lucky you forced me into a marriage with a woman as fucked up as I am."

I swallow hard and step back from him, knowing everything he's saying is true. I learned to be a father from a bad example, despite how much I hated my childhood. I should have strived to be different, but the damage done to me not only by my father but by my uncle was too great to overcome and my rage consumed me. The cycle repeated, but from the sounds of it, if he and Livia have children, then they'll do it differently.

"I'm glad to hear it, Maxim. You can break the cycle with your child." I turn to face him. "But if Livia is like you, then you get it. The moment I looked into Imalia's eyes, I knew she was the only one who could truly love me. I saw it, deep down in her soul."

Maxim shakes his head, still angry. "Whatever. You do what you want, like you always do." He stands and turns away, walking toward the door.

"I'm sorry, son. For everything."

He stills, glancing briefly over his shoulder. "It's too little, too fucking late." He walks out and I slump against my desk, knowing he's right.

I dragged my children into my mess, forcing them to endure pain and heartache all because I can't overcome my own. I knock back the rest of my vodka and then sit back down behind my desk, rubbing my face in my hands.

Perhaps I've already lost my son without realizing it. Everyone I care about leaves soon enough, even Imalia. I must do this differently and give her the choice to love me if she wants, otherwise I'll make the same mistakes as always and push her away.

I'll still go to the party, but only to speak with her. It's time I learn from my mistakes and stop taking things by force. Love can't be forced, and that's something I'm realizing after countless mistakes with my family, starting with my wife.

She never saw the real me until after we were married. I thought I could force her into loving every part of me, but it wasn't possible. In the end, she resented me for not being open with her from the start and allowing her to make her own choice and she died regretting our life together.

I can't make that mistake again with Imalia, and I need to rebuild my relationship with my son.

MAXIM LOOKS furious as Livia leads him into the dining room. "What's this all about?" he asks.

Livia squeezes his arm. "I told you. Your father wishes to make amends."

"Let him speak," he growls, glaring at me.

"Your wife is right. I want to make a start in repairing things between us. That's what this dinner is about."

Maxim's eyes narrow. "You want something. That's all this is about."

"Yes, I want your forgiveness for being such a terrible father lately."

He raises a brow. "Only lately?"

I sigh. "Fine, most of your life. Would you have a seat?"

He eyes me warily, but sits at the table in his usual seat to the right of me at the head. Livia takes the only other seat to the left, opposite her husband. It's surprising she doesn't hold our first encounter against me, since I did get my son to bend her over and spank her ass. Ever since, she's been relatively tame toward me.

"How are you healing?" I ask, meeting Maxim's furious gaze.

"You asked me that yesterday." He crosses his arms over his chest, wincing slightly as he does. "I'm fine."

I clench my jaw and nod in response, as Olga brings the first course in. We remain silent until she leaves, and that's when I turn my attention to my daughter-in-law. "How have you been, Livia?"

Her eyes widen slightly at the question, but she shrugs. "As good as can be, considering my husband was shot."

"Why don't you cut the bullshit and tell us what you want, Father?" Maxim says.

I shake my head. "I told you there's no ulterior motive to tonight's dinner." I grab my spoon and taste the soup, which is as delicious as always. "I was wrong not to visit you after they shot you."

"You already said that yesterday. I don't need to listen to anymore of your half-hearted apologies." He glances at Livia and then stands. "Let's go home."

"Olga has gone to a lot of trouble to prepare dinner." Livia shakes her head. "We will eat it, whether you like it or not."

My son's eyes flash at Livia's brazen refusal to leave, and after a few beats holding her gaze, he backs down and sits.

I never thought I'd see the day when a woman could speak to my son like that. He's always been rather controlling with the opposite sex.

He notices me smirking and glares. "What are you smirking at?"

"Nothing." I lift my glass of wine up and sip it. "Livia reminds me so much of your mother."

There's a flash of surprise in my son's eyes, as if my mention of his mother disarmed him. After all, I've always been so cagey when he brought up her up in the past, and it's because of my guilt. My guilt for forcing her into a marriage she didn't truly want. It's been eating at me for years, but I've seen the error of my ways.

Livia clears her throat. "I'll take that as a compliment, as I believe she was a formidable woman."

"Indeed, she was one of the few women I respected." I knock back the rest of my wine. "A rarity."

Livia smiles at me and I notice Maxim's jaw clench. He's possessive of his wife, who at first he didn't wish to marry. I'm thankful that I forced him to, as I feel she's the best thing for him.

Olga enters with the next course, setting it down in the center of the table. "Enjoy," she says, before leaving.

"What is this?" Livia asks, brow furrowing. "I haven't had this before."

"Pelmeni," Maxim and I say in unison.

Maxim clears his throat as our eyes meet. "It's delicious. Russian dumplings. You will like it."

She smiles and takes a large helping. "It smells divine."

Maxim helps himself next, and then me.

I hope that the bridges between us aren't forever burned, but I fear my actions going forward might anger him more. I intend to win back Imalia fair and square and make her my wife, which he won't agree with.

Imalia is an Allegro, and she is related to the Morrone family. The action will only flare tensions between our families, but I intend to give Imalia the choice this time.

It will be her choice if she returns to me, which I know she will. After all, you can't keep soulmates apart forever. He would call me crazy, but I don't care about anyone's opinion of me, except for hers.

17

IMALIA

A knock echoes through my room.

"Who is it?" I ask.

"It's me," Camilla calls.

I smile wistfully into the mirror. "Come in, birthday girl."

She opens the door and sweeps in toward me. "Wow, you look gorgeous." She kisses my cheeks in greeting. "How are you doing?"

I turn around and face her, taking her hands in mine. "I'm fine. Stop worrying. What's it like being an adult?" I sigh, recalling the past. "I can't believe you're eighteen years old. I remember so well when you were four, running around the garden."

She laughs, shaking her head. "Don't be so silly. You're not even that much older than me."

I raise a brow. "I'm eight years older than you."

She waves her hand dismissively. "I love this dress."

She touches the fabric in her hands. "I thought your luggage got lost?"

I nod. "Uncle Remy bought me it for tonight. It's because of his guilt that the Russians had me for so long me."

She sighs. "Probably, as he's never bought me a dress as nice as this."

I roll my eyes. "You have tons of beautiful dresses, including this one you're wearing."

She's wearing a stunning deep blue Dior dress that must have cost a small fortune. "Yes, but I bought it yesterday at the mall with Mia." She twirls around. "Does the color suit me?"

"Perfectly. You look stunning." I sit down on the edge of the bed. "It's been so long since I last saw you. How is school?"

She huffs, shaking her head. "It's alright, but I'm glad this is my last year."

"Don't wish your life away, as it's pretty boring once you finish. After all, a woman's role is to be beautiful at all times and attract a husband who can increase the wealth of our family."

Camilla tilts her head. "You're lucky, though. As your mom has no intention of forcing you to marry anyone."

"I wouldn't be so sure." I drag my fingers through my hair. "In the end, she'll want me to marry someone suitable."

"Not from what I heard. She and Father were

discussing it and your mom said it was out of the question. There's no way she's forcing you into an arranged marriage." Her face falls as she swallows hard. "My father, on the other hand, insists both Mia and I will be married by arrangement."

"All the more reason to enjoy your last year of freedom, then." I shove her playfully in the ribs.

She gives me an irritated glare. "It's not funny. I want to marry a man I like, not because I'm forced to, but because I want to."

"Maybe Uncle will change his mind," I suggest, trying to keep the conversation light. "Now no more moping. You only turn eighteen once. Let's have fun tonight and forget about everything else." I hook my arm with hers and drag her toward the door. "You can't be late for your own party."

She rolls her eyes. "This party isn't even for me, and you know it. My father took advantage of my birthday being around the same time as his annual ball and combined the two. Do you have your mask?"

I reach into my clutch and pull out the ornate eye-mask. "Yes."

She smiles and pulls hers out, which matches her dress perfectly. "Me too. Let's have some fun."

We walk out into the corridor and down the stairs together, where the entire family is gathered. It makes no sense having the party at a casino when their house is so magnificent, but Uncle Remy always likes to hosts his parties there.

Camilla goes to talk to Mia, who is also wearing a stunning dress.

Massimo approaches. "How are you doing?"

I shrug. "As well as I can be." The truth of it is it's like I've been drowning since I got back here. Every moment alone, the man I escaped from consumes my thoughts, making me wonder why I ran. When I was with Spartak, for the first time, someone truly understood me. He made me feel safe and protected, despite his brutal and sadistic ways.

My mom was hysterical on the phone when we first talked, unable to stop crying. I sense Remy told her what happened to me from some of the things she said, but she didn't come outright and tell me. I spoke to Gio and Fabio, who both vowed to return and string Spartak up by the neck once they'd dealt with his forces in San Diego.

All the while, all I can think about is returning to the monster's arms.

Remy clears his throat as he approaches. "Let's go." His eyes linger on me for a few beats, as if considering whether to ask how I'm doing. Ever since I told him that things with Spartak became sexual, he doesn't look at me in the same way anymore. Instead of stopping, he heads toward the door, leading the family out to the cars.

Mia hooks her arm with mine. "You can ride in the car with us," she says.

Camilla smiles as Mia leads the way toward the town car we're taking.

Even as I slide into the back of the car, I can't get my head straight. It's like every single second of every single day I can think of nothing other than Spartak Volkov. The way he touched me consumes me. I long to have his body against mine again and to kiss those lips of his. My stomach churns as I even long to call him daddy as much as he wants while he fucks me repeatedly.

It's so wrong that after everything he put me through, I still want him. Perhaps that's exactly the reason I want him. Because all along he was right. I'm desperate to be taken against my will and controlled during sex.

"Imalia?" Mia says my name, both of them staring at me.

I shake my head. "Sorry, what?"

Camilla's brow furrows. "We were asking if you spoke to your mom today."

"I was in another world," I admit, shaking my head. "No, why?"

They both exchange uncertain glances. "Father says the war in San Diego isn't going well. The Volkov Bratva got a head start and they've been battering the Allegro Mafia on all sides," Mia says.

Camilla sighs. "In three days alone, they've lost four million dollars of product and countless men."

"Fuck," I say, running my fingers through my hair. "Perhaps I should head back."

Mia squeezes my hand. "What could you do? I know your mom was hoping my dad could back her up, but unfortunately, he can't spare any men here in Chicago."

Camilla shrugs. "I don't know what that man did to you, but can he be reasoned with?"

I raise a brow. "Spartak Volkov reasoned with?" I ask, laughing lightly. "I doubt it."

Their expressions turn grave, but I know the only way he would listen to reason is if I returned to him willingly. Perhaps if he believed I was happy to be his forever, he'd call his men off and spare my mom and brothers.

"Rumor is, he's insane," Mia says. "Like clinically insane."

I swallow hard, as it's probably true. And what does that say about me wanting to be with him? "Yeah, it wouldn't surprise me."

Mia's face turns sympathetic. "What exactly was it like? Did he torture you?"

My stomach churns as I break their gaze, looking down at my lap. "To be honest, I'm not sure I want to talk about it."

Camilla nudges Mia. "Leave her alone. No doubt Imalia is scarred by her time in captivity."

Scarred isn't really the word I'd use. Broken, perhaps. I mean, what else could explain why every waking second of every single day, I'm consumed by fantasies of my kidnapper. Stockholm Syndrome at its finest. It's as if he's captured my mind and even though I've escaped physically, there's nothing I can do to escape the effect he had on me.

"Sorry," Mia says, shaking her head. "I can be such an idiot. All that talk about arranged marriages the other week. Will Father set us up tonight?"

"I hope not," Camila says, shaking her head. "I'd kill him if he did that on my eighteenth birthday."

I'm thankful for the change in subject as my two cousins chat about who will be in attendance. Their talking fades into the background as I watch the world go by, unable to keep my mind off of Spartak. Is it possible that he was right all along and I couldn't see it?

He was holding me captive, but in some ways I've never been more free. Not in the physical sense, but in the emotional sense. He didn't judge me for my tastes. In fact, he encouraged them. The car comes to a stop outside of the casino and the driver opens the door. Camilla and Mia get out first, and I follow them like a third wheel.

Massimo approaches me and offers me his arm. "Shall we?"

I smile at my eldest cousin, who has always been like a brother to me. "Sure." I take his arm, but even as I walk into the casino alongside my family, I can't shake the deep-rooted unease inside of me.

"If you get tired or it's too much for you, I'm happy

to skip out. After all, I've never liked these parties," Massimo says, leading me through the grand entrance, which has more guards on it than I've ever seen before.

"Thank you, Massimo." I squeeze his arm, as I'm sure that I won't be able to hack an entire night at this thing. "How late does it normally go on?"

He shrugs. "Early hours of the morning, I'd suspect."

I sigh, as there's about zero chance of me wanting to stay here much longer than a couple of hours. "I'll see how I get on, but I can alway grab a cab."

He shakes his head. "No fucking chance. Father wouldn't allow it, not after last time. It's too dangerous." He leads me over toward the bar, which is heaving. "What would you like to drink?"

"Double Vodka and Coke," I say.

He nods. "Wait right here, and I'll get you it."

I'm thankful for my cousin, but in all honestly, I want to disappear into a quiet room somewhere in the back and fade away. Before my ordeal with Spartak, I would have been excited to party with my cousins. Now, all I feel is despair that I ever ran from his arms.

The arms of a monster are more inviting than returning to my old life, because he has given me a taste of true freedom to be who I am.

I fear that I'll never be able to get over it or him, which is part of the reason I can't face leaving for San Diego. As soon as I leave Chicago, it means the fantasy between Spartak and I is really over.

18

SPARTAK

"Aren't you worried, sir?" Osip asks, brow furrowing.

I glare at my obshchak. "Am I ever?"

He shakes his head. "No, but you're about to attempt a suicide mission."

"Suicide mission?" I laugh. "Do you really believe me so incompetent that I can't sneak in and out of a party?"

He looks so serious as he meets my gaze. "You're the most competent man I know, but we're in the middle of war. The security at the party is three times what they normally have on." He runs a hand across the back of his neck. "I don't want to lose my pakhan tonight."

I pat Osip on the back. "Don't worry, I have a way in and out." I wink at him.

"Care to share?"

I smirk. "I never share my finest secrets."

The fact is, I can't share how I'm getting in and out, because I'm using a source I have on the inside. One of Remy Morrone's high-ranking men feeds me information from time to time, but part of the agreement is that only I can contact him or know of the arrangement. Maxim is also in the dark about this.

He's agreed to leave a service door open for me so that I can get into the party and blend in as one of the staff. Conveniently, Remy is throwing a masquerade ball, which makes going unseen that much easier.

"Did you know it's a masquerade?" I hold up my mask.

Osip nods as I slip it on. "Well, that's something I guess."

"Quit worrying and relax." I shrug. "If it goes south, try to get me out. Leave me if it's too dangerous."

I adjust the bug on my lapel of the worker's uniform my source supplied me, before opening the door to the surveillance van. "How's the camera working?"

Osip nods. "Perfectly. Be careful, sir."

I give him a salute and then head down the alleyway behind the old library toward the back of the Casino. I'm exactly on time, which means that Dante should have removed all the guards from the back to rotate them, giving me two minutes to slip inside.

As promised, there's not a guard in sight as I get to the cracked open fire door at the back and slip in. I adjust my mask, making sure it covers my face entirely, and walk casually into the back service corridor. Dante gave me the instructions to get to the kitchen, which should be straight ahead. I intend to grab a tray of canapes and circle around the room, searching for Imalia.

Once I find her, I hope I can convince her to speak with me alone. There's only one way to find out. She could just as easily throw me to the wolves the moment she realizes who I am.

My veins pump with adrenaline as I walk into the kitchen, where many staff members are working. "Hey you," the manager shouts.

I nod. "Sir."

"Take those canapes and circulate. I don't want to see you without a tray for the rest of the night. You hear me?"

"Of course," I say, grabbing the tray and heading out of the kitchen toward the main event.

No one even looks twice at me as I make my way through the busy casino toward the main events room, which is where the ball is. My first portal of call to find Imalia, as I would expect the Morrone family are keeping her close.

The ballroom is dimly lit and lavishly decorated as I make my way through the crowd, occasionally stopping to offer guests a canape. After all, I've got to fit in.

"Mia, come here," Remy's voice cuts through the

air and I freeze, realizing how close I am to my enemy right now, hiding in plain sight.

Clearing my throat, I offer the nearest person to me a canape. As I turn to meet their gaze, my heart skips a beat. As Imalia's dark brown eyes are staring right at me through a half-face mask that matches her exquisite dress perfectly. The moment our eyes meet, recognition flashes through them. "Would you like a canape?" I ask, trying to keep my accent as neutral as possible.

Massimo, her cousin, nods and takes one.

"Miss?" I ask.

She shakes her head. "No, thank you." Her attention moves to her cousin. "If you'd excuse me, I need to use the restroom."

"Sure, I'll wait here for you," he replies.

Our eyes meet again, as if she's asking me to follow her. At first, I move in a different direction away from Massimo before changing course and following her through the crowd toward the restrooms.

I follow her into the corridor, but she doesn't go into the bathroom. Instead, she carries on and opens a door further up on the right, glancing back at me before disappearing inside.

Blood thrums through my veins as I set the canape tray down on a console against the wall and then march toward the door, swinging it open.

Imalia has removed her mask, and she's standing there with her hands on her hips. "What the hell are you doing here?"

I step into the supply closet and shut the door behind me, smirking. "I would have thought the last thing you'd do upon seeing your kidnapper would be to take him into an isolated closet away from your family."

"If they recognized you, they'd kill you," she says, shaking her head. "You really are insane."

"Why do you care what happens to me, baby girl?"

Her eyes dilate, and she clenches her thighs the moment I call her that. "I don't want you killed."

I move toward her, my cock hard and straining against my zipper. Is it possible a few days apart made her realize how right we are for each other? "And why not? After all, I'm a monster who kept you locked away."

Her throat bobs as she backs away from me until there's nowhere else to go and I have her cornered. "Because I'm not like you."

"What's that supposed to mean?"

Her chest heaves as she breathes in deeply. "It means, I don't believe killing people is the way to make amends."

I set my hands on either side of her against the wall, caging her in. Inhaling deeply, I savor her sweet scent of strawberries and jasmine, groaning as my cock hardens. "I've missed your smell," I breathe, gazing down at her as her eyes dilate with desire.

She licks her bottom lip, searching my eyes. "It's

been three days since I escaped you, but I haven't really escaped."

I tilt my head and lower my lips closer to hers. "What do you mean, baby girl?"

"I'm going fucking crazy." She sets her hands on my chest, shutting her eyes as she feels the warmth of me beneath her fingers and sighs. "Ever since I ran, all I can think about is you." Her eyes open and pin me with a stare that's enough to stop my heart. "What did you do to me?"

"You're such a good girl, Imalia," I murmur, moving my lips to her neck. "I've not been able to stop thinking about you either."

Has she finally accepted what I've known from the moment I set eyes on her?

"I did nothing to you, other than set the part of you that you hide free, little lamb."

"Don't call me that," she snaps, brow furrowing. "It makes me sound like prey."

"Aren't you, prey?" I ask, moving my hands from the wall to her hips and yanking her perfectly curvy body flush against me. "I do so very much want to eat you, malishka," I breathe, letting my lips tease over hers gently. "I've missed you." I move my lips to her neck and inhale her scent again, more deeply. "So fucking sweet."

"Spartak," she moans my name as I kiss her neck. "This is insane."

"Insane and so fucking right," I say, hitching up the

skirt of her dress and sliding my finger into her panties, which are soaking wet. "I've missed your pretty little cunt."

She claws at my shoulders. "Fuck," she murmurs as I slide a finger inside of her.

"I've missed everything about you," I continue, tearing apart her panties as they're getting in the way. "I need to be inside of you right now."

Imalia whimpers and slides her fingers into my hair, yanking my lips to hers. Her tongue delves hungrily into my mouth as she kisses me more desperately than she ever has before. "Fuck me, daddy," she breathes when she breaks away breathlessly. "I need you."

"You are such a good girl, Imalia. Which means you deserve daddy's cock in that greedy little pussy." I yank my finger out of her and lift her against the wall, forgetting where I am and how insane this is. It would take one of her family members to find us and I'd be a dead man. My cock teases against the soaking wet entrance of her pussy as I hold her gaze. "Never leave me again, malishka."

She shakes her head. "Never."

I thrust into her the moment she says that, overcome with desire and emotion. "Good girl," I breathe, holding still deep inside of her as she claws her fingernails into my back. "Tell me how badly you've missed me."

She looks into my eyes as I lift her up and down slowly on my cock, teasing her with long, soft strokes.

"I've missed you so fucking much," she murmurs, whimpering as her back knocks against the wall. "I haven't been able to think about anything but your thick cock stretching me day and night."

"Such a good girl for me," I murmur, thrusting into her so hard she cries out loud. "Do you like it hard?"

Imalia's eyes roll in the back of her head. "Yes, daddy."

"Of course you do, as you're my dirty little slut." I tighten my grasp on her and thrust into her so hard she moans like a whore. "Have you been touching yourself and picturing me?" I ask, increasing the tempo as I fuck her against the wall.

She nods, struggling to breathe enough to speak. "Yes, every day, multiple times."

My cock swells inside of her, hearing she's been so insatiable for me. "Fuck, I want you to come on my cock. Can you do that for me, baby girl?"

Her body shudders against me as I pound into her harder.

"Take my cock and come for me while I fuck you against the wall."

I claw my fingernails into her hips, thrusting harder and slamming her body into the wall.

"Fuck, yes, daddy," she cries, tumbling over the edge for me just like that.

I groan as I sink my teeth into her neck and come apart myself. "That's it, take daddy's cum. Every single drop deep in that pretty little pussy."

She moans as I keep her pinned against the wall, thrusting over and over until I've released every drop deep inside of her. The desire to get her pregnant still ruling me as it would be the ultimate claim over her. Once she has my baby growing inside of her, no one could refute that Imalia Allegro belongs to me.

"Imalia?" Massimo's unmistakable voice cuts through the air as he walks down the corridor. "Are you down here?"

Imalia's eyes widen and she tries to push me out of her, but I hold still.

"He won't check in here, little lamb. Stay quiet," I whisper.

She bites her bottom lip, looking utterly adorable as her cheeks flush.

"Imalia?" Massimo calls again, before huffing. "Where the hell is she?" His footsteps rush away and once she's certain he's gone, she bursts out laughing. It's the most beautiful sound I've ever heard.

"Fuck, that was close," she says, shaking her head.

I laugh along with her, stunned by how beautiful she looks while she's laughing. This is the first time I've seen her look so genuinely happy.

"It makes it even more thrilling, doesn't it?"

She shakes her head and punches me playfully in the arm. "If you're insane, yes."

I raise a brow and slide my cock out of her, dejected about leaving her body.

Imalia clears her throat and slides up her torn panties before adjusting the skirt of her dress.

"You look so fucking beautiful tonight."

Her cheeks flush as she avoids my gaze. "I'd better get back before they wonder where I've gone." She moves to step around me, but I step into her path.

"Not so fast." I slide my hands onto her hips and pull her against me. "I want you to come home with me, where you belong."

She tenses in my grasp. "I can't live the way you made me live those three weeks, Spartak." She shakes her head. "I'm not an animal that can be caged."

"I know that, little lamb." I press my lips to hers, kissing her softly. "I was wrong to keep you locked up for so long." I inhale her scent, memorizing it as I sense she won't come as willingly as she just came on my cock. "You deserve to be my equal." I press my lips to her neck and kiss her. "My queen," I breathe. "If you feel the way I feel, I want you to come to live with me and be by my side. You'll be free and never caged again."

Her eyes are wide as she searches mine, as if looking for a lie. "And what about my family?" she asks.

"What about them?" I ask.

She tilts her head slightly, looking irritated. "I heard you're causing a real stir for my mom. Will you leave her alone if I come with you?"

Backing down now in San Diego wouldn't make any sense. I search her beautiful brown eyes and know in an instance I can't deny her anything. "If that's what you want, I'll back down." I narrow my eyes. "The same can't be said for here in Chicago. I'm afraid the war will continue and you'll be on the opposite side of it to your uncle and cousins."

Her throat bobs as she swallows. "They'll believe I betrayed them."

"Perhaps, but does it matter?" I tighten my grasp on her hips. "After all, they don't let you be who you want to be, do they?"

Imalia shakes her head. "Can I have a couple of days to decide?"

I clench my jaw, as the idea of leaving her here tonight drives me mad. "How will I get to you after tonight? This was the perfect opportunity."

She reaches into my pocket and pulls out my cell phone. "I'll give you my number and we'll arrange a meeting point if I decide to come and stay with you."

I unlock my cell phone and she puts her number in, ringing her own phone so she has mine. And then she passes me the phone and walks away, glancing over her shoulder as she reaches the door. "Be careful. If you get caught leaving, I don't need to tell you what my family will do to you." With that, she walks out of the closet, leaving me on edge.

Normally, I would have insisted she was coming with me, thrown her over my shoulder and dragged her out like a neanderthal. However, this has to be her choice if I'm going to avoid making the same stupid mistakes as I did in my past.

I head out of the closet and make my way back through the party toward the exit. Where there are now guards stationed. One of them speaks to me, "Hey, where are you going?"

"My shift is over. The manager dismissed me."

His eyes narrow and for a moment, I wonder if he's going to force me to reach for my gun. Finally, he nods and mutters something in Italian, allowing me to leave.

I walk away, quietly optimistic about Imalia returning home to me. Despite being disappointed that she didn't want to leave with me tonight, I sense she won't be able to stay away long.

My cell phone buzzes and I pull it out.

Imalia: Did you make it out okay?

I smirk, amused by how worried she is about me.

Yes, baby girl. It's so sweet of you to care so much.

She sends back an eye roll emoji and I slide my phone back into my pocket and head toward the van where Osip is waiting.

I wonder if he enjoyed our little show.

19

IMALIA

*M*y heart is practically beating out of my chest the rest of the night, as I try to focus on anything but Spartak fucking me in the supply closet.

Did that really happen?

I clench my thighs, knowing without a doubt it did. As I'm still sore and his cum is dripping out of me into my torn panties. My stomach flips as I can't stop replaying the moment in my mind.

Massimo swears he was going insane trying to find me, but I told him we must have missed each other.

Spartak got in and out of this party so easily, which is a little concerning considering we're at war. If my uncle's enemies can get into his casino that easily, it's possible they could repeat the disaster at Le Stelle with his entire family inside, ending the war.

And yet, Spartak came here seemingly alone with

the sole purpose of seeing me. Perhaps winning me over would be a victory and nothing more. It's why I asked for a few days to decide, as I can't work out if he's just saying the right things to get me to come willingly.

Does he truly care about me, or is it all a game for a man like him?

It's the dilemma I can't solve. My feelings, although fucked up, are clear. I'm falling for the brute of a man who kidnapped me, tied me up and took me against my will.

"You seem distracted," Camilla says, leaning on the bar counter nearby.

"I'm tired, is all." I sigh. "How are you enjoying the party?"

She wrinkles her nose. "It's fucking boring, isn't it?"

I laugh at that.

"Honestly, I'd rather ditch and head to the pizza place around the corner."

I shrug. "Why don't we?"

She raises a brow. "Because Father will kill me."

"Seriously? You've just turned eighteen. Officially an adult and you're worried your dad will kill you for sneaking off to get some decent food." I scrunch my nose up as I look at the half-eaten canape that tasted of smelly socks. "Seriously, what is with this food?"

Camilla laughs. "Okay, let's get Mia and go." She hooks her arms with mine. "You seem better. Perhaps it was a good idea to get you out of the house."

The reason my mood is so improved is my tryst with

Spartak, which my family would kill me for. Spartak's proposal is tempting, but it means losing my family forever. It was easier when he didn't give me a choice.

"Mia, we're going to sneak out to the pizza place around the corner. Do you want to come?"

Mia smirks. "Of course, when do I ever say no to doing things I shouldn't?"

Camilla rolls her eyes. "Never."

"Exactly, let's go." She hooks arms with me and leads us toward the exit. "We'll have to make sure Massimo doesn't see us, as he'd stop us for sure."

"What about Luca?" Camilla asks.

Mia's brow furrows. "What about him?"

"He'll be very disappointed we didn't invite him, especially when pizza is involved."

Mia laughs. "He'll get over it."

Both of them were so engrossed in the conversation, they didn't even notice Luca approaching us. "And where is it you ladies are going?"

Mia and Camilla straighten suddenly, plastering on false smiles. "For pizza around the corner. Care to join?"

He groans, holding his stomach. "Thank fuck someone suggested it. The food at this event is awful." He runs a hand through his hair. "Does father or Massimo know?"

We all exchange uncertain glances. "What do you think?" Mia asks.

He makes a tutting sound, but a smirk spreads onto

his lips. "Count me in. We better get out quick before Massimo catches us."

We all rush for the exit and head out of the heavily guarded doors, where none of my father's men bat an eyelid. It helps that Luca is with us as we head around the corner to the small pizza restaurant. It's quiet when we enter and the server tells us to choose a seat.

Luca selects a table by the window and grabs a menu. "So, how did you enjoy your eighteenth birthday party, little sis?"

Camilla glares at him. "It was never a party for me and you know it, Luca."

He nods. "Yeah, it was bullshit."

Mia glances at me. "You disappeared for a while during the party. Where were you?"

I shrug. "I needed some time alone."

A flash of rage enters Luca's eyes. "I tell you, if I ever get my hands on Spartak Volkov, I'll break his neck."

Guilt floods through me as they're all so angry at what happened to me, and yet I snuck off with him tonight at the party. I'm lying to my family and considering betraying them to return to a man who doesn't care about free will. The decision isn't an easy one, even if I'm pretty sure I'll never be happy again if I don't give in to the connection I have with Spartak.

The waitress smiles at Luca as she approaches. "What can I get you?"

"I'll have the deep dish pepperoni pizza," Luca orders.

Camilla nods. "The same for me, please."

Mia's brow furrows. "I'll have cheese and tomato."

The waitress jots down Mia's order and then glances at me. "Bacon for me, please."

She nods. "Can I get you any drinks?"

"A bottle of your finest prosecco and four glasses," Luca says, flashing the waitress a smile. After all, both Mia and Camilla are underage.

She looks a little uncertain, but nods and writes it down on her notepad. "Coming right up." She collects the menus and leaves us.

Camilla laughs. "This is so much more fun than that boring party. I'm definitely ordering ice cream after."

"There's no way you'll be able to finish an entire pizza here, so how are you going to fit in ice cream?"

Mia rolls her eyes. "There's always room for ice cream, Imalia."

Luca laughs. "Yeah, it melts anyway."

"True," I say, laughing with my cousins.

I'm thankful for this distraction. At least while I'm here with my family, I can try to put the life-changing decision looming over me to the back of my mind, and enjoy their company.

Tossing and turning, I find it impossible to sleep. The decision I need to make weighing heavily on my mind.

Family has always been my number one priority all my life. You stick with your family no matter what, especially having Italian roots, and yet I can't sleep because I'm considering betraying them.

My cell phone dings and I sigh heavily before turning over and grabbing it off the nightstand.

When I see who the text message is from, my heart skips a beat.

Spartak.

I unlock the phone and my body heats when I see the photo of him naked in bed, up to his hip line. Along with the message.

I can't sleep, because all I can think about is you, baby girl.

My body turns to molten lava as I clench my thighs, wishing I was beside him right now in his bed. I bite my bottom lip, knowing how sick I am to even be thinking like that. The bastard kidnapped me and all I should hate him and yet I can't find anything other than desire when I look at the picture.

I slide my hand between my thighs and rub myself through the fabric of my panties, groaning. Moving the covers, I snap a photo of my hand between my thighs and send it to him, continuing to touch myself. My nipples harden as the phone buzzes again and Spartak has sent me another picture with his hand wrapped around his thick shaft as he jerks himself off.

Such a good girl, touching your pretty little pussy for daddy. I want you to make yourself come for me. Can you do that?

I moan, unable to believe sexting can be this damn hot. Sliding my panties off, I reach into my nightstand and grab my dildo out, positioning the head of it at my soaking wet lips and taking a photo.

I wish this was your cock, daddy.

I send the photo and slide it inside of me, groaning when I do. It helps quench the deep ache inside of me for more, rubbing my clit with my other hand.

Fuck your pretty little cunt with that dildo for me. I want you to video it and send it to me.

I bite my bottom lip and turn on the video recorder, positioning it at the foot of the bed, pointing toward me. Slowly, I fuck myself with the dildo and continue to rub my clit as I shut my eyes and picture my kidnapper moving above me, sliding in and out of me.

"Fuck, daddy, just like that," I moan softly, not wanting anyone to hear outside the walls of my room. "You make me so fucking wet." I bite my lip and then set my eyes on the camera, so aroused right now. The wet sounds as it moves in and out of me are so loud as I moan again. "I wish it was your cock buried inside of me." And then I grab the phone and turn off the recording, editing out the bits at the start and end before sending it.

Is this what you want?

I see the bubbles ignite as he texts back.

Yes, now make yourself come for me watching this.

A video pops through of him lying on his bed with his hard cock in his hands as he strokes himself up and down. "You are such a good little girl, Imalia, fucking your pretty little pussy for daddy."

My muscles tighten hearing his voice as I move the dildo in and out faster and harder, watching as he stares at the camera and strokes himself.

"Such a good girl who should be sitting on daddy's cock, but you will be soon. Soon, you won't be able to stop sitting on this cock morning, noon and night."

His dick looks huge at this angle as I watch him, making me long for it more.

"Now come for me, baby girl. I want you to make your pretty little cunt come as if I were balls deep inside of you."

It's all it takes as I moan loudly, coming apart as I thrust the dildo in and out of myself harder, shuddering around it. "Fuck," I breathe, unable to believe the power this man has over me. I come on fucking command from him and it's so damn hot.

My phone buzzes with a message.

Did you come for me?

A picture comes through with the message of his abs sticky with his own cum.

I shift in the bed and take a picture of the wet patch beneath myself on the sheets.

Yes daddy. I came so hard for you.

The cell phone rings and my stomach dips as I see it's him calling. "Hey," I answer.

"I need to fuck you as soon as possible, Imalia," he growls down the phone, sounding more animal than man.

"I told you I need—"

"Bullshit, what you need is my cock deep in your pussy," he murmurs. "What you need is my cock inside of you and the dildo buried in your ass."

I moan at the filthy thought.

"Do you like that idea, little lamb?"

I swallow hard. "Yes," I breathe, knowing how dangerous it is to reveal that to him. I've never had anal sex, but I've played with my dildo alone. It's something my ex was never interested in trying, but something I've wanted to do for ages. "Or the other way around," I murmur, my heart pounding in my ears.

He makes a deep groaning sound, which sets my blood on fire. "Would you like that, baby girl? My cock deep in your tight little ass?"

I shudder, finding it impossible I could be so turned on after climaxing moments ago. "Yes, daddy," I purr.

"Fuck, baby girl. I'd like it too. Have you ever put the dildo up your ass?"

I groan softly. "Yes, I love fucking my ass with it."

"Good," he says, his voice raspy. "I'm going to pop your anal cherry and once I do, you won't be able to stop riding my cock with your tight little asshole."

I moan, rubbing my hard, painful nipples. "Fuck, I want you so bad," I breathe.

"Perhaps you should have come home with me earlier."

I swallow hard as his comment pulls me back to reality. "It's not a snap decision I could make. I need time."

He groans. "I wish you would accept the inevitable. No matter what you do, you'll never be able to forget about me."

"That's a cocky statement."

He chuckles, and it's such a rich sound. "Because I know you, Imalia. I know what makes you tick and you'll never be happy in a normal, vanilla relationship."

"How do you know that?" I ask, hating how right he is.

"Because you crave pain and domination and filthy fucking sex. The kind of filthy sex that would make most people's skin crawl."

I swallow hard.

"I saw the desire in your eyes when I walked into that knife in my dungeon. The idea of being cut turns you on, doesn't it, little lamb?"

I clench my thighs, knowing without a doubt there has to be something wrong with me, as he's right. The idea of being cut during sex turns me on, as pain does like when he branded my ass with that paddle. "Yes," I breathe, so quiet.

"Good girl for telling me the truth," he breathes. "I can't wait to explore every dirty little kink you have."

I swallow hard, as he's assuming I'm going to go back to him. Unsurprisingly, I guess after everything that I've admitted to him tonight. The fact is, deep down, it's what I want, but it means forsaking my family. I wish I didn't have to choose between my family and being happy with a man who gets me like no person ever has. "It's late," I say.

"Indeed," he replies. "Get some sleep. Sweet dreams." He cancels the call, leaving my head spinning.

I'm more confused than ever as I stare up at the ceiling in the bedroom, rubbing my thighs together. When I hear his voice, it does something to me I can't explain, especially when he calls me a good girl. It's as if I crave his praise like a fucking kid, but it's what he does to me. Turns me into someone I don't really recognize and yet I know better than anyone in this world.

The part of me I've been burying for years, trying to fit into the social molds he told me he'd break me out of. Perhaps Spartak was never my enslaver, but my salvation.

20

SPARTAK

"Sir, I've been informed the Callaghan clan targeted Poldoka."

I sit up straighter in my desk chair, narrowing my eyes. "When?"

"Thirty minutes ago." Osip taps the toe of his foot on the floor. "They stole the shipment from last night."

I slam my fist down on my desk and stand, pacing the floor. "Motherfuckers have taken advantage of the fact the Italians have distracted us." I pin Osip with a glare. "How the hell did they get past security?"

Osip's throat bobs. "It appears the men on the night shift weren't taking their post seriously enough." He runs a hand across the back of his neck. "They were drunk."

I grab hold of a vase off the dresser next to me and throw it at the floor to ceiling glass windows. It smashes into hundreds of pieces as I turn around and glare at my obshchak. "Who was on guard that night? I want every name."

Osip bows his head. "I will find out for you, sir."

"We're at war, and my men are getting drunk rather than do their jobs?" I shake my head, feeling the rage spiral out of control. "I'll have blood for this, Osip."

He nods. "I thought as much, sir. Those responsible will be brought to you."

I slump down behind my desk, loosening my tie from my neck. "The problem is we can't afford anymore fucking losses. We're thin on the ground as it is." I swallow hard, as Imalia hasn't decided yet. I promised her that I'd pull my men from San Diego and leave her family alone if she comes to me willingly. Perhaps a show of early good will might encourage her to return to me sooner. "Contact Timur and pull him back to Chicago. We've taught the Allegro family a lesson. Ask him to send a message that if they return to Chicago, we won't hesitate to strike again."

"Sir, is it wise to pull back when we're making such headway in San Diego?" Osip asks.

I clench my jaw. "We can't have the brotherhood split forever. Pull him back." I glare at him, knowing that despite his penchant for questioning me, he won't question me twice.

"Very well. I'll ask Timur to make the arrangements and return to Chicago as soon as possible." He lingers, shuffling his feet. "This isn't about Imalia Allegro, is it?"

I narrow my eyes. "What are you saying?"

He shrugs. "The ultimatum she gave you, sir."

I grind my teeth, as I'd forgotten that Osip listened to that conversation and our fucking in the supply closet. "It does not. Imalia hasn't made her decision. We need more men here if we're going to hold off the Irish and Russians."

"Fair enough. Is there anything else you need, sir?"

"Get Kirill to strike at the Irish. I want their next shipment stolen." I run a hand through my hair. "We can't let it go unanswered."

"Of course." He bows his head. "Have you considered approaching the Estrada family to see where they stand?"

"I've already had discussions with them." I shrug. "They're happy to supply us with arms, but they're not taking a side in the war. Hernandez was pretty clear on that."

Osip grimaces slightly. "Any word on whether Vito can help?"

I sigh, pacing the floor. "He's struggling to get his men to move across the Atlantic. He's got fifteen men here." I shake my head. "The deal is lucrative to give us a foothold in Europe, but it will not help us win the war." I pace the floor. "Our only hope is to solidify our forces here in Chicago and make sure we split our efforts between the Callaghan Clan and the Morrone family."

Osip nods. "I agree, sir."

I nod. "Good, now make sure those Irish pay."

He understands that I wish to be left alone, turning and walking out of my office. I slam my fist down hard on my desk, a glass tumbling over and rolling onto the floor, shattering into pieces. Anger coils through me as I glare out of the window, knowing somehow I need to put the Volkov Bratva back on top in Chicago. Peace has made us weak all these years, and now I need to shake the city to its core.

My cell phone buzzes and I pull it out of my pocket, my stomach fluttering when I see Imalia's name on the screen.

What are you doing?

I groan, as this isn't the time to text the niece of my enemy. She's distracting me as much as the Morrone family in this war. I know she's the reason my eye has been off the ball, but I can't resist indulging her.

I just had a business meeting. It didn't go well.

I take a picture of the smashed glass and vase on the floor and send it to her.

Oh, well, I don't see any blood, so it can't have gone that bad.

I smile at her candid response. A response which suggests she knows me better than I thought. A knock behind me draws my attention, and Maxim pokes his head through the door. "Can I come in?"

I draw in a deep breath and stow my cell phone away. "Of course."

He eyes the smashed glass warily before taking a seat opposite my desk. "I have a request for you."

"Request?" I ask, raising my brow as I sit in my chair behind my desk. "What kind of request?"

He runs a hand across the back of his neck and I sense he's anxious, which isn't like Maxim. "I need you to give me Vito Bianchi."

"Give you him?" I shake my head. "I'm not sure I understand."

Maxim's jaw clenches. "I want him strung up in our basement."

His statement surprises me as I sit up straighter. "What exactly did he do?"

Maxim glares at me.

"I can't help you if you don't enlighten me, son."

He sighs heavily. "He has been abusive to Livia all her life, and it came to light recently that he's been poisoning her mother." He raises a brow. "I guess you noticed she's not exactly normal?"

I nod in response, as it was clear at the wedding reception she was not sound of mind. "Yes, I did."

"He's been drugging her, and that's why." He shrugs. "Besides, you love any reason to torture a man to death."

"And Livia wants this?"

Maxim nods. "She hasn't asked me to do it, but she declared she wished she could string him up and do her worst."

I smirk at that. "She was with you when you tortured Daniel. Does she have a penchant for violence like us?"

"Yes." He adjusts his jacket. "So what do you say?"

I consider the proposal, knowing that it would rock things but it would be manageable. Maxim is set to inherit the Bianchi family throne along with Livia, so it makes sense that removing Vito would only benefit our own goals. "It's a tempting proposal, as we'd gain sole control over his empire across the Atlantic, but it would mean more resource we can't spare."

I stand and walk to the dresser housing my decanters. "Would you like a drink?"

Maxim's eyes widen, perhaps because I never offer him one when he's in here. "Sure."

I pour him a whiskey, which I know he prefers, and myself a vodka.

He gives me a nod as I pass it into his hand. "I can head up the operations on the other side of the Atlantic. Me and Livia."

I nod. "Allow me to reflect on it, but I'm very open to the idea." I sip my vodka. "Vito hasn't delivered on a lot of his promises, such as one-hundred extra men to help in the war." I set my tumbler down, stepping around the broken glass on the floor. "It appears his men aren't so willing to move with him to America." I sigh. "It's why I've had to bring back Timur and our men from San Diego."

"Wise move," Maxim says simply, nodding his head. "It makes no sense to split our efforts."

"Did you hear about the Callaghan's hit on Poldoka last night?"

Maxim shakes his head. "No."

"They stole a large shipment. It means I'm going to regroup and rethink our strategy. Too much effort has been going on scuppering Remy's plans that I've forgotten to keep my eye on the Callaghan Clan." I narrow my eyes as I wonder what he'll think of my plan with Imalia if she returns to me. "I saw Imalia the other night and asked her to return of her own free will."

Maxim sits up straighter, cupping his tumbler in both hands. "And?"

"She said she needs a few days to decide, but was keen if you catch my drift."

Maxim rolls his eyes. "Surely not at the party?"

I nod. "In a supply closet."

"Crazy bastard," he mutters, shaking his head. "You could have gotten yourself killed."

"If she returns to me, Maxim. I need you to know that I intend to marry her."

"Marry her?" he scoffs, eyes widening. "Are you insane? She's a Morrone."

"She's an Allegro."

"Whatever, she's related to your arch nemesis, Remy

Morrone." His eyes narrow. "Do you even care about her, or is it about snatching something from him?"

I growl, my son questioning my intentions angers me more than it should. Normally I don't give a shit what anyone else thinks of my actions, but this I'd hoped he'd understand. "I told you I love her. She's mine, and I intend to seal that with a marriage contract. It has nothing to do with who she is related to."

"Doesn't look that way to me," he mutters.

I move toward him, ready to grab him by his collar out of his seat and slam him against the wall, but that's when I remember I'm trying to build bridges, not fucking burn them. Clenching my fist by my side, I shake my head. "You can believe what you want. I'm going to be better to you from now on. I fucked everything up with your sister, and that's on me, but I don't wish to do the same with you."

His eyes narrow. "It's a little late to turn back the clock."

I clench my jaw, wishing I could be more open with my son and make him understand why I am how I am.

Maxim's expression turns unreadable as he stands. "I'm leaving."

I set my hand on his shoulder before he turns. "I am sorry for everything I did to you as a child, Maxim."

There's a flicker of emotion in his ice-blue depths, but it extinguishes quickly. "So am I," he says, before turning and leaving the room, slamming the door behind him.

I stare at it blankly for a little while, realizing that the way I treated him as a kid to toughen him up broke him. It wasn't a patch on what I went through, but it was bad. Brutality doesn't breed strength, it breeds a person who is broken and damaged beyond repair.

I've known for a long while I'm damaged beyond repair, but I never believed I'd done the same to my son. I thought I was easy on him. Turns out I fucked him up almost as bad as my family fucked me up.

21

IMALIA

I sneak down the stairs, my heart hammering at a thousand miles an hour.

Spartak is meeting me at a twenty-four-hour diner to discuss arrangements. As I've finally agreed to return to his side, even though it's utterly insane.

Who the hell agrees to return to their captor?

"Where are you going?" Massimo asks from behind me, making me jump out of my skin.

I turn around and shrug. "I'm hungry." I try to school my features despite the mess of nerves twisting together inside of me. "I'm going to rummage something up."

His brow furrows as his eyes take in the outfit I'm wearing. "Overdressed for rummaging in the kitchen, Imalia."

Fuck.

"Fine, I'm going out to meet a friend, as I can't sleep."

"Like hell you are," he growls, rushing toward me. "We're at war with the Volkov Bratva, Imalia. You can't sneak out in the early hours of the morning."

"Do you realize I'm twenty-six, Massimo?" I tilt my head. "A grown woman who can make her own choices. I'm only going around the corner to the local diner." I swallow hard, hating lying to him. Although I'm going to a diner, it's not around the corner.

"How long will you be?"

I shrug. "A couple of hours, I'd expect. Why?"

He sighs heavily. "If you haven't returned in two hours, I'm coming to fetch you myself. Understand?"

I clench my jaw, but nod. "Sure." Two hours should be long enough, and he won't find me even if he does try to come and get me.

Spartak has asked me to take a cab and meet him in a diner in his territory, as he could get killed if anyone from the Morrone mafia saw him within the boundaries of our territory.

Massimo holds my gaze for a few beats. "Just be careful, okay?"

"I will be." I give him a smile, but it's forced. "See you later."

It's been five days since my last encounter with Spartak, and I'm going insane. I need to touch him, to kiss him, and have his hands on me. Our late night sexting was only driving me more insane until I finally snapped tonight and demanded we meet up in person.

I walk away from my cousin burdened with both guilt and relief to have made it away without him stopping me. Massimo is renowned for being a stickler for the rules. He almost lost his shit when he found us at that pizza place the night of the party, because he takes on far more responsibility than his siblings being next in line to the throne.

My phone buzzes and I check it.

Waiting for you, baby girl. Hurry!

My stomach churns as I type back.

On my way. Almost got stopped by Massimo.

I rush out of the front door and down the winding driveway, knowing the guards will be on duty at the gate. Once I'm close to the gate, I take a left and head toward the hole in the fence that all my cousins have used in their lives to sneak off the premises. Quicky I dash onto the street and away from the gates toward a car with its engine on, which I hope is my Uber.

"Hey, Uber for Imalia?"

He nods. "Yeah, you're late."

"Sorry," I say, getting into the back. "Charge it to my account."

The driver nods and then drives toward the diner where I'm meeting Spartak. All the while, my heart is thundering against my rib cage at a thousand miles an hour. I've definitely lost my mind as I watch the building and street lights rushing past the window.

It's a fifteen minute drive across the city at this time of night when the driver finally pulls up outside of the diner. I open the door. "Thanks," I say, passing him a ten-dollar bill as a tip. "And sorry about the delay at the start."

He takes the cash and makes a grunting noise before rushing away from the curb.

When I turn around, Spartak is standing right behind me, looming over me. "Hey there, little lamb."

Goosebumps prickle over every inch of my body at the look in his eyes. It's predatory and raw and it makes me want to jump his bones. "Hey, daddy," I breathe quietly.

Those beautiful gray eyes flash with desire as he groans. "Come with me."

He pulls me in the opposite direction of the diner.

"Where are we going?"

He smirks at me, the most wicked smirk I've ever seen. "It's a surprise."

I shudder, realizing that despite my inescapable desire for this man, I don't trust him, not really. He's a psychopath who I shouldn't even be meeting with. The extent of his depravity I've probably not yet witnessed, and that smirk scares me. "I don't like surprises," I say, hugging my arms tightly around myself.

"This one you will." His hand lands on the small of my back as he pulls me closer to him. "Trust me."

I grind my teeth and allow him to lead me along the dark street, knowing that Massimo will lose his shit if I'm not back in two hours. "By the way, Massimo gave me a curfew."

Spartak raises a brow. "I'm surprised he let you leave at all."

I shrug. "I'm a grown woman."

"We're here," he says, stopping outside a building and facing it. "Come on." Spartak walks up to the door and opens it as the faint sound of music travels up to the street.

I narrow my eyes, unsure about entering this nondescript looking building with him. "I'm not sure about this."

He rolls his eyes and grabs my hand, yanking me into his muscular body. "Stop thinking so much." With that, he pulls me into the stairwell and we descend into God knows where. The music is heavily bassy and grows louder the further we descend.

"I feel like I'm descending into hell."

Spartak smirks. "Perhaps you are, baby girl." And then, he opens the door at the bottom of the stairwell and all the air from my lungs escapes at the sight in front of me.

The place is a sex club. People are walking around half-naked or dressed in leather, and the sounds of people fucking echo around me. My stomach clenches as I try to take in the crazy scenes in front of me. "What the hell," I mutter, my eyes landing on a woman tied to some kind of swing being fucked by one man and the other has his cock down her throat.

Spartak's breath teases against my earlobe. "I thought you might learn more about yourself and what you like, malishka."

I swallow hard and glance at the man who brought me here. "This is insane."

He pulls me against him, his hard cock pressed against my ass cheeks. "Yes, but don't worry, you don't have to do anything if you don't want to. Let's find a table." Guiding me from behind, he steers me toward a table near the back cloaked in darkness.

I clench my thighs tightly as I sit down. Right now, I'd actually consider having sex with him here in the middle of the club. The thought hardens my nipples and soaks through my panties as I shift uncomfortably in my seat.

Spartak slides in close to me, his hand resting on my hip as he pulls me against him. "I'm so fucking hard for you right now. Do you want to touch me?"

I look into those blue-gray eyes and nod. "Okay."

"Good girl," he purrs, unzipping his pants and freeing his huge length.

I swallow hard, as I can't believe I'm doing this in a fucking sex club, of all places.

He grabs my hand and wraps my fingers around him. "Touch me, baby girl."

I groan at the hard, velvety feel of him beneath my

fingers as precum pools at the tip. "I've missed touching you," I breathe.

Spartak's eyes flicker shut. "I've missed everything about you."

I swallow hard and tighten my grasp, stroking the length of him more firmly. The ache between my thighs becomes unbearable as I rub them together, trying to get friction.

Spartak notices my movement and smirks, sliding his hand beneath my skirt and rubbing me through my panties. "So fucking wet, Imalia. Would you like to ride daddy's cock here in the club?"

My heart skips a beat as I stare at his huge, pulsing length and then glance around the darkened room. No one is paying attention to us. They're all too caught up in their own acts, as men and women fuck around us. I never believed I'd be into getting off in such a public place, but it's thrilling. "Yes, daddy," I breathe.

"You're such a good girl." He grabs my hips and lifts me off the bench next to him, forcing me to straddle his thighs. The hard length of his cock presses against my soaking wet lips. "I want you to fuck yourself on my cock and come for me like my dirty little whore right here, where anyone could see us."

My nipples are so hard they hurt like hell, as Spartak yanks down the front of my dress and pulls one into his mouth, groaning. "I've been going fucking insane without you."

I grind myself on his hard length, hardly able to

believe we're about to do this. "I thought you already were insane."

He grips my hips so hard it hurts, biting on my nipple and making me yelp. "Careful, malishka. You wouldn't want me to punish you right here in front of everyone, would you?"

My pussy gushes at the idea of being made an example of in such a public place.

He chuckles. "Or perhaps you would the way your pretty little cunt just soaked my cock at the thought." He lifts me and frees his length. "First, I need to be inside of you." He pulls me down over his huge cock, impaling me on it.

I moan so loud, forgetting about where we are. "Fuck, yes," I breathe, finally feeling him quench that ache that's been there since Camilla's birthday party. The last time I had him inside of me.

"That's it, baby girl. I want you to bounce up and down on my cock like that." He helps me, his rough hands guiding me up and down as we fuck in the back of a sex club like a couple of crazed animals, and I know I've never felt more free in all my life.

"You feel so good inside of me, daddy," I moan, clawing my fingers in his dark, messy hair.

He captures my lips, kissing me deeply and stealing the oxygen from my lungs. When he breaks free, he murmurs, "I never want to go another day without this tight little cunt wrapped around my cock. Do you understand?"

I pull back, continuing to bob up and down harder on his length, looking into his beautiful eyes. "Yes, daddy. I want your cock every day," I reply.

He groans, eyes rolling back as he sinks his fingernails into my hips hard enough to break the skin. "I can't stand it any longer." He lifts me right off his cock, making me whimper as he throws me down on my back onto the bench as if I weigh nothing. "I need to fuck you hard."

My nipples are so painful right now as he sinks every inch as deep as he can physically go, bottoming out inside of me. "Fuck, daddy," I cry.

Spartak growls above me, moving in and out of me with forceful thrusts, as if he's trying to split me in half.

The roughness only drives me toward the edge faster as he fucks me like an animal, holding my eye contact with such intensity.

"Take it just like that," he groans, muscles straining in his neck as he increases the pace.

I can hardly find time to breathe as he fucks me faster and harder, driving me right toward the edge. He holds himself up with one arm and wraps his other hand tightly around my throat, cutting off my oxygen.

"Do you like being choked, Imalia?" he asks.

I can't answer as he tightens his grasp, eyes holding mine.

"Because I enjoy choking you, and your pretty little pussy is getting wetter."

His hips roll more viciously and erratically as his

eyes dilate further. "Fuck, I'm so damn close to coming deep inside you, Imalia. I want you growing big and round with my baby."

"Fuck, that's hot," I hear someone say nearby, drawing my attention to a group of people who have gathered to watch us. Three guys and two girls, all of them pleasuring themselves and watching us fuck.

The guys have their cocks out and are shamelessly stroking themselves, while the girls finger themselves. Spartak finally releases my throat, allowing me to draw in a deep gulp of oxygen.

"Oh my God," I breathe, returning my gaze to Spartak. "We have an audience."

Spartak smirks down at me. "Do you enjoy having an audience, baby girl?"

I swallow hard as the answer shocks me. I do like it, it's so fucking hot and I know I won't last much longer.

"That's it, baby girl," Spartak breathes. "You're doing so well. Make that pussy come on my cock."

"Fuck, yes, daddy," I cry, tumbling over the edge as he ruts into me. It's the most spine tingling and earth-shattering orgasm I've ever had, as a flood of liquid squirts around his cock.

Spartak roars above me, muscles straining as he comes apart deep inside of me, filling me with his cum.

I hear the men and women watching us grunting and groaning too as they come to climax as well. As I glance over, I see two of the men shoot their cum across the floor shamelessly. My entire body shudders with the intensity of my orgasm and the overwhelming sensation of being watched.

One guy gives me a wink as he shoves his cock back into his pants. The onlookers move away from us, leaving us alone.

"That was definitely the craziest thing I've ever done." I meet Spartak's intense gaze. "And I kind of loved it."

He smirks. "I knew you would, because you're just like me, little lamb." He nuzzles his nose against mine in an oddly tender caress. "I've missed you so fucking much." He pulls back and searches my eyes. "Are you ready to come home with me?"

I swallow hard, staring into his blue-gray eyes and knowing that my decision is going to be the most life-changing decision I've ever made, either way.

"Yes, I'm ready." I've never meant those words more than I do right now. There's no going back once I return with him. I've made my choice and I'll live with it for the rest of my life, whether it's the right or wrong one.

22

SPARTAK

She chose me over her family and I'm honored by her decision. My little lamb has accepted what I've known since the day we met, but I want to be sure she's certain about this. Once she's mine, there's no going back. I won't repeat the same mistakes I made in my youth.

Imalia follows me into the chamber where I first tied her up, nervously tangling her fingers together. "Why are we in here?"

"If you're going to make this decision for certain, you need to learn the depths of my depravity and if you can handle it."

Her throat bobs as she swallows hard. "I see."

"Are you willing to try?"

She nods in response.

"Good, because this will either break you or make you." I walk toward the bed and sit on the edge, patting

229

the space next to me for her to join. "Few can survive me."

She shudders as she sits a little distance away from me. "What do you mean?"

"They break mentally." I shrug. "Sometimes physically."

Imalia winces at that. "You've killed girls?"

I swallow hard, as there's been one time when things got out of hand in this dungeon, and I did accidentally take her life. "Accidentally, yes." I place my hand on the small of her back, gently caressing her. "That was a long time ago, though. I'm more experienced now."

There's a flash of what looks like jealousy in her eyes. "Right, because you've had so many women in here?"

I smirk at the angry tone of her voice. "Does that annoy you?"

She clenches her jaw and shakes her head.

"Don't lie," I murmur, moving my lips to her neck and kissing her. "Clearly, my baby girl has a jealous streak, but don't worry, daddy is all yours forever, malishka."

She shivers as I unhook the buttons on the back of her dress and peel it off of her. "Do we need some kind of safe word?"

I stop and look her in the eye. "Yes, how did you know?"

"Curiosity led me to porn." She shrugs. "I have had

an obsession with BDSM for as long as I started watching it."

"Of course you have, because you're a dirty little girl, but none of what you've watched would have got close to what I intend to do to you."

I notice Imalia shudder as I stand and walk toward the implements on the wall. "What shall I use on you today?" When I glance back at her, she looks scared, which only turns me on more.

I select the paddle with daddy on I used the first time and the same knife she threatened to stab me with off of the wall. "These will do," I say.

Imalia stares at me with wide eyes as I place them on the bed and then meet her gaze, clenching my jaw. I rarely give a woman a safe word, but this has to be different. "Safe word will be red." I tilt her chin up with my finger to get a better view of her. "If you want me to stop at any point, then you shout it out. Do you understand?"

Imalia nods in response, but I'm not satisfied with it.

"Answer me, malishka."

"Yes, I understand." She twists her palms together in her lap, clearly nervous. "Are you going to cut me?" she asks, glancing at the knife on the bed.

My cock throbs in my boxer briefs as I can't wait to make her bleed, teach her how good different methods of pain can be. "I want to. Would you like that?"

"I honestly have no idea." She places the pad of her

finger against the blade, testing the sharpness. "I like pain."

She more than likes pain from what I've witnessed. "This isn't all we're going to experiment with." I walk toward a cabinet on the far side of the room, opening it to reveal an array of sex toys. "I'm going to blow your mind and pop that anal cherry of yours." I glance over at Imalia to see her squirming on the bed, needy at the prospect.

I remember how she shamelessly told me she wants my cock in her ass and a dildo in her pussy, and that's exactly what she'll get. I chose a medium-sized flared based dildo, a bottle of the best lube and a vibrator that can be used handless since it fits inside her cunt.

"Now get on all fours for me like a good girl."

Imalia sinks her teeth into her bottom lip, driving me inside. Her hesitation melts as she scampers onto the bed on all fours, arching her back toward me. The sight of her so eager has me ready to fuck her, but I need to control myself.

I part her ass cheeks with my hands, making her groan. Grabbing the thin lace fabric of her Brazilian panties, I tear them apart with my bare hands and toss them to one side. "You're so wet," I murmur, dipping my finger into her soaking wet pussy. "Wet and ready to learn whether you're truly as kinky as I am."

Imalia watches me as I walk to her left and fix the restraint around her wrist. Slowly, I circle her, fixing the restraints to her two ankles and then her right wrist last.

And then I walk behind her and enjoy the image of her splayed out and ready for me.

I notice her shudder in anticipation, which only makes my cock throb harder. "Now then, whare shall I begin?" I muse, picking up the paddle I used on her before.

I sense Imalia is about to say something, but she doesn't get a chance as I slam the paddle with intense force into her left ass cheek.

She screams, and it's like music to my ears. Her arms and legs attempting to crawl away from me, despite being clamped in place with the restraints. The sound of her scream is so piercing and yet erotic as I take her left ass cheek in my palms and massage it, easing the sting from her flesh.

I sense it's a little too much for her to handle, so I grab the vibrator and turn it on, pushing one end inside her so it remains pressed against her clit. Her body shudders in response to the sudden pleasure and I pick the paddle up again, ready to imprint the word daddy on her other cheek. A gush of liquid rushing down her thighs from her pretty little cunt is proof enough that's she enjoying this.

With the same force, I slam it into her right ass cheek and this time the scream is a half-moan. The vibrator doing its job as she accepts the pain willingly, arching her back so her ass is higher, begging for more. Her entire body shudders and I'm sure she's getting close, so I pull the vibrator out and turn it off.

She whimpers in response. "No, please."

"All in good time." I caress her skin. "I can't have you coming too fast."

And then I slam the paddle into her ass cheeks in the same place two more times, making sure I embed my brand on her skin.

"Fuck," I breathe, caressing her ass cheeks. "Your ass looks so fucking pretty with daddy in welts on it," I murmur, massaging the red skin. "What if I cut it into you as well?"

She turns a little stiff beneath me. "I'm scared."

"Don't be scared, baby girl. Remember the safe word."

She nods in response, her body shuddering from either fear or anticipation.

I'm protective of this girl, something I've never felt before when I'm in the dungeon. "I'll never let anything bad happen to you." I pick up the knife, knowing that I'll have to go slow with her, maybe just graze the word into her skin. Softly, I drag the serrated edge of the blade along the red welts in her skin, making her whimper.

The red marks it leaves in its wake drive me wild as I long to see her bleed for me. Instead, I continue my gentle assault with the knife as she shudders before me.

"Please," she breathes, her body shaking more violently.

"What do you want?"

I stop grazing her skin and wait for her response.

"Cut me," she murmurs, so quiet I can only just hear it.

I groan at her desire for more pain, struggling to control the urge I have to slide into her tight little cunt while I cut her perfect skin. I grab the vibrator and shove it back inside of her, turning it on. My body shakes with desire as I press the knife into her slightly harder and drag the blade along the red marks already on her skin, cutting only the surface.

She moans, her back arching as the red blood trickles down her creamy soft skin.

"Fuck, I'm so damn hard for you, Imalia."

Her thighs are quivering now as I cut the word into her right ass cheek, not going too deep. She's moaning and panting as the pleasure from the vibrator and pain from the knife drive her toward the edge. And this time I want her to come. "That's it, baby girl. You're doing so fucking good, getting turned on while I make you bleed."

"Daddy, it feels so good," she pants, her thighs shaking more violently as I finish carving the word into her flesh on her right ass cheek. "I don't know how long I can last."

I groan, knowing that one ass cheek will do for now. As I'm not sure that I can last much longer without shoving every inch of my cock in her. "Good, because I want you to come for me. Can you do that? Can you come for daddy?" I shove three fingers alongside the vibrator into her soaking wet pussy and finger fuck her toward climax.

"Fuck, yes," she cries out, her entire body shuddering with an intense orgasm. "Don't stop," she pants, rolling her hips to get more from me.

I pull my finger out of her and the vibrator, turning it off.

Imalia lets out an utterly adorable frustrated sound at the loss of pleasure.

"Now, it's time for me to fuck that tight virgin ass of yours."

"Oh God," she mutters, her fingers digging into the bedsheets below. "I don't know how it will fit."

"Believe me, I'll make it fit." I grab the bottle of lube and squirt it onto her ass, making her gasp.

"That's cold," she mutters.

I work it in with one finger, surprised how easily it goes in. "How often do you fuck your ass with that dildo?"

She tenses slightly, glancing at me over her shoulder. "Quite a lot."

I groan, knowing this is going to be so damn good if she's that into anal. "Do you ever come when you do?"

"Every time," she says, her brown eyes so dilated they look almost demonic.

I shove three fingers inside, working the lube in and loosening her hole. After a while, I can fit all four inside without trouble and I'm certain she'll be able to take me. "Have you ever had something in your pussy at the same time, though?"

She shakes her head, biting her lip. "No, but I want to."

"Fuck, you're perfect." I lean forward and pull her head back, kissing her at an odd angle. "I can't wait for you to come with my cock in your ass." I unzip my pants and free my heavy, throbbing cock. It drips all over the bed as I squirt some lube on and work it up and down my shaft, making sure it's well lubricated.

Imalia watches me over her shoulder, licking her lips at the sight. "I'm so ready, daddy," she murmurs, eyes shamelessly holding mine. "I'm ready for you to fuck my ass." Her eyes flicker shut. "I've wanted this for so fucking long."

I position the head of my cock up with her stretched hole and push forward slowly but firmly, groaning when the tip pops through her tight ring of muscles. "I'm happy to make your fantasy come true, malishka."

She moans, wriggling her hips as I sink further into her hole until I'm half-way. "Fuck, I'm so full."

"Only half-way yet, baby girl," I murmur, grabbing her cut up ass cheek and smearing the blood over her skin. "You look so fucking pretty with my cock in your ass and daddy cut into your skin."

She moans, arching her back more and allowing my cock to slip another inch inside. Slowly, I move my cock in and out, working more of it in each time until I'm buried to my balls inside of her.

"How does that feel?" I ask.

"So damn good," she whimpers, her thighs shaking.

"Good girl," I praise, grabbing her hips and forcefully pulling my cock almost all the way out of her. Only to slam back in with force, making her scream. "I want you to take it rough for me," I say, grabbing a fistful of her hair. "Can you do that?"

"Yes, fuck, yes."

I swell inside of her, increasing my pace as I fuck her as hard as I can. Our bodies coming together in a rough clash of passion and Imalia enjoying every single second. It's almost impossible to believe she can be so fucking perfect for me.

"Oh God, I think I'm going to—"

Her body spasms and she can't even finish her sentence as a gush of liquid squirts out of her pussy, soaking the bed beneath and me.

"Fuck, that's so damn hot," I murmur, dragging my fingers through the wetness between her thighs. "You just squirted for me."

She moans, arching her back even more. "Don't stop, please don't stop."

I reach for the dildo. "Are you ready to be stuffed in both holes?"

Imalia looks at me over her shoulder, licking her lips. "Yes, please."

I position the head of the dildo at her entrance and push, groaning at the tightening channel around my cock. "That's it, baby, relax," I encourage, allowing more of it to sink inside. Once It's firmly wedged inside of her, I move again and it's the most heavenly sensation. "Holy shit, that's tight as hell."

"Fuck me harder," she pants, arching her back and taking it so damn well.

I grind my teeth and grab her hips, ignoring the incessant need to explode inside of her as I pound into her tight hole, groaning as the dildo makes it so much tighter. She's so wet that I can hear the dildo squelching as I move against it. "I don't know how long I can last in this tight fucking hole," I growl, sinking my fingernails so hard into her hips I know I'll break the skin.

"Please, I never want it to stop," she groans.

I grit my teeth and fight every part of my being that wants to release, giving her what she wants. My cock swells harder as I fuck her with all my strength, stretching her virgin ass with my cock like she's got all the experience in the world. She really must have fucked herself with that dildo a lot.

"I want you to be a good girl and come for me. Can you do that?" I ask, my voice hardly recognizable to my own ears. "Can you come for me, baby girl?"

Imalia shudders, glancing over her shoulder at me and making eye contact. "Yes, daddy, I'm so fucking close."

I spank her cut up ass cheek and she whimpers, her entire body spasming as her orgasm inches ever closer.

"Oh fuck, daddy, I'm going to—"

She doesn't finish as a gush of liquid floods her pussy, forcing the dildo out in a mess on the bed as she comes apart, making the most beautiful sounds I've ever heard come from a person. Her body spasms around me, and I increase the pace, chasing my own release.

Four thrusts into her tight little hole and I explode, shooting my cum deep inside of her. "That's it. Take daddy's cum in your ass just like that," I groan, thrusting erratically as I drain every drop from my heavy balls. We both collapse, her on her stomach and me on top of her, spent by the single most erotic experience of my life.

"I think I died," Imalia murmurs.

I chuckle, rolling off of her and pulling her against me. "Trust me, you're very much alive." I press my lips to her forehead. "And the most perfect woman I've ever fucking met."

It turns silent between us as we remain wrapped up in our fantasy a while longer. I hold her like I've never held anyone, scared she's going to disappear.

A man like me can't be so lucky to find the woman who makes him whole after all these years, especially not after all the shit I've done. It makes no sense, and yet it's happened. The question is, how long will the dream last?

23

IMALIA

I wake the next morning and groan deeply, wondering if I've been in some kind of accident.

And then I see Spartak lying by my side, watching me. "Good morning, malishka."

I place my hand against my forehead and sigh heavily. "So, it wasn't a dream?"

He tilts his head slightly, giving me a quizzical look. "If you mean what happened at the sex club and then after in my dungeon? No, it wasn't."

My body is so sore as I sit up suddenly, realizing that Massimo is going to be losing his shit. "Fuck." I reach for my cell phone on the nightstand, which I switched off at the club last night.

He grabs my wrist rather forcefully. "Bad idea."

I yank my arm away from him. "What do you mean? I have to tell my family what I've decided."

"Do you really want to hurt them like that?"

I'm taken aback by the question and unsure how else this is going to work. I can't feign being kidnapped for the rest of my life. Spartak searches my eyes, his hand still clenched around my wrist. "Wouldn't you prefer to pretend I kidnapped you again, like the monster I am, and forced you to marry me?"

I stare dumbfounded at him, wondering what the fuck he's talking about. "Marry you?"

Spartak moves and grabs a small black box off his nightstand, making my head spin. "Imalia Allegro, will you marry me?" he asks, flipping open the lid to reveal a stunning vintage ruby ring set in solid gold adorned with smaller diamonds around the gem.

"This was my grandmother's ring, which I never believed I'd give to anyone." He shrugs. "After all, my first wife, Maxim's mother, wanted a huge diamond and didn't like the ruby." There's an uncertain look in his eyes. "If you would prefer a diamond, then—"

"No." I shake my head, tears forming in my eyes. "It's beautiful, but this is crazy."

"Crazy, but right. I don't want you to burn bridges entirely with your family." He shrugs. "The Morrone family are always going to be my enemy, but I see no reason for the Allegro family to be."

I swallow hard, pain clawing at my throat. "But my mom is a Morrone."

"Semantics," he says, dismissing the fact that my mom was born a Morrone and has loyalty to her brother, Remy. "Some would say I'm not capable of love, but I knew the moment I saw you strung up in my warehouse that I loved you, Imalia."

A fluttering ignites in the pit of my stomach, hearing him say that. Although, his treatment of me between then and now doesn't suggest he loved me. "You've got a funny way of showing it."

His eyes narrow. "I had to be sure you were as filthy minded as me. I had to be sure I was right about you." He glances at the ring. "So, what do you say?"

"I say you're insane." Tears I'd tried to hold back flood down my cheeks. "And I am too, as I want to say yes."

"Then say yes, malishka." He grabs my hand, squeezing. "Let's be dirty together forever. Fuck society."

The tears spill and trickle down my cheeks, probably making my face all puffy. "Okay, yes."

Spartak looks at me, confused. "Why are you crying?" He pulls the ring out of the box, sliding it on to my ring finger. It's a little snug, but it fits. "You don't have to marry me, if you don't want," he says, looking a little surprised by his own words.

"I'm so mixed up right now." I shake my head. "I'm sad because I'm betraying my family, but I think I love you, which is wrong on so many levels."

He cups my face, shaking his head. "It's not wrong, Imalia. We're consenting adults that want each other." I wrap my arms around her and pull her against me. "We may not have had a traditional start to our relationship, but what matters is we're being honest with each other." He clears his throat, looking a little guilty. "I admit keeping you captive for so long was wrong, but now it's your choice."

I nod, silently staring at the ruby on my finger. One question that has been bugging me for a long while I have to ask him. I bite my lip. "Is it also wrong that I kind of enjoyed being held captive by you?" I stare into his brilliant gray-blue eyes and know the answer before he says it.

"No, I think it's further proof how right we are for each other." He presses his lips to mine softly, kissing me more tenderly than he's ever done before.

It makes a fluttering ignite between my thighs, even though I'm in no state to even move out of this bed right now. I'm so damn sore.

"We can role play it in my dungeon sometime, if you'd like?" he asks.

"Role play what?" I ask, sitting up straighter and immediately regretting it.

"Nonconsent," he says simply.

My thighs clench involuntarily. "Like rape fantasy?"

He nods. "Sort of, yes. I'll walk you through it some time," he murmurs, yanking me closer and sliding his hands down to my hips. "I can't fucking wait."

I shudder against him, partially from the pain of moving. "Me neither, but I'm so sore right now I feel like I've been in an accident."

"Shit, of course you are," he says, gently removing his hands from me. "Let me run you a bath. You wait here. It will help, I promise."

I groan. The idea of trying to get myself into a bath right now seems impossible.

Before I can protest, he's in the bathroom and I hear the faucet running. I stare at the ruby on my finger, trying to process all the crazy shit that has happened since I arrived in Chicago just over a month ago.

There's no way in hell I thought I'd be engaged to my uncle's arch nemesis. I always told Spartak he was insane, but perhaps I'm the one that's not right in the head. Most women would have run as far away from their kidnapper as possible, and yet I ran into his arms, desperate to be protected and wanted. It's all I've ever wanted, to find someone who can care for me the way he does.

Spartak returns and pulls the comforter off of me. "I'll help you." He reaches down and wraps his arm around my back. "Hold on to my neck."

I wrap my arms around his neck and allow him to carry me into the bathroom, where a bathtub full of bubbles awaits. "I used non-scented bubble bath, as the cut will sting."

I swallow hard, remembering that he etched daddy into my right ass cheek with a knife last night, and I practically came from the pain alone. There's something very off with the wiring in my brain. Carefully, he eases me into the bath and I sigh heavily, the warmth of the water soothing the aches. A soft stinging from my ass only makes me needy, another sign I clearly like pain as much as pleasure.

"I'm fucked up," I murmur, not only meaning physically but mentally.

When I look at Spartak, he actually looks guilty. "Sorry, I think I was too rough for your first time."

I shake my head. "No, I mean, yes, I'm physically sore, but I'm not right in the head." My brow furrows as I try to articulate my thoughts. "How can pain turn me on so much?"

He crouches down so we're at eye level, pinning me with those unique gray eyes. "There's nothing wrong with you. It's actually natural for everyone to find some level of pain erotic and arousing." He shrugs. "Some more than others. That's just how it is."

I search his eyes, wondering what made him the way he is. "What was your childhood like?"

A wall shutters over his expression at the mention of his childhood and his jaw clenches, making a vein more prominent on his temple. "It was bad, Imalia." He stands and turns his back to me, pacing the bathroom. "As bad as it could be."

I worry my sore lip between my teeth. "Can you tell me about it?"

He turns and looks at me, such turmoil blazing in those beautiful eyes of his. "I've never spoken to anyone about it."

I nod, glancing at the bubbles and placing my

fingers through them. "It's just I've agreed to marry you and I hardly know anything about you or your past."

He sighs heavily and walks back toward the bathtub, kneeling down next to it. "My childhood was brutal." He runs a hand across the back of his neck. "When I was very young, my uncle abused me... Sexually." He winces as if it pains him to say it. "Thankfully, a couple of years on, my father caught him and murdered him right in front of my eyes."

"That's terrible—"

"Quiet, little lamb. If you want to hear it, listen."

I nod and fall silent.

"His abuse fucked me up more than the physical beatings I took from my father, but neither helped. I guess it's what made me so formidable as a leader. It's what gave me the nickname psycho, as I never understood what morals were. I was never taught the meaning of the word." He looks me in the eye. "You're the only other living soul who knows about the abuse."

My brow furrows. "What about your brother?"

He shakes his head. "He's younger, and I made sure my uncle's attention remained on me and never shifted to him." His jaw clenches. "Although, if it hadn't been for Father finding out when he did, I'm certain it was only a matter of time." He places a finger under my chin and lifts it gently. "This must stay between us. Promise me, baby girl."

"I promise." Unshed tears collect in my eyes. "I'm so sorry that happened to you."

"Hush, now," he murmurs, kissing the tears as they spill from my eyes. "It made me the man I am today. Even if that's a bad thing."

"It's a bad thing that you had to endure that, but it's not a bad thing that it made you who you are. As I love the man you became, despite everything you went through." I move my mouth so that it connects with his, kissing him softly. "I love you so much it hurts." It's hard to believe that this man, a man who I believed was insane, and who most likely is, trusts me enough to tell me the deepest, darkest secret he kept locked away, weighing him down. It explains so much.

He deepens the kiss, his tongue thrusting into my mouth as he tangles it with mine. "I love you too, little lamb," he breathes, kissing my cheek and then dragging his tongue right down it. "So fucking much." He chuckles softly. "Turns out the lion fell in love with the lamb, after all."

I shake my head, rolling my eyes as the ache inside of me deepens, even though I know can't take anymore, not after last night. "Are you really a lion, though? Underneath it all." I meet his gaze. "Deep down, I don't think you are."

"Quiet, or someone might hear you." He moves back away from me and kneels by the side of the bathtub. "Let me wash you," he murmurs, grabbing a loofah and soaping it up. "Relax."

I sit forward and allow him to wash my back with it, enjoying being looked after by him. It's an oddly platonic moment, as he doesn't try to touch me sexually once. Merely cleaning me gently and thoroughly. Most of our encounters have been sexual and yet it's natural being taken care of by him like this.

"Is your ass bruised?" he asks once he finishes washing me.

I nod, shifting a little. "Pretty sure it is."

He grabs my hand. "Stand up. I've got something to help."

I use him to help myself climb out of the bathtub and he wraps me in a huge, plush white towel. And then he goes to the bathroom cabinet and opens it. "This stuff will help heal the bruises." He holds up a bottle of something. "It's a gel." He walks back over to me. "Turn around."

I do as he says, turning around so my back is to him.

He lifts the bath towel, groaning under his breath, when he sees the state of my ass.

I'd be lying if I said I didn't fear looking in the mirror at the damage.

He squirts some of the liquid onto his hand and then gently massages it into my aching buttocks. "This will help, but you might want to ice the skin, too. I'll get you an ice pack later."

My stomach flutters as his fingers skate dangerously close to my pussy, which is wet and needy. I moan involuntarily and Spartak's fingers stop moving.

"Don't tell me you're horny, malishka." He gently

parts my lips, growling when he feels how wet I am. "I wish I could take you right here and now, but you need time to heal, baby girl." He kisses my shoulder and then up my neck. "You need to rest."

I know he's right, as I'm aching and tired. "Okay." I let him usher me back to the bedroom and tuck me under the comforter.

He kisses my forehead. "Get some sleep. I've got some things to deal with, but I'll bring you lunch in a couple of hours." He heads out of the bedroom door and, for the first time, he doesn't lock it.

I shut my eyes, thankful he's sticking to his word about not keeping me caged. Within minutes, I can feel myself drifting to sleep.

24

SPARTAK

*M*axim storms into my office. "So, you're going ahead with it?" he asks, waving the invitation I sent up to his apartment this morning. It's been three days since she agreed to the wedding, and we've set a date this Saturday, in four days' time.

I raise a brow. "Yes, Imalia said yes." I glance over at my beautiful fiance who is sitting in the corner reading a book. "In fact, why don't I introduce you both now?"

It's clear my son hadn't realized she was in the room as he straightens, his attention moving to her. The expression in his eyes is one of rage.

Imalia looks a little uncertain as she stands and walks toward us, smiling. "It's nice to meet you, Maxim," she says, holding out a hand to him.

He just looks at it with disgust. "What has he threatened you with?" he demands.

I lean my ass against the desk and cross my arms over my chest, waiting for Imalia to answer.

"He hasn't threatened me with anything." Her lips purse as she senses the animosity in the room. "I returned here because…" She looks at me and then back at Maxim. "Because I'm in love with your father."

He wrinkles his nose, taking a step away from her. "He's old enough to be your father," he spits, shaking his head. "What the fuck is wrong with you?"

Imalia's eyes flash with hurt and anger as she takes a step back. "I don't appreciate being talked to like that. You can't choose who you fall in love with."

"And that means you should both rush into marriage after knowing each other all of what? Five weeks?" he presses.

Imalia crosses her arms over her chest and glares at him.

I push off the desk. "Marriage was my idea. What's stopping her family from trying to steal her back again if there's not a very good reason not to?"

He looks at me and then at Imalia before throwing the invitation to my feet. "Thanks for the invite, but I'll have to decline." He marches out of the room, slamming the door behind him.

An awkward silence falls between us, as I can sense the encounter upset Imalia. The look in her eyes is one of pure anguish, probably because she's been doubting herself and her feelings since the start. Now Maxim has questioned them openly.

She turns silently and walks back to the chair in the corner where she had been curled up reading.

I chase after her, wrapping my arms around her waist and forcing her to face me. "Ignore him. He's angry because I'm remarrying."

She opens her mouth to ask something but then shuts it, looking a little uncertain.

"What is it?" I ask.

"What was your first wife like?"

My heart pounds hard against my rib cage as I stare into Imalia's beautiful brown eyes. She differed greatly from Imalia. "She was beautiful and strong and totally wrong for me."

Her brow furrows. "Oh, why's that?"

I usher her over to the sofa, and we sit. "I made a mistake. I think I've been making the same mistake all my life that I made with Maxim's mother." It's rare that I admit when I make mistakes, but it's a revelation I only recently became aware of. "When we met, I knew I loved her almost instantly. The problem was, I kept a lot of myself hidden from her. She never knew the real me before she agreed to marry me, which meant once my depravity became apparent to her, she was trapped in a marriage with a man she didn't really know."

Imalia nods in understanding. "Is that why you gave me a choice?"

"Yes, as I realized I was about to repeat the mistakes of my past with you." I squeeze her hand. "And you don't hate that part of me."

"Did she know about your past?"

I shake my head. "No, I've kept that buried and secret from everyone all my life."

"Except for me."

"Except for you, little lamb," I reply, shifting closer to her on the sofa. "How is your ass healing?"

Her throat bobs at the question. "It's a lot better now. And I'm not so sore anymore."

"Good, because I've been dying to be inside of you again." I kiss her lips, groaning at the pillowy softness of them.

Imalia tenses slightly, glancing at the door. "Surely not in here?"

I smirk. "Why? are you worried someone will walk in on us?" I raise a brow. "That didn't worry you at the club the other night."

"The doors are not locked and your family live here. That's different."

I nuzzle my nose against her neck as it bobs softly. "Stop worrying. Maxim won't return."

Her lips purse as I capture them with my own, groaning as she willingly opens them. It's been over three days since I last had her and I've been going out of my mind. I slide my palm around her throat and squeeze softly. "I want to watch you ride my cock." Roughly, I grab her hips and position her above me, forcing her thick thighs to straddle my hips.

Desperate to feel her wrapped around me, I free my cock through the zipper of my pants and tear apart her panties, making her gasp. Without warning, I pull her down over my shaft, making her cry out in a mix of pain and pleasure.

"Ride me, baby girl."

Her eyes dilate as she looks down at me, placing her hands on my chest. "Okay, daddy." She pulls her bottom lip into her mouth, sucking on it as she rolls her hips in slow, sensuous movements.

I groan, linking my fingers behind my head and admiring the way her body moves above me. She's like a fucking siren, mesmerizing me. Her tits jiggle in her tight dress, making my cock swell inside of her. I reach up and grab the fabric, tearing it apart and popping all the buttons off.

"Fuck," she breathes as I cup her pert breasts in my hands, rubbing my thumb over her hard nipples.

It's rare that I'm comfortable with a woman being in control, but with Imalia, I'll make an exception. Gently, I tease the palm of my hand higher to her throat and cup it, groaning at how good she looks with it around her neck like a fucking collar.

"Choke me," she murmurs, eyes holding mine with a fiery look that turns me into molten lava.

I smirk and move my other hand to her neck too, squeezing only gently. "Is that what you want? You want me to choke that pretty little throat while you ride my cock?"

Imalia nods, eyes flickering shut. "Please."

"Since you asked so nicely, baby girl," I murmur, clamping my fingers tightly around her throat.

She moans, eyes rolling back in her head as she moves harder up and down my shaft, rolling her hips with such force. The lack of oxygen makes her wetter as she fucks me harder, faster, driving herself toward the edge.

"Fuck, daddy," she gasps, struggling to speak with my hand fixed tightly around her throat. "I'm going to come."

"Good girl," I purr, lifting my hips to meet her thrusts. "Come on my cock while I choke you, just like that."

She screams as best she can, considering I'm still restricting her airways, her tight little pussy clenching my dick so damn hard it feels like she's trying to milk me. I can't hold out as I explode deep inside of her, releasing her throat and grabbing her hips so that every drop shoots deep inside of her.

"That's it, baby girl, takes daddy's cum," I growl, pulling her forward and sinking my teeth into her shoulder.

She moans, trying to roll her hips as I come apart inside of her.

"Stop moving," I order, slapping her ass.

I love that she obeys me so easily, turning limp above me. Quickly, I flip her over so she's on her back on the sofa and then pull out of her. "I don't want a drop coming out of you. Do you understand?"

Her brow furrows, and she glares at me. "Not that again. Surely it's enough that you're marrying me."

I raise a brow. "Don't you want to have kids?"

She purses her lips as if thinking about it. "Yes, but I just didn't think I'd want them yet."

I kiss her and then pull just an inch away. "Well, get used to it, because I want you pregnant with my baby as fast as possible."

She groans, but doesn't protest as she remains on her back for me, like the good girl she is. I tuck my cock back into my pants and return behind my desk, admiring the view of her splayed out for me on the sofa. It's going to be a long day if she keeps hanging around my office. I fear I won't get any work done.

I WAKE on my wedding morning with my bride nestled against my chest, her hand pressed over my heart.

It's hard to believe such a delicate, beautiful creature loves me. And, I fear that the darkness that infects my blood and soul makes it impossible not to destroy everything around me. I can't destroy her. I won't. Although she's seen a part of my depravity, she doesn't truly know the violence I'm capable of when it comes to my enemies or people who cross me.

My cock turns hard as I watch her sleep, knowing I've never felt this way about anyone before. We were destined for one another from the moment my men dragged her into my warehouse.

Today we'll cement our bond in stone in the eyes of the law, making sure no one can take her from me. I won't lose her again, not for a second time.

Imalia groans and tries to roll away from me, but I hold her firmly. Her eyes flicker open and then they widen. "You're supposed to be sleeping in your own room," she says, pushing my chest with all her strength.

I smirk, as last night she went to the guest room over some silly belief about the groom not seeing the bride in the morning. "Sorry, I couldn't resist."

"It's bad luck to see the bride on the morning of the wedding."

I kiss her lips. "That's a bullshit old wives' tale."

She glares at me, shaking her head. "I don't like to tempt fate."

I grab hold of her tightly and press the length of my hard cock against her thigh. "How could I stay away when I'm this damn hard all the time?"

Her eyes dilate, and she purses her lips. "I don't know," she mutters.

I shift away from her, despite my rock solid, throbbing dick protesting. "Let's get showered and dressed as you overslept." I nod toward the clock on the nightstand, which shows that it's eleven in the morning. I have booked the ceremony for one o'clock this afternoon downtown in a quaint little church.

Her eyes widen. "What the hell?" She scrambles out of the bed. "Why didn't you wake me?"

"Because you looked so peaceful."

She rushes toward the bathroom, stopping at the threshold and glancing over her shoulder. "Are you coming?"

"It's bad luck for the husband to fuck the bride on the wedding morning."

She rolls her eyes. "I meant to shower, and I told you it's bad luck to see the bride, so you've already fucked that one up."

I chuckle and climb out of the bed, glancing down at my cock tenting my boxer briefs. "If I shower with you, there's zero chance of you not getting fucked, malishka." I walk toward her and grab her hips, pulling her firm ass against my cock. "The next time I have you, I intend for you to be my wife. Tonight, I'm going to blow your fucking mind with all the kinky, dirty things I do to you."

Her head falls back against my shoulder. "Please, daddy," she moans, eyes connecting with mine.

"So needy, little lamb," I murmur, squeezing her hips. "Now get in the shower."

Imalia turns and gives me an irritated glare as she pulls off her shirt and then panties, dropping them to the floor. "Fine." She turns around, giving me a perfect view of that beautiful ass of hers. "I'll just get myself off."

I growl and catch her around the waist before she

takes a step. "No, that pussy belongs to me and only I get you off," I groan, my hard cock now only separated from her skin by my thin boxer briefs. "You make me so fucking insatiable."

She giggles, and it's the most beautiful sound I've ever heard. "Then get me off, daddy."

I groan and lift her off the floor, carrying her into the bathroom. "You're going to make us late."

"You already made us late, not waking me up earlier."

I breathe in the scent of her, memorizing it like a work of art. "It's not my fault you can't make it until tonight without my cock," I murmur.

She elbows me in the ribs. "Cocky pig."

I growl softly and spin her around to face me, crashing my lips into hers. Slowly, I walk her backward toward the shower, reaching in to turn on the faucet. There's no stopping this raging inferno inside of me. This strong desire to claim her over and over until there's no refuting who she belongs to.

"We're going to have to multi-task," I murmur against her skin. "Get in."

She does as she's told, walking under the spray of the warm water and sighing. I walk in after her, grabbing the soap off the caddy and lathering my hands, before soaping her up as my cock nudges against her ass.

Imalia moans from my touch, even though I'm not

going anywhere near her cunt. She's such a horny little devil and I can't wait to call her my wife.

"Part those ass cheeks for me, malishka."

She glances over her shoulder at me and eagerly parts them so I can see her tight little hole and wet pussy between her thighs.

My cock falls between them and I nudge at her entrance, groaning as she practically swallows the head. "Now fuck yourself on my cock," I order.

She moves her hips, impaling herself on me as I continue to wash her body. "Oh god," she groans, reaching forward to steady herself on the wall. "You feel so good, daddy."

I grab a fistful of her hair and pull her hard against me, so I bury every inch of my cock inside of her. "Not as good as you feel, baby girl. You drive me fucking insane with this pretty little cunt." I grab her hips and plow into her hard, making her whimper at the sudden change in intensity. "Do you like being dominated?"

"Yes," she gasps, glancing at me over her shoulder. "I love it."

"Good," I say, tightening my grasp on her hair and using it to push and pull her up and down my cock. "Because I'm going to dominate you every damn day of your life, and you're going to submit to me like the good girl I know you are."

"Yes, daddy," she moans, arching her back. "Every day."

I groan, fucking into her with brutal thrusts. These

past few days, we could not stop fucking. It's as if the more I have her, the more I need her. It's impossible to quench my hunger for my beautiful little lamb.

Although we haven't returned for a visit to my sex dungeon, as I want to make sure my bride can stand at the altar. The bruises and cuts on her ass have now fully healed, but tonight I intend to consummate our marriage in that dungeon, learning more about what makes her tick.

"Fuck, daddy," she moans, making my balls draw up. "You're going to make me come."

"Good," I growl, pulling her toward me and flattening my palm against her stomach, so her head rests on my shoulder. "I want you to come for me. I want that tight little cunt milking every drop of cum out of my balls. Do you understand?"

She can't reply as she comes apart, screaming Daddy over and over.

I tease my hand over her throat and squeeze, which only makes her shudder move violently. "You're such a good girl," I murmur into her ear as my balls draw up and I flood her pussy with cum.

She tries to move her hips, but I hold her firmly, keeping her where I want her.

"Don't let a drop escape and lie down on the bed for me," I breathe.

She shudders as I release her throat and spank her ass. "But, we'll be late."

"Now," I order, as my cock slips from her.

She puts her hand between her legs and rushes for the bedroom like a good little submissive who can't deny me.

I smirk as I wash myself quickly, knowing that if we don't get a move on, we will be late. And I can't find it in me to give a fuck. If we're late, the officiant will have to wait.

25

IMALIA

I spin around in front of the mirror, hardly able to believe I'm about to get married to a man who took me captive.

A part of me is a little sad that I don't have my cousins and family here to support me on such a happy day, even though I know they'd do anything to stop me. That's the only thing missing. A bridesmaid or maid of honor by my side and someone to walk me down the aisle, but it doesn't matter. All that matters is I'm marrying my soul mate. A man so unlikely at yet so perfect for me.

It's just over five weeks since I arrived in Chicago, but this place has turned my life upside down. There's no hiding from the part of me that Spartak has unleashed, and he gives me a safe space to enjoy my kinks, which makes me love him all the more. I think there's nothing I could say or do wrong in his eyes, and that makes me feel special.

Perhaps it's that he fills the role of a caregiver that I've longed for since I was little. A man who will protect me no matter the costs. After all, he's fucking crazy, but if he loves me, then he'll never hurt me.

The hardest part of this is that my family can't share in my happiness. They can't find out the truth. That I left with Spartak of my own free will. As he's right, it would burn too many bridges. This way, they believe I had no choice but to marry him.

Olga, who I still can't stand, was forced to attend to help me get ready. Although, she hasn't been much help. "Can you help me with the veil?" I ask her.

She nods, walking toward me. "You wanted to escape, so why are you marrying him?" she asks, speaking to me properly for the first time since we stepped in here twenty minutes ago.

I swallow hard, watching her assessing gaze in the mirror. "Because I'm insane," I say, blowing out a dejected breath. "Despite everything he did, kidnapping me, holding me hostage, I love Spartak," I say simply.

Her brow furrows. "Forgive me, but it's hard to believe, considering how badly you wanted out of that room."

I clench my jaw. "I needed to be given my freewill back to realize that I wanted him. I chose to return to him."

She raises a brow. "Really?"

"Yes, he gave me the option at my cousin's birthday party, and a few days later, I agreed."

Olga nods, as if satisfied by my answer. "Fair enough. I just don't want to see my boss hurt. He's been through enough in his life." There's an odd look in her eyes, and I wonder if she knows about his childhood.

After all, she has to be about twenty years older than him. "How long have you worked for the Volkov family?" I ask.

She shrugs. "Since I was eighteen years old. They've been very fair and kind employers. Initially, it was Spartak's father who employed me." Her jaw clenches as if she's remembering him.

"What was he like?" I ask.

"A vile man." She shakes her head. "If you thought Spartak's treatment of you was bad, you would have begged for mercy from his father, Vadim. He's a pussycat in comparison." She waves her hand in the air. "Thankfully, those times are past us." She smiles, and it's the most genuine smile she's given me since the first day we met. "Here, let's get this veil on." She takes the clip out of my hand and fixes it into my hair at the back. "Perfect."

The officiant pops his head through the door. "Are you ready?" he asks.

Maxim has stuck to his word and hasn't turned up after throwing the invite back at Spartak. Olga is here as a witness and to help me get ready, and Timur, Spartak's right hand-man, is here as his best man instead of his son. He's disappointed that Maxim didn't change his mind.

I nod. "Yes, I'm ready."

He smiles, but it doesn't reach his eyes.

I sense that Spartak probably blackmailed the officiant into marrying us, as he has been on edge since we got here. My heart pounds hard in my ears as Olga and I follow him out of the back room and toward the main church, where Spartak is waiting for me. There's been a few times I've questioned whether I've lost my mind.

The man I'm marrying wasn't exactly clear on consent from the start and was pretty brutal in his treatment of me, and yet I love him. It's proof that perhaps I'm as insane as he is. Fuck society and what it dictates. He's right, I'll never be happy with someone like my ex, Jamie. I need a man who's not afraid to push the boundaries, someone as crazy as Spartak is.

The wedding march plays over a stereo, since they couldn't arrange a band at such short notice. The officiant goes through the doors first, followed by Olga, who takes her seat near the front. I peer through, my stomach churning when I see the altar.

Marriage.

It's not something I'd given much thought to, especially as I knew I would never marry Jamie. I walk onto the aisle and my heart skips a beat when I see Spartak dressed in the most immaculate three-piece designer suit in a light gray. His hair is neater than I've ever seen it and he looks devastatingly beautiful, like an older male model who has aged so damn well. Half the time I forget about our significant age-gap as it's hardly noticeable.

When he smiles, my world stands still. I remember the first time I set eyes on him, and the insane thoughts I had about how handsome he was, rather than freaking out that I'd been captured. None of this makes sense and yet it feels right. As if it were set in the stars for us.

Once I get to the end of the aisle, Spartak takes my hands in his. The warm, callous feel of them against my skin sets my soul ablaze, flooding my veins with electricity. That intoxicating, manly scent of him overwhelms me as I take a deep breath, pursing my lips together and trying to ignore the ache he ignites deep within me. I've never known chemistry with anyone that's so electrifying before.

The officiant clears his throat before starting what appears to be a shortened version of the wedding ceremony. He seems in a rush, but I don't care as I stare into the blue-gray eyes of the man I know I want to spend the rest of my life with. Never have I been so in awe of another person.

Learning the truth about his past and the abuse he endured explains a lot, but learning he's kept it buried and not told a single soul all his life explains even more. He's harboring a darkness that's eating away at his sanity, and I wish I could take it away from him.

I wish I could help him heal the wounds that are so deeply inflicted. Although, I can't deny that one reason

I'm so drawn to him is his utter lack of care of what society deems normal. He is insane and acts crazy, but he owns it in a way that few people could. It suits him and it's part of what I love about him.

"Do you, Spartak Volkov, take this woman, Imalia Allegro, to be your wedded wife?" he asks, clearing his throat. "To have and to hold for the rest of your life until death do you part?"

Spartak's lips lift up a little at the corners and he looks so handsome it makes my chest ache. "I do."

My stomach flutters at the way he looks at me, like I'm the only other person on this planet.

"And do you, Imalia Allegro, take this man, Spartak Volkov, to be your lawfully wedded husband?" he asks, glancing hesitantly between us, as if perhaps I'm not marrying him of my own free will. "To have and to hold for the rest of your life until death do you part?"

There's not a moment of hesitation. "I do."

Spartak's smile widens.

"Then, by the power vested in me by the state of Illinois, I now pronounce you man and wife." He glances at Spartak. "You may kiss the bride."

A wicked flash ignites in his eyes as he steps forward, wrapping an arm around my waist. He yanks me against his hard, muscular body and then kisses me with such passion.

I wrap my arms around his neck and kiss him back, drowning in how happy and free I feel. There's no doubt I've never been so connected to another person in my twenty-six years of life. It may be unconventional, and I may have lost my family, but I can't imagine my life without him.

Spartak's right-hand man, Timur, claps. "Congratulations, sir," he says.

We break apart and Spartak smiles. "Thanks."

Olga stands and approaches us, stopping in front of Spartak. She says something to him in Russian and then pulls him in for a hug. I'm surprised Spartak allows it, as he doesn't seem like the hugging type. However, I sense Olga is like a mother figure to him, considering she's known him since he was a child.

"So, what next, sir?" Timur asks.

Spartak meets my gaze, a wicked glint in his eyes. "Next I take my bride home."

Timur smirks and Olga looks a little uncomfortable as she shuffles from one foot to the other, since it's clear what he means.

"No honeymoon?" Timur asks.

My husband, God, that sounds weird, shakes his head. "Unfortunately not. I can't afford to leave town, not with the war heating up with both the Irish and the Russians. There isn't a day that goes by that we don't have an attempted attack, and it's only going to get worse."

Timur nods in agreement. "Indeed."

Spartak turns to me and cups my face in his hands. "We'll celebrate properly with a honeymoon once things are a bit more stable. I promise."

I shake my head. "I don't need a honeymoon. I just need you."

Timur groans as if sickened by my response and Olga smiles widely.

"Well, if that's all, sir. I have a lot of jobs to get done back at the house," Olga says.

Spartak shakes his head. "You can have the day off, Olga. There's no need to work all the time. I've told you this countless times before."

"I like to keep on top of things."

"Take the day to yourself. Relax," Spartak says, nodding toward the exit.

She bows her head. "Yes, sir."

I watch as she walks out of the church, leaving me and my husband and Timur.

Timur clears his throat. "I best be off, too."

Spartak nods. "I wish you could take the day off, but unfortunately, there's no respite in the war."

He claps his boss on the shoulder. "Congratulations again. I'll be in touch soon."

Once he's gone, Spartak grabs my hips and spins me to face him. "We're alone in here right now…" He raises a brow.

I punch him softly. "No chance in hell, unless that's exactly where you want to end up."

He chuckles. "Don't tell me you're religious."

"No, just not completely insane enough to fuck you in the middle of a church."

He nods. "Fair enough. I want to get you home

anyway, where we can be as loud as we want." His hand lands on the small of my back as he steers me toward the exit.

It's hard to believe I'm actually married, and about to spend the rest of my life with the most dangerous man in Chicago.

SPARTAK

I lead my wife back down the aisle, eager to return home with her. If she'd been up for it, I'd have fucked her over the altar, however she seemed shocked by my suggestion of having sex in a church.

The honeymoon, unfortunately, will have to wait, as the bratva is in chaos, trying to fight on two fronts. There's no way I can swan off somewhere with my new bride, not at the moment.

"How are you feeling, malishka?" I ask, holding her close to me.

She smiles at me and it's possibly the most genuine smile she's given me yet. "Happy," she says simply. "So happy."

I smile and pull her against me, unable to resist kissing her again. "Me too," I breathe against her lips. "I never thought I'd be this happy."

"Stop this madness," a deep voice booms ahead of

us from the doorway of the church. A voice I know all too well.

Remy.

We both turn at the sound, clutching onto each other's hands. My enemy has somehow taken me by surprise, and my mind runs wild as the only people who knew about this wedding were my son, Olga, and Timur. My gun sits against my ribs holstered in the inside of my jacket, but I can't reach for it because Remy and two of Imalia's cousins are aiming their guns right at me.

Slowly, I lift the palms of my hands up in surrender. "How did you find us?" I ask.

Remy ignores me, glancing at his niece. "Imalia, come here."

She opens her mouth and then shuts it again, glancing at me as if searching for guidance.

"What are you waiting for?" Massimo snaps, looking irritated.

"I'm married to Spartak," she says simply, looking his dead in the eye. "I can't go with you."

Remy growls. "What have you done to my niece?"

I tilt my head. "You didn't answer my question. How did you find us?"

He sneers at me. "After we got Imalia back, we anticipated that you might try to steal her again, so we put a tracking device in her neck."

Imalia gasps, grabbing her neck. "You did what?"

"It was for your own safety, Imalia." Remy moves

closer, his gun still fixed on me. "Now, come here and let's go home."

She steps closer to my side. "I'm sorry, uncle. I can't do that."

The look on his face is priceless as Imalia steps in front of me, guarding me with her body. There's a tug at my insides that she'd put herself in front of a gun for me. No one has ever cared enough to protect me like that.

"I'm in love with Spartak and we're married." She moves her attention to Massimo. "When I snuck out that night, I was going to meet him."

Remy glares at his eldest son. "What's she talking about?"

Massimo grinds his teeth. "I let her go the night she disappeared, as she told me she was meeting a friend at the diner around the corner."

"Foolish boy," he quips, shaking his head. "Can't I trust any of you?" His attention move to Imalia. "I never thought you would betray me, piccola mia."

Imalia stiffens slightly. "I'm not betraying you, Uncle Remy." She shakes her head. "I can't help who I love."

"How will you mother react to this?" He glares at me hatefully. "A Russian."

Imalia shakes her head. "I don't know, but I'm a Volkov now." She holds her hand up, showing them the ring. "There's no turning back."

"Bullshit, you've not consummated the marriage," Remy says, starting forward.

Imalia shakes, pressing into my chest for support.

I wrap my arm around her waist and lean down to whisper in her ear. "It'll be okay, little lamb. I won't let anything happen to you."

Imalia folds her arms over her chest. "Uncle, please don't do this."

Massimo steps forward. "He's manipulated you, Imalia. Can't you see?"

I tighten my grasp around her and glare at the son of my rival. "No, Imalia made this choice by herself."

"Bullshit," Remy says, moving ever closer. "We're not letting you leave with her."

"Then you'll have to kill me, Uncle, if you want to get to Spartak," Imalia says bravely, making pride rise in my chest.

Other than my men, who protect me out of a sense of duty, there's not a soul alive who would lay their life on the line for me. This is out of love, pure and simple. It makes me love her even more. "Don't be foolish, Imalia," I murmur into her ear, tightening my grasp around her waist. "Let me handle this."

"No," she says back, shaking her head. "They'll kill you if I move."

"Damn right we will," Massimo growls.

Remy, on the other hand, remains silent, as he knows killing me would bring hell down upon him. If he were to kill me, my men would be out for his blood. It would be carnage, and we both know it. He shakes his head and places a hand on his son's arm, lowering his gun. "No one is killing anyone today, it seems."

Massimo looks enraged as he glares at his father, but he doesn't question him in front of us. "So, we're going to let him take Imalia?"

Imalia steps forward, the gap between us instantly making me nervous as I move with her. "He's not taking me. I'm choosing to go with him."

Remy glares at his niece. "You've betrayed our family and for that, I don't want to see you crawling back when it all goes wrong. Do you understand?"

"Perfectly."

He nods. "Then leave now out the back."

I am wary of Remy's sudden decision to let us go. It doesn't sit well with me. There's something off about it. "Why the back?"

Remy's eyes narrow. "Because we're at the front, and if you walk past us, I might decide to shoot you after all."

I nod in response and Imalia turns away from them, unshed tears clear in her eyes. This is exactly what I wanted to avoid, but the son of a bitch put a tracker in his own niece. A tracker that I'll remove the moment we get home safely.

As I turn along with her, I hear a gun cock behind me. My spine stiffens and before I can turn around a shot sounds, pain shooting through my midsection as I glance down at my rather expensive Amani suit and see blood staining the fabric.

Imalia screams, so loud as she drops to her knees by my side. Her hand quickly covering the wound as she tries to stem the blood loss. "You fucking bastard," she shouts, glaring at her family behind.

I move my head enough to see who shot me, and it appears the youngest son, Luca, was the one to shoot. He obviously wasn't so inclined to let this go.

"Grab her," Remy says, his eyes cold and devoid of all emotion as his niece cries over me.

I grit my teeth, clinging onto her hand. "It's okay, baby girl," I murmur, kissing her lips softly. "I'll find you."

"You're dying," she cries, looking down at her bloodied hands.

I laugh, but it hurts. "It'll take a lot more than a gunshot to bring me down. Now go, and I'll find you. I promise."

She doesn't move, but Massimo is the one to lift her away from me. His eyes meet mine and there's pure hatred burning in them. I watch as he disappears out of the back with her.

Remy crouches down over me. "My son shot, not under my direction. I will have your man contacted to help you. It was not in my interest to escalate this war into fucking carnage."

"You should have kept your mutt on a tighter leash then," I spit. "You've shot me and my son in the space of a month." I hold my hand over the wound, knowing that Timur should be back any second. I called him the moment Remy stepped in here on speed dial, knowing he'd hear the conversation.

"Get the fuck away from him," he growls, flanked by a few of our men. All of them have guns.

"Perhaps I should repay the favor?" I say, smirking at my nemesis. "After all, we have your son and you here. Might as well even the odds."

I nod at Timur, and he shoots Luca in the leg. Luca, like the coward he is, cries like a little girl and falls to the floor. At least my son had dignity when he got shot.

Remy holds his hands up in front of him. "Come on, surely we can work this out?"

The door at the back of the church opening sets everyone on guard as their attention moves to a couple of Remy's men entering. They hold their guns up and aim them at my men.

"Well, it looks like we're at a standoff," I say.

Remy nods. "Let's agree a ceasefire for twenty minutes to get everyone out of here. That way, no one else has to get hurt."

I nod in response to Timur, who lowers his gun.

Remy's men also lower their guns, tucking them away. Everyone scatters, the Morrone men rushing out of the building at speed.

Timur is quick to get to my side. "Fuck, sir. We need to get you to a doctor right away." He and Vitaly help me to my feet. "I'll ring the private hospital and tell them to expect us." He glances around. "Where's Imalia?"

"Gone," I say, struggling to put one foot in front of the other from the pain.

His brow furrows, but he doesn't question me. Instead, he helps me get into the back of the van, where I press my fingers to the wound. My head swims as I try to cling to the last threads of consciousness. "I don't think I can stay awake," I say.

Timur nods. "Vitaly will stem the blood flow. We'll get you fixed up in no time, sir."

Vitaly slips in beside me, pressing a large rag against the wound firmly. "Relax, you need to conserve as much energy as you can."

I let my head fall back on the headrest as I shut my eyes, knowing that I have to make it through this. Otherwise, Imalia is at the mercy of her family, a family she just tried to betray. I won't leave her captive in a world where she can't be herself, where she can't be happy.

I WAKE in a clinical operating theater with one of the private doctors staring at me.

"Perfect, you're awake," he says, glancing at the glass screen where Maxim is standing. "Your son would like to speak with you."

My memory is a little hazy as I try to sit up, wincing

at the pain radiating through my stomach. "What happened?"

"You were shot. Maxim will explain everything to you." He nods at him to enter.

I'm surprised he's bothered to visit me, especially since I didn't do him the same favor when he was shot.

The doctor clears his throat. "I'll leave you to talk."

Maxim approaches the bed. "How are you feeling?"

"Fucking awful," I reply.

He nods. "Not surprising. The doctor said you were damn lucky that the bullet missed vital organs by about two centimeters." He runs a hand across the back of his neck. "I've instructed Timur to hit the Italians as hard as he can for this." He crosses his arms over his chest. "He was on board and is formulating a plan."

"Good," I reply, struggling to sit up straighter. "What about Imalia?"

His brow furrows. "What about her?"

"They took her, and I need to get her back."

Maxim sighs heavily. "I'll ask Timur to locate her. For now, you just need to rest."

"Could you rest if it were Livia who had been taken?" I ask, hating that my son doesn't take my feelings for her seriously.

"No," he says. "But I'd have to if I sustained your injuries. Not to mention, her family has taken her, so at least you know she'll be safe."

I relax into my pillows as he's right. Although Remy

is my enemy, he's not about to harm his niece. They will probably chalk it down to Imalia being brainwashed by me and won't blame her for what happened. "That's true," I say, glancing at the dresser next to the bed. "Where's my cell phone?"

He sucks in a sharp intake of breath and reaches into his pocket, pulling out my cell phone, which the bullet seems to have gone right through. "The surgeon reckons it saved your life, as it changed the trajectory of the bullet, but the phone is fucked."

"Shit." That was my single way of communicating with Imalia and if it won't turn on, I can't get her number.

Maxim chews on the inside of his cheek. "I'm sorry I wasn't there. Perhaps I could have—"

"Don't apologize. I'm thankful you weren't there, otherwise it might have been you in this bed instead." I clench my fists by my side. "Remy Morrone is a bastard, but he told them not to shoot. It was Luca that got trigger-happy as we were trying to leave." I rub a hand across the back of my neck. "Although I sensed they had another trick up their sleeve, telling us to leave through the back of the church."

"You think they had men waiting for you?" Maxim asks.

I nod. "Yes, as Massimo took Imalia that way after Luca shot me."

"Son of a bitch." He paces the floor. "I can't see an

end in sight for this war, not the way it's going. We're heading for self-destruction at this rate."

I hate to agree, but it's getting out of hand. The war was supposed to be between us and the Irish, but someone it's the Italians that we've escalated it with. I know it's partially my fault for snatching Imalia.

"We need to plan an exit strategy, and consider peace talks again." I tilt my head slightly. "Obviously not when we're stealing from them and also on neutral ground. I won't go back into their territory again."

Maxim nods. "I agree. We need to open up communication before one of us ends up dead."

It's not often that we see eye to eye, but I'm thankful we do on this. After all, there's no way we'll win a war if we can't agree amongst ourselves. "I'll leave you to come up with a strategy." My brow furrows. "Have you seen Artyom lately?"

Maxim shakes his head. "No, why?"

A sense of unease prickles at the back of my neck. "Me neither. It's odd that he's not lurking around like he normally is."

"Do you want me to check in with Timur on his movements?"

I nod in response. "Yes, and try not to talk to your cousins about any of this."

"Got it. I'll get to work now." He turns to leave.

"Maxim," I say, stopping him in his tracks.

"Thank you." I run a hand through my hair. "I

think it's clear you are ready for more responsibility. You are in charge while I'm in here."

His eyes flash with surprise. "Okay, I won't let you down."

I nod in response and he walks out, leaving me alone with my chaotic thoughts. All I can think about is Imalia and the fact my enemy snatched a happy occasion away from us. I can't deny that I want revenge, but I know that if we continue down the path of escalation, we could lose everything. Imalia is my world, and I won't risk her safety all because of my ego.

27

IMALIA

*M*y entire world is being torn apart, as Massimo drives me away from the church. All I can see in my mind is the image of my new husband splayed on the ground, a pool of blood forming beneath him.

Massimo hasn't said a word since he forced me into the back of the car and drove away. All my life I've cared only about my family and doing what is right, but now they've torn me away from my chance of happiness. Spartak's wound looked bad to me, even though he seemed certain he'd survive it.

I press my hand to my neck, wondering when and how they implanted a fucking tracking device in it.

"We did it the night of Camilla's party," Massimo says, looking at me in the rearview mirror. "You passed out in the back of the car and Luca shot it into your neck."

I glare at him. "Well, I want it out," I spit.

"Imalia, you'll come to realize we did this for your own good, no matter what you think you feel for that monster."

I cross my arms over my chest. "The only monster here is you."

He sighs heavily, his jaw clenching. "The man kidnapped you. How can you feel anything but hatred toward him?"

"You'll never understand," I say, breaking his gaze and staring instead out of the window.

"Try me."

I shake my head and ignore him, as there's no explaining to my cousin the inner-workings of my relationship with Spartak. It's dirty and messy and complicated. I'm not entirely sure I understand it, not fully.

Massimo sighs. "For what it's worth, Luca wasn't supposed to shoot him."

I can't look at my cousin right now. In fact, I can't stand being in the same damn car as him. "No, but he did anyway. What was the plan?"

"We had a couple of men waiting at the back door to snatch you. They were supposed to knock Spartak out."

I grind my teeth. "Why couldn't you listen to what I wanted?"

He growls. "You wanted to remain with a man who kidnapped you, Imalia." His nostrils flare as he glances over his shoulder at me. "What people would leave their own flesh and blood in the hands of a man so brutal, so fucking crazy?"

"He's not crazy."

My cousin releases a defeated sigh. "You'll understand in the end."

"How would you like it if someone made your own decisions for you?" I ask, knowing that despite Uncle Remy's constant pushing for him to marry, he'd never actually force the issue. As a man in this world, he has all the power. Women are expected to do as they're told and marry who is selected for them.

He huffs in response as he comes to the gates of the Morrone family residence. I can't stand the thought of being trapped now in another cage, as my family won't let me out. In fact, they'll probably ship me back to San Diego the first chance they get. It's the only way they could keep Spartak away from me.

The gate opens for us and he drives up the long, sweeping driveway. Once there, my heart almost stops beating when I see my mom waiting near the doorway. "Great, why the hell is she here?"

"Because she's your mom, and she's been worried sick about you." He glares at me. "Not that you care."

Pain claws at the sides of my throat as I stare at her, realizing somehow I've got to explain. The fact I wanted to marry Spartak. He tried to protect me from this, but it turns out my uncle was one step ahead of him, this time with the tracker implant.

I get out of the car and my mom rushes toward me, tears streaming down her face.

"Oh, thank God!" she says, wrapping her arms around me.

I hug her back, as this may be the last time she'll want to hug me once she hears the truth.

"Are you okay?" she asks, and then she gasps when she sees the blood on my hands. "Who's blood is that?"

I can't hold the tears back now. They stream down my face unrelentingly, but not for the reason, she thinks.

"It's okay, you're safe now."

I shake my head. "I was safe with him," I say, taking a step back. "The truth is Mom, I love Spartak Volkov." I hold my hand up to show her my ring. "I married him, and Massimo dragged me away from him." I can't hold back the tears and it's beyond embarrassing. "Not to mention Luca shot him. This is my husband's blood."

My mom looks shell shocked for a moment, staring at me with her mouth open. "Come inside, sweetheart," she says, putting her arm around my back to steer me toward the house. "You need to get some rest."

I don't have the energy to fight her as she ushers me into the house and leads me up to my bedroom. Inside, I'm utterly shattered, not knowing whether the man I love is alive. If he dies, I'll kill Luca. I honestly would murder him for it.

Once we're behind closed doors, my mom fixes me with an odd look. "Do you really love Spartak Volkov?"

I nod in response. "Yes, that's why I left the other night, because he asked me to come back to him and I chose to."

She blows out a shaky breath. "You realize he attacked our family in San Diego?"

I nod. "Yes, one condition I gave him if I returned was that he had to pull his men out of San Diego."

"That was your doing?" she asks, eyes widening.

I'm surprised she's not shouting at me yet. "I want to be with him and make sure he's okay."

"I'm sorry, Imalia. Your uncle won't allow it."

"I don't give a shit what he'll allow. I'm married to him." I cross my arms over my chest. "He's my husband, and you can't tear me away from him."

She smiles, but it's a sad one. "Unfortunately, your uncle has already fueled the jet, ready to take us back to San Diego tonight." She shakes her head. "I understand you think you love this man, but he kidnapped you." Her brow furrows. "Perhaps some space away will help you learn whether your feelings are genuine."

Unbelievable.

Everyone is treating me like a victim, as if Spartak somehow brainwashed me into thinking I love him. He was right all along. I've been trapped by social norms and what my family expects of me. My mom expected me to marry someone like Jamie. A nice guy, despite the fact he's from this criminal world too, but he's not for me. "I know my feelings are real, Mom. Are you suggesting that I'm some kind of idiot who can be manipulated?"

She shakes her head. "Of course not, I'm merely suggesting that spending such a long time locked away with him may have swayed your judgement."

"I won't leave Chicago."

Her expression turns severe. "You'll do as your told Imalia Alicia Allegro, so help me God."

I glare at her. "I'll escape the first chance I get."

"Well then, I guess that means we'll have to keep you locked up until you come to your senses." She turns around and heads toward the door. "I expected better from you, Imalia."

I grind my teeth. "And I expected better from you, Mother, than locking away your daughter like she's some animal."

"Much like your so-called husband did to you," she snarls, looking border line feral as she glares at me over her shoulder. "You need to have a long, hard think about where your loyalties lie. Family is everything to us and always has been. It's time you remember that." She walks out of the room before I can retaliate and slams the door behind her, locking it.

A flood of rage hits me as I stare at the shut door. How are they any better than Spartak if they lock me away?

It's hypocrisy at its finest.

I stand and walk to the adjoining bathroom, hoping

the window is unlocked. The building is only two storeys and if the window were open, I could scale the side of it pretty easily. Especially since I've been rock climbing since I was eight years old. I try the windows, but they're locked with a key.

"Fuck's sake."

I glance around the room, looking for something to try to bust the lock open with. Although it didn't work at Spartak's home, I'm desperate to get out of here. I don't even know if he's alive or dead. All I can see in my mind is that terrible image of him in a pool of blood. There was nothing I could do as Massimo dragged me away.

I pull my cell phone out of my pocket, wishing I had Maxim's or Timur's number. The only number I have is Spartaks, and he's probably not going to be very responsive.

I write a text anyway.

Are you okay? They're keeping me locked up and sending me to San Diego tonight. I don't know what to do.

It sends but there are no ticks to say it's delivered. I call the number, but it goes straight to messaging. My stomach sinks as hopelessness sets in and I drop to my ass on the bathroom floor.

The tears come hard and fast, streaming unrelentingly down my face. Until my uncle walked into that church, today had been the happiest day of my life. It quickly turned into the biggest nightmare.

Tears flood down my cheeks as I wonder if I'll ever see my husband again. He has to make it through and survive his injuries. The alternative is too hard to bear, and in time, we'll find each other.

I have to play it smart with my family and convince them they were right. I was brainwashed and I've come to my senses. Only then will my family allow me enough freedom to find my way back to him.

28

SPARTAK

"*I* highly advise against you leaving this facility, sir."

I glare at the surgeon. "I've been in here five days while people hold my wife captive." I cross my arms over my chest. "Do you think I'm going to sit around any longer when I'm fine?"

His jaw clenches. "You may feel fine, but that's probably all the drugs in your system."

That's when I snap as I grab hold of the collar of his white scrubs and lift him off the floor. "Are you suggesting that I don't know my own capabilities?" I ask, staring him in the eye. "This isn't the first gunshot wound I've sustained. Far fucking from it and I know what I'm doing." I release him and he almost collapses. "Now get out of my way and grab my release papers before I do something I regret."

He adjusts his jacket. "Of course. I'll get them now."

I watch as he scurries out of the room and down the corridor, running a hand through my hair. The happiest day of my life turned into a fucking disaster and I need to right everything that went wrong. Imalia is in her uncle's clutches and, knowing my luck, she's probably already back in San Diego. Remy wouldn't risk keeping her here where she can easily find her way back to me or vice versa.

Timur has been tracking her down for me and text me earlier to say he's located her and he's on his way to get me, which is why I'm so eager to leave. I've wasted enough time lying in a hospital bed. Imalia means the world to me and I won't put off rescuing her any longer than I already have.

I spin around and stare at the hospital bed, knowing that I shouldn't be taking on such a dangerous task right now. The meds will help with the pain, but once they wear off, I'll be struggling. Gunshot wounds can take years to heal fully. Five days isn't enough time, but I don't care. I've had my fair share of gunshot wounds in the past, although none were as near to fatal as the one Luca hit me with. If it weren't for Timur returning when he did and getting me to this clinic, I would have died.

"Sir, how are you?" Timur asks, appearing in the doorway.

I tense at the sound of his voice as I owe him my

life, which I don't like. Debts unpaid make me uncomfortable. "Fine." I turn to face him. "Thank you for saving my life, Timur. I'm in your debt."

He shakes his head. "Never, sir. It's my duty as Sovietnik to protect my pakhan no matter what."

I inhale a deep breath and nod. "Well, if I can ever do anything for you, you tell me. Okay?"

He nods in response, but I know Timur. He'd never ask anything of me.

"Where is Imalia?" I ask.

He winces. "San Diego, I'm afraid."

"Motherfuckers."

"I've requested that the jet be ready to take off in an hour."

"Good." I nod. "How did you find her?"

He smirks, shaking his head. "The idiots left the tracker device in her, and we hacked into the system and used it to track her." He holds up his cell phone, which has an app with what looks like a GPS map. "Once we're there, this will lead us directly to her."

"Perfect." I walk toward my Sovietnik and clap him on the shoulder. "Good work, with this and again for saving my life."

Timur bows his head. "It's my pleasure, sir."

The surgeon has returned and clears his throat. "Here are your release papers. I need to get your signature." He approaches me.

I snatch them out of his hand and the pen, signing

the form and thrusting them back at him. "There. Am I free to go?"

"Yes, but I recommend you take these meds with you." He holds up a paper bag of prescription painkillers. "You'll need them when the drugs in your system wear off."

I take the bag. "Thanks." I glance at Timur. "Let's get the hell out of here."

He turns to leave. "Follow me."

I follow him out of the facility, knowing that getting Imalia back is going to be the biggest challenge of my career yet. Also, the most important one, as I can't live without her. She's my everything and my reason for living.

I won't sit idly by while she slips away from me.

THE PLANE DESCENDS toward the private airstrip on the outskirts of San Diego. One which the Utkin Bratva of San Diego has assured us the Allegro mafia have no control over or insight into who lands. It means they won't anticipate us coming.

I shift in my chair to look out of the window, wincing as the movement sends a shooting pain right through me.

"Should you take some meds before we land, sir?" Timur asks, noticing my discomfort.

I clench my jaw, glancing at the bag of drugs the

doctor gave me. "Perhaps, but I don't want to be slowed down by drugs when we try to rescue her." I grab it and check out what drugs he prescribed. There's a range of pain meds, including fentanyl, which is too fucking strong.

I take a few less potent pills and knock them back with a bottle of water. Over the five-hour flight, the effects of the drugs I had in my system before I left Chicago have slowly worn off. It's as if someone has beaten me up from the inside out. There's no doubt that this is the worst gunshot I've sustained

I brace myself as the plane rocks from side to side, suffering from turbulence as it comes in to land. The plane jolts onto the ground, sending a wave of pain through me. I grit my teeth and try to ignore it as the plane steadies and then taxis down the runway.

"Check the app. Where is she?" I ask.

Timur pulls his cell phone out of his pocket and powers it on. After a few moments, he has the GPS locator loaded and pulls up Imalia's location. His brow furrows. "It looks like she's at the train station, possibly."

"Shit, do you think she's leaving the city?"

Timur shrugs. "We best move fast to catch up with her before she gets on a train."

If it's not one thing, it's another. The surprising thing is I didn't expect her to be allowed out of the Allegro residence, unless she's changed her mind about being with me. A knot forms in my stomach at the prospect. I couldn't accept a sudden three-sixty from her, as my heart won't give her up.

Once the jet comes to a stop, we're quick to get off and get into the SUV parked on the tarmac courtesy of the Utkin Bratva's Pakhan, Dimitry. "So straight to San Diego train station?"

Timur nods. "Hold on, sir." He puts the vehicle into gear and speeds out of the private airstrip, which is about a twenty-minute drive from the station.

"Can I borrow your cell phone?" I ask Timur.

He nods, passing it over.

I call up the trains leaving the station, checking through the times and locations. Most are leaving within the next twenty minutes, which doesn't bode well for us. "I think we'll miss her."

Timur's brow furrows. "Why?"

"A hunch," I say, pulling up the tracking app on Timur's phone. "Huh."

"What is it, sir?"

My brow furrows. "It looks like she's leaving the station, but not by train. This suggests she's in a car heading in our direction on the road."

"Really?" Timur asks. "Perhaps she got off a train.

"Perhaps." I nod, certain that I've got it right. "We'll have to follow her. I'll direct you once necessary. At the moment, she's heading toward us."

Timur steps on the gas, speeding down the road. "Hopefully, she stays the course. That'll make it easier."

I keep my eye on the symbol like a hawk, waiting for it to turn off this road. Unfortunately, once we're close, it does just that and turns left. "Fuck, she just turned."

"Where?" Timur asks.

"For us, we need to take the fifth right turn to follow her."

"Got it." He focuses on the road, going as fast as he can as he weaves in and out of traffic. His brow furrows as he pulls into the lane to turn right. "San Diego International Airport?"

A tug pulls at my chest as I wonder if we've caught her trying to make her escape, trying to get back to me. Or perhaps that's just hopeful.

I check the flights due out of the airport on Timur's phone, smiling when I see there's a domestic flight to Chicago in about an hour. "I reckon she may be trying to get to Chicago."

"Why's that?" Timur asks.

"There's a flight in one hour." I pull up the tracker. "And she's just stopped at the airport."

He sighs heavily. "Turns out we didn't need to come all this way after all, then."

I glare at my sovietnik. "She's a fool if she thinks her mom's men won't find her before the flight takes off. Thankfully, we're here to save the day."

He nods and continues along the road into the airport, heading toward the short-stay car park, which is closest to the lobby. "Is she still in the lobby?" Timur asks.

I nod. "It looks like it."

"Good," Timur says, as he gets out of the car. "We can't let her get through security." He rushes off toward the terminal building and I have to clench my jaw at the pain radiating through me as I keep his pace. I manage to catch him and place a hand on Timur's shoulder. "Calm down and let me lead this."

He bows his head and slows his steps. "Sorry, sir. I forgot about your injury."

Silence falls between us as we travel the last hundred yards to the building. I walk into the entrance of the lobby, scanning it. The place is large and I don't see her. The tracker suggests she's further into the building. As we walk through the lobby, she gets further away.

"Are you sure this thing is working?"

"May I?" Timur asks.

I pass it to him, and he turns the phone around. "It was the wrong way, sir." He nods toward the direction we came. "She's somewhere in that direction."

"Fuck," I say, noticing that's the direction of the security clearance. Once she goes through there, we could lose her and have to buy a ticket to get through. A time delay we can't afford, not if our assumption is correct and Imalia is trying to make an escape. It means her family could almost be upon us.

We move quickly back the way we came, Timur holding the tracker to navigate to her. He comes to a stop and nods ahead. "There she is," he says.

My heart stops beating for a few moments when I

see her from behind, glancing up at the security desk where she's about to join the queue. There's no rush, not now I've found her. She's at the back of the queue, which buys me some time, so I watch her from afar for a moment, knowing without a doubt that I've never felt so strongly about anyone before.

"What are you waiting for, sir?"

I glance at Timur, shaking my head. "Nothing." I walk forward and close the gap between us, my heart pounding at a thousand miles an hour.

The last time I saw her, she was being torn away from me and I was bleeding on the floor of the church. It feels almost surreal that she's right here, a few feet away.

"Imalia," I say her name and notice the way her entire body stiffens.

Fear coils through me as I wonder if perhaps she isn't here to get back to Chicago. Maybe she has changed her mind, and she's about to break my heart. I can't face it if she does.

IMALIA

I tap my foot nervously, waiting at the platform to get the train to Chula Vista. It's a little delayed, which I'm hoping will aid my plan. Alonzo, my bodyguard, has to come everywhere with me, but I intend to skip off the train at the last minute and ditch him.

The sound of a train approaching the terminal makes my heart rate speed up. If I don't get this right, then all my planning is for nothing, including purchasing a one-way plane ticket to Chicago. I bought the ticket last night and know that once I'm on that plane, they can track me with the device they put in my neck, which I hope I can remove once at the airport.

San Diego International Airport is only a ten-minute cab drive from the station. I then have about an hour and ten minutes until my flight is due to take off, so it'll be cutting it fine.

I have been going out of my mind for the past few days, still unaware of whether Spartak is dead or alive. My mom insists that if he were dead Uncle Remy would know about it and rumor is they patched him up at a private hospital. I don't trust rumors, though. I need to see he's alive for my own eyes and feel the warmth of his skin beneath my fingers.

"Imalia, the train is here," Alonzo says, breaking me out of the daze I fell into.

I shake my head. "Oh yeah, sorry, I was miles away." I grab my bag and he heads toward the door of the train as the whistle blows to signal it's about to leave.

He sighs heavily. "I wish you would have let me drive rather than taking the train."

"I enjoy taking the train," I say, moving behind him toward it.

He jumps on first and turns around to help me on. Before he can, I slam my hand into the button to shut the door, closing it between us.

His eyes widen as horror dawns on his face. "What the fuck?" I hear him shout through the glass as the train rolls away from the platform.

I mouth the word sorry before rushing in the opposite direction and out of the station.

Alonzo is a good guy and he'll get a lot of flack for losing me, but it's not my problem. Now, my only issue is that damn tracker in my neck, the tracker my mom promises she'll have removed. Despite having doctors and surgeons on call, she still hasn't. It means my mom could get people to the airport and stop me before I get on the plane.

I knock into some guy, making him spill his coffee as I try to rush away.

"Watch where the fuck you're going."

I hold my hand up as I continue running. "Sorry."

The entrance to the station has a cab rank on the other side, which I jog to. One cab has its light on, which means it's free. Quickly, I jump in and slam the door, thankful to be inside.

"San Diego International Airport, please," I say.

The cab driver's brow furrows as he assesses me in his rearview mirror before nodding. "Sure."

My nerves settle a little as the car moves toward my destination. I check my watch and I have exactly one hour and five minutes until my plane to Chicago. It's only a ten-minute cab ride to the airport from here, as long as the traffic is alright.

I glance out of the window, knowing that if I pull this off, it might be the last time I'm in the city I grew up in. All my life I was sure I'd never want to live anywhere else, and then Spartak came along.

Chicago is very different from San Diego, but it's home because it's where the man I love is. Or at least, I hope it is unless Luca's shot killed my uncle's arch nemesis.

"We're here," the driver announces, eyeing me in the mirror. "That'll be thirty bucks."

I dig my hand into my pocket and pull out a fifty-dollar bill, thrusting it at him. "Keep the change."

His eyes widen as he thankfully pockets the money and I get out of the cab, staring up at the international airport terminal.

I slip into the first bathroom I see as I enter the lobby of the airport, and check there's no one in there. Once I'm sure it's clear, I lock the door behind me so no one walks in as I try to slice my neck open. My stomach churns as I reach into my pocket and grab the surgical knife I stole from the clinic in the basement of our home. The tracker is raised and just beneath my skin at the back of my neck as I run my fingers over it. My hand shakes as I bring the blade to my neck, trying to keep it steady.

I press the knife into my skin and blood trickles down my neck. "Fuck," I say, pulling it away and shaking my head.

There's no way in hell I'm going to cut out the little tracker without catching an artery. Not when my hand is shaking this much. It means I've got to chance it and hope that my mom's men don't find me before the plane takes off in under one hour. I grab a bandaid out of my bag and put it over the cut, not wishing to draw attention to myself.

I sigh heavily and lean forward over the sink, staring at my reflection in the mirror.

Am I insane thinking I can escape?

If this goes wrong, then they'll end up locking me

up for eternity until my mom marries me off to some guy she approves of. I shudder at the thought of ever being touched by anyone other than Spartak. My mom has been trying to find out how to get my marriage annulled, but it turns out it's not as easy as she expected. It means if I can get back to him today that I can stop her in her tracks.

I leave the bathroom and head for my airline check-in desk, knowing it's not long until it will close. It's quiet, and I walk straight up to a man behind the desk. "Hi, I'd like to check in, please," I say, grabbing my passport and ticket and putting it on the counter.

"Certainly," he says, grabbing my documents and typing into the computer. He glances up at me as he checks my passport, nodding.

"You're sorted," he says, passing me my boarding pass. "Gate 12 for boarding. Get over there fast, as they'll close it in twenty minutes."

"Thank you," I say, grabbing my documents and rushing in the gate's direction. I'm about to walk up to the security desk when I hear a voice I never expect.

"Imalia."

I stiffen, wondering if I'm going insane, hearing his voice when he can't possibly be here. When I spin around, my heart almost bursts the moment I set eyes on him. My husband is standing behind me, very much alive. Tears prickle my eyes as I blink a few times, wondering if I've finally flown off the handle and I'm hallucinating.

A smug smirk twists onto his lips as he moves toward me. "Where are you going, little lamb?"

It's all it takes to unravel me as the tears flood relentlessly down my cheeks and I rush toward him, wrapping my arms around him.

He grunts, wincing in pain.

"Oh shit," I say, stepping back. "The gunshot. I totally forgot." I shake my head. "How are you here? How did you find me?"

Timur lingers a little way behind, watching us like a hawk.

"My Sovietnik hacked you uncle's tracking device. We followed you here, as the cab you took crossed our path on the way from a private airstrip."

"You came for me," I say, wiping the tears away.

He grabs my hips and pulls me close. "Of course. I promised I'd find you."

"I thought you might have died." I shake my head. "I don't know what I would've done without you."

He cups my cheeks and kisses away my tears, so similar to the way he did the first day we met. "You would have been fine, baby girl, but I'm here. You don't have to worry."

"The tracker," I say, suddenly panicking. "My mom has probably sent guys over here already."

Spartak looks wicked as he smiles more widely. "And why don't we send them on a wild goose chase?"

I raise a brow. "What did you have in mind?"

He pulls me close to whisper in my ear. "Let me cut you and you'll find out."

My stomach pulls up and I nod in response, assuming he intends to cut out the tracking device. "Where?"

He nods toward a door which says airport personnel only. "Supply closet?"

I clench my thighs as I remember the last time we were alone in a supply closet together. "Okay."

He grabs my hand and drags me toward it, checking there's no one to see us before dragging me inside. The door shuts and plunges us into darkness.

"How will you see in here?" I ask.

A click sounds and the closet lights up. "That better?"

I nod in response, kind of struggling to believe he's actually here in San Diego and alive. "Shouldn't you be recuperating in hospital?"

He shrugs. "Probably, but I couldn't spend another day lying in a hospital bed while you weren't with me."

I wince that he'd risked his health to come and find me. "Did the doctor say you were okay to leave?"

He shakes his head. "No." He grabs my hips and pulls me toward him. "But a little gunshot wound couldn't keep me from you, malishka. Now turn around."

I swallow hard and turn my back to him.

"Did you already try to remove it?"

I nod in response. "Tried and failed spectacularly. I was shaking too much."

He chuckles softly, brushing the hair away from my neck. "So you have a blade on you?"

I pull the surgeon's blade out of my pocket and hold it up. "Yes."

"That'll work a lot better than my switchblade," he says, taking it out of my hand. As he does, are fingers brush together and electricity pulses through my body.

"I've missed you," I murmur softly.

"Not half as much as I've missed you." He places a firm hand on my shoulder and then pulls the bandaid off.

I feel the knife slice into my skin as he proceeds without warning. After a few seconds, the blade retreats. "Done."

My eyes widen as I spin to face him. "That was fast."

The smirk on his face widens, and his eyes flash with amusement. "Sorry, little lamb. Was it not enough pain to turn you on?"

I grit my teeth, as that's perhaps part of the reason I'm disappointed. "No. Now what's the plan?"

"First, I'm going to kiss you." He pulls me against him and presses his lips firmly to mine, parting mine with his tongue.

I moan and claw at his back as he deepens the kiss, swiping his tongue in erotic caresses against my own.

When he breaks away, we're both breathless. "I've

missed you so fucking much it hurts," he pants, clawing at my hips with such force. "I wish I had time to fuck you right here and now."

I lick my lips, wishing he did too.

"Unfortunately for the both of us, time is of the essence." He pulls a handkerchief out of his pocket and cleans up the tracker so it's no longer bloody. "Let's plant this on someone."

I smirk at the idea of my mom's men searching aimlessly in this airport for me when I'm long gone. "Good thinking."

He holds out his arm to me. "Shall we, Mrs. Volkov?"

I take it. "I love you," I say.

He smirks at me and leads me out of the supply closet in search of a mule. It should buy us enough time to escape San Diego and return to Chicago.

30

SPARTAK

I drag Imalia onto the plane, knowing that it's only a matter of time until the Allegro Mafia catches up to us. By now, they'll know that Imalia no longer has the tracker in her neck and will probably check the airport CCTV.

Once they do, they'll also know that I have to fly out of the city somehow. The only possible ally that would help me in this city are the Russians, and this is their private airstrip.

It doesn't take a genius to work it out. All I can hope is that we take off before they piece it all together.

"We made it," she says, slumping down into a chair.

"Don't get too complacent, Imalia. We haven't taken off yet."

Her brow furrows. "Then get the pilot to take off fast."

I chuckle at her eagerness as Timur joins us on the plane.

"We're all set to go, sir."

I nod in response. "Good. Make sure we take off in the next five minutes and no later."

He heads toward the cockpit of my private jet to instruct the pilot.

"Do you really think they'll try to stop the plane?" Imalia asks, twisting her fingers together nervously.

I clench my jaw. "It's unlikely they'll be able to piece everything together that fast, but I wouldn't rule it out."

She worries her bottom lip between her teeth.

"Come here," I say, patting my lap.

Imalia stands and walks toward me, sitting on my knee.

I hold her close to me, inhaling her intoxicating scent of strawberries and Jasmine. "You smell divine," I breathe, groaning as my cock grows hard under her. "I've been going out of my mind these past few days, wondering where you were."

"You have?" She says, sounding shocked. "How do you think I've been not knowing if you were dead or alive?" Her beautiful brown eyes glare down at me. "Why didn't you text me back?"

I raise a brow. "Unfortunately, the bullet went through my phone." I pull it out of my jacket and show it to her. "Although, it's probably fortunate, as the surgeon believes my cell phone was the only thing that stopped the bullet from hitting vital organs."

Her face pales. "Shit, I…" She shakes her head. "I don't know what I would have done if you'd have died."

The engine of the jet fires up, warning me we're preparing to take off. That's when Timur returns from the cockpit, a grave expression on his face. "The pilot is getting us into the air now, but they're here."

"Who?" Imalia asks.

Spartak's jaw clenches. "Your family."

The hostess quickly shut the door to the jet as the jet taxis down the runway.

"Surely they can't stop us now?" Imalia asks.

"They can try to shoot our engines so we can't take off."

Timur nods. "He's getting us in the air as quick as he can."

The far off sound of gunshots makes me tense as I stand to gaze out of the jet's window. "Motherfuckers," I murmur, running a hand through my hair. "I'll give your mom one thing. She's determined to stop you, no matter what." I glance at my wife. "I'm surprised they'd shoot at a plane housing their boss' daughter, though."

Imalia stands and comes to gaze out too, paling slightly. "Are we going to make it?"

"How good are your mom's men at shooting a moving target?"

She shrugs. "I wouldn't have a clue."

"Then I'd say cross your fingers and hope."

Imalia jumps out of the way as a bullet hits the bulletproof glass window of the jet. "Fuck."

The jet pulls up as it gets near the end of the runway, but the barrage of bullets increases, ricocheting off the carcass of the jet. We shakily move into the air and I grab Imalia by the waist, pulling her toward a seat and sitting with her on my lap. "Relax, malishka. There's nothing we can do but hope they don't hit the engine."

Imalia buries her face into my chest. "I'm scared."

I move my hand in soothing circles over her back, trying to calm her as we rise higher and higher into the sky and the bullets stop hitting the jet. "It's okay, little lamb. I think we're safe."

Timur comes back from the cockpit, smirking. "Bastards were lousy fucking shots."

Imalia sighs in relief. "So, we're safe?"

He nods. "Yes, sit back and enjoy the flight." He gives me a wink and then returns to the cockpit.

"Looks like Timur is giving us some privacy, baby girl."

She bites her bottom lip, searching my eyes. "Surely you shouldn't be doing anything but relaxing." Her hand lingers over the spot where Luca shot me. "How are you even walking around?"

"Pain killers," I say simply. "And I intend to relax while you ride me." I link my hands behind my head and rest back, raising a brow. "So, what are you waiting for?"

She crosses her arms over her chest. "I don't want to hurt you."

"Believe me, you couldn't do anything to hurt me." I unzip my pants and free my cock from the zipper. "Now hop on and make me proud."

Her eyes dilate as she looks at my hard cock, shifting as she becomes increasingly more aroused. That is when she hops off of my lap and teasingly undoes the buttoned front of her dress to strip for me. "Is this what you want, daddy?" She asks, dropping it to the floor and pulling her panties down. "Do you want my pussy?"

I groan. "Stop fucking about and sit on my cock before I put you on it."

Imalia drops her bra to the floor before straddling my thighs, her perfect cunt inches away from my cock.

I grab her hips and force her down over my length in one harsh movement, burying myself to the hilt in her.

She gasps, eyes wide as she gets used to the sudden invasion. "You're supposed to relax, now let go," she says, prizing my fingers off her hips.

And then she moves above me like a goddamn sex goddess, rolling her hips in the most exquisite way. Slowly, she moves her hands over her own breasts, touching her stiff nipples and moaning.

I watch her in awe, knowing that I would have gone to the ends of the earth for this woman. She's what makes all the shit I've been through worth it. Finding my soul mate after all these years. The other half of my whole.

"That's so fucking good, malishka," I say, knowing how much it turns her on when I praise her.

Her hips roll faster and harder, spurred on by it. "Do you like that, daddy?" She asks, eyes flashing with desire.

"Fuck yes, malishka. I love watching you ride my cock like a good girl who wants to please me."

Her lips part slightly as she moans and I have to grind my teeth to stop myself from coming apart from the mere look on her face. Imalia Volkov is the most stunning woman on this planet, a woman I can't live without. In that moment, I know I would lay everything on the line for her. She has a power no one else has ever had over me. A power to bring me to my knees.

I mold my hands to the side of her body, memorizing every curve and dip as they skate over her hips. The panic I felt when she was torn away from me by her family will stay with me forever. I never want to feel so utterly powerless ever again.

I tighten my grasp on her hips, guiding her up and down with more force. The need to take control growing stronger as I watch her. Adrenaline pulses through my veins as I lift her off of me and set her down on the sofa opposite, groaning at the ache in my abdomen.

"What are you doing?" she gasps, eyes wide.

"I need to fuck you, baby girl."

"You could hurt yourself."

I bite her lip hard enough to break the skin and lick the blood from it. "Don't question me." I grip her throat with my hand and squeeze, before slamming my hips forward and burying myself deep inside of her. My eyes shut at the sensation of being in control, of fucking her the way I craved these past five days. "I need to consummate our marriage, little lamb."

"That's what I was doing," she mutters, pursing her lips in annoyance.

"And you were doing such a good job that I couldn't resist taking you harder," I murmur, capturing her lips. "I've missed this so much." I graze my teeth over her nipple before sucking it into my mouth.

She hisses in pleasure, back arching as her muscle clamp around my cock, making me grunt.

"That's it, take daddy's cock like a good girl," I purr, thrusting with more brutally into her. There's a desperate, primal aspect to our fucking as we both lose control.

Imalia plays with her nipples for me and it's the most erotic thing I've ever seen.

"Good girl, play with yourself for me." I dig my fingertips into her hips, hard. "I want you to come on my cock. I want your tight muscles gripping me hard as you fall over the edge."

She moans, eyes dilating so much she looks otherworldly.

"And once you do, I'm going to fill you with my cum so it's dripping out of you for hours," I growl.

"Yes, daddy, I'm going to come," she cries out, driving me wild.

I explode deep inside of her tight pussy as I continue to fuck her into the sofa below with brutal thrusts, making sure I spill every drop inside of her. The desire to have Imalia growing big and round with my baby drives me. Her muscles clamp around me as she trembles beneath me, her beautiful dark eyes rolling back in her head.

I slide my palm around her throat and squeeze, attempting to prolong her pleasure. As we both come down from our mutual climaxes, I become more aware of the pain shooting through my abdomen.

Imalia's eyes widen as they fix on my shirt, which is stained with blood. "Shit, you've overdone it." She tries to scramble out from underneath me, but I keep her pinned with my hand around her throat.

"Don't move," I order, pulling my cock out of her pussy and grabbing her panties, sliding them back on. "Stay on your back. I don't want a drop wasted, do you understand?" I glance down at my bloodied shirt. "I'll handle this."

She bites the inside of her cheek and I know she wants to argue, but instead she nods.

I stand and zip my pants back up before unbuttoning my shirt and peeling away the bloodied fabric, glancing at the dressing over the gunshot wound. It will need changing and we have a medical kit in the cockpit. "Stay here and don't move."

Her eyes narrow. "Where are you going?"

"To get a first aid kit."

She doesn't reply as I walk toward the cockpit, knocking on the door.

Timur answers, eyes widening when he sees the bloodied bandage over my stomach. "What happened, sir?"

"I may have slightly overdone it. Can you give me the first aid kit?"

He nods and goes to fetch it. "Do you want me to help?"

I shake my head and take the kit. "No, I've got this. Thanks." I return to the main part of the plane to find my naughty little brat of a wife has disobeyed my order. She's sitting in a different seat opposite the one I fucked her on. "I thought I told you not to move."

She glares at me. "You may be my husband, but it doesn't make you my boss."

"Is that right?" I ask, walking toward her.

She nods and stands. "Let me sort that out."

I consider arguing, but she looks determined. "Fine." I sit down in the opposite chair and she kneels in front of me, slowly peeling away the dressing.

"Shit, this doesn't look good." Her brow furrows. "I think it needs new stitches."

"Just stem the blood flow with a new dressing for now."

She nods and chucks the bloodied dressing and bandage into a paper waste bin before grabbing a fresh one. "I should clean the blood from the wound with a saline solution."

I raise a brow. "Is that right?"

She nods and soaks some gauze with saline solution, gently dabbing clean the wound.

Even though she's careful, it hurts like hell. Once she's finished, she dries the area and then affixes the new dressing over the wound. "It should help, but you'll need to see a surgeon the moment we get back."

I grab her around the waist before she can move away and force her onto my knee. "Thank you, Nurse Volkov." I search her eyes. "For patching me up, but also for fighting to get back to me."

"Always," she murmurs. "Thank you for coming for me."

"Always," I reply back.

"I love you, Spartak. There's nothing that can ever change that."

I smile at her, knowing without a doubt I didn't know what love was until I met this girl. "I love you too, Mrs. Volkov."

31

EPILOGUE

IMALIA

*O*ne year later…

"I'm so glad I can finally take you on our honeymoon," Spartak says, his hand firmly grasping my bare thigh. "The place I rented is so isolated, no one will hear you scream."

I shudder at the thought, my panties getting damp. "Good," I say.

Ever since we got married, I've become obsessed with role-playing consensual non consent with my husband. It gets me going like nothing else can.

We're heading to Colorado into the mountains for a week away. A late honeymoon since things are finally settling in Chicago, even though things aren't perfect. We finally found out who the rat in his ranks was and it wasn't who he had suspected. It was a family member, but that's a story for another day. The warring gangs of Chicago had to find common ground to defeat a larger threat that a member of Spartak's own family posed to all of them.

I know I'll never repair the bridges I burned with my family, but my mom is more open to having a relationship still, especially now I'm going to have her first grandchild.

He places a hand on my growing bump. "How are you today?"

I smile at him. "Great. I can't wait to be a mom."

He kisses me softly. "There was no way I ever thought I'd get another chance at being a father."

"But you're going to do things differently this time, right?" After hearing the horrific stories of what he put Maxim and Viktoria through as children, I honestly considered getting sterilized. There's no way in hell I'd allow my child to be put through that.

"Yes, definitely."

I smile, thankful that he's seen the error of his ways. His relationship with his daughter is understandably irreparable. Maxim is slowly but surely coming around to his father's constant apologies. The SUV takes a sharp turn off of the main road and up a mountain pass.

"Hold on," the driver says, glancing back at us. "This might be a bit bumpy."

He isn't joking as he slowly makes the ascent up the mountain track, jolting us around the back of the car aggressively. I glance at my husband, who looks a little uncomfortable. Even after a year since Luca shot him in the stomach, he's still not fully healed from it. Although the wound has long closed up and healed, it bothers him when he moves a certain way or if we're driving over particularly bumpy terrain.

I set my hand on his and squeeze gently. "How far up the track is it?"

He sighs heavily. "About a mile, at least."

I nod and focus on the road ahead, watching for our isolated cabin to come into view. When it finally does, I gasp. The place is more like a mansion than a cabin, even if it's clad in wood.

"Wow, this looks expensive," I say.

Spartak leans toward me, his breath teasing against my ear. "Only the very best for my baby girl."

It's crazy the way his words can turn me into a pool of desire. I smile at him as the driver pulls the SUV into the driveway and parks in front of the door. "I'll get your bags and bring them up," the driver says.

"Thanks," Spartak says, grabbing my hand and leading me up the steps into the huge cabin.

The warmth hits me the moment we enter, as a gigantic fireplace is already lit and roaring in the center of the double height vaulted living room. "Wow, this place is nice."

"It even has a jacuzzi." He nods toward the deck, which you can see through the floor to ceiling glass windows. There is a huge jacuzzi on there, steaming away and lit up.

"That will be fun," I say, smirking at him.

The driver clears his throat behind us. "If that's all, I'll be back to collect you in one week's time."

Spartak nods. "Yes, thank you." He moves forward and tips him with a bill.

The driver smiles and then takes his leave.

Spartak walks after him and locks the door, securing us inside. "This is going to be fun," he says, a glint of mischief burning in his beautiful gray-blue eyes.

"Is it?" I ask, pretending not to understand his meaning.

"Yes," he murmurs, walking toward me. "I can't wait to play with you, little lamb." He wraps his arms around me and pulls me against him, pressing every hard inch of his cock into me. "Wait here and don't move."

I do as he says, biting my bottom lip in anticipation.

A rustling sounds behind us and I'm tempted to look, but I know not to. He returns and spins me around.

"Mrs. Volkov, are you ready to play?" he asks, holding up a blindfold and a set of handcuffs.

My thighs clench at the thought as I nod. "Yes, sir."

He groans and moves toward me, pushing me down onto the chair he dragged into the center of the room. "Good girl," he purrs into my ear as he fixes the blindfold over my eyes. And then he fixes the handcuffs on my wrists behind my back, making it impossible for me to move.

"Now, what am I going to do with a pretty little prisoner like you?" he muses.

I shudder in anticipation. "Please don't hurt me."

He chuckles. The sound of his laugh is wicked, and it sends shivers down my spine. "Hurt you?" I can sense him circling me like a shark circling its prey. "I won't hurt you. No, I'm going to fuck you."

My nipples harden against the fabric of my shirt. "No, please don't."

He grabs hold of my throat, flexing his fingers around it gently. Ever since he found out I'm pregnant, he's less forceful with the choking in particular. "You're my prisoner and I'll use you how I see fit."

I whimper, the desire building inside of me becoming almost unbearable. I'll never fully understand my desire to be taken against my will, or at least playing that part. It makes no logical sense, but every time we roleplay it, I'm wetter than ever.

"Open that pretty little mouth," he murmurs.

I do as he says as he slides his thumb into it, groaning. "Such a beautiful mouth, perfect for fucking."

"Fuck you," I say, biting down on his thumb softly.

He hisses and pulls it out of my mouth, grabbing my chin. "If you're going to use your teeth, I guess I'll have to ensure you can't."

My stomach flips as I realize he's talking about the open mouth gag he'd recently purchased. One that had become a favorite of his to use during our non consent role play since it renders me mute and pliable.

"Please, just let me go," I plead as my pussy gets wetter and my desire heightens.

Suddenly, he forces the gag into my mouth and fastens it. "Let's see if you can bite me now, princess."

I whimper as his zip comes down and then the thick head of his cock slides through the ring in the gag. When he hits the back of my throat, I gag instantly.

"Such a pretty little throat for fucking," he growls, sliding all the way to the back again. "That's it. Take every inch." Saliva spills down the length of him as I gag.

He robs my senses, removing my ability to touch and to see, and I combust for him. It's an oddly illogical reaction to such domination and yet I love it. Every second. Focusing on my breathing, I take his thrusts more easily as he slides in and out of the back of my throat brutally.

I want to see him and look into those feral blue-gray eyes as he takes what he wants from me, but I have no control here. My husband is in complete and utter control and it drives me wild.

"Such a good girl taking that cock so well," he groans. "Perhaps it's time I try out some of your other holes."

I groan as he removes his cock from my mouth and then pulls the gag off of me. "Please, don't do this."

"Shut it," he growls, gripping my jaw firmly and

forcing my mouth open with a finger. "You'll do what I say, because I own you," he growls, making my nipples so hard they hurt like hell. I need friction. I need him to touch me.

He pulls the blindfold off and glares down at me like an angry God. "I'm going to fuck your tight cunt and then that tight little asshole, and there's nothing you can do to stop me."

"No, you can't." I push at him. "I'm pregnant, please don't—"

"Don't think I'm going to listen to any bullshit from you. If you're pregnant, then you'll love this even more once you get my cock in that pretty little cunt."

My heart skips a beat as he grabs hold of my chin.

"Open those lips for me."

I do as he says, and he spits into my mouth, making me groan.

"Was that a moan? I think you're already coming around to the idea of getting fucked." He kisses me, his tongue thrusting in and out of my mouth viciously. "I can't wait to be inside of you."

"You're a sick bastard," I spit back.

He smirks and chuckles, that evil yet sexy laugh I've grown to love. "You haven't seen nothing yet, little lamb."

He parts my thighs forcefully and pulls my panties down, teasing his fingers through my wet entrance. "So wet, and such a naughty little lair." He moves his lips inches from mine. "Begging me to stop when really you're gagging for my cock."

He thrusts his finger inside of me and I bite my lip hard, trying not to moan as I want to keep the fantasy alive a little longer. "So damn wet and ready."

He pulls his finger out of me and I can hardly stop the whimper escaping my lips, which entices another deep chuckle from him. "It seems you keep telling me to stop, but deep down, you want it all."

"No, I—"

He doesn't give me a moment to find my sentence as he slams his cock all the way inside of me with one thrust.

I scream at the sudden invasion. The pain and pleasure morphing into one as he stretches me around his thick length.

"That's it, scream for me," he growls into my ear, looming over me. "No one can hear you." He pistons his hips hard and fast, taking me brutally. Even if he's more gentle since I got pregnant, he's still rough the way I love it.

"So fucking wet, which suggests you love being fucked against your will," he breathes, placing his palm over my throat but not squeezing. "Tell me how much you love it."

I glare at him, despite loving every second. "Never."

He groans, eyes rolling back in his head. "I can feel you getting close, no matter how much you deny it."

I moan, forgetting my role was to be not into this. "Please stop." It's hard to keep up the pretence when it's so damn good.

He lifts me suddenly and carries me over to the large sofa in the center of the room.

I gasp as he lowers me to the sofa and then positions me on all fours before slamming every inch back inside of me.

He spanks my ass with the flat of his palm hard. "I can't wait to fuck that tight little asshole."

The clash of skin against skin echoes around the cavernous living room. His grunts becoming more animalistic by the second.

"Oh, fuck," I cry, knowing that any second I'm going to come apart. There's no way I can hold out.

"Good girl, come on my cock just like that."

His command is all it takes for me to come apart. My body spasms uncontrollably as a flood of liquid gushes around his length.

"Fuck, yes, daddy," I cry, touching my nipples as he fucks me through it.

The violence of the orgasm is intoxicating, but he doesn't give me a second to adjust as he spits on my asshole. I know he's going to fuck me hard and rough. I feel him spreading my juices onto my ass and then his fingers dip inside with not much effort, especially when I've just come the way I did. I'm so turned on he could probably fuck my ass dry and I'd love it. After all, pain is my kryptonite.

And then the heavy press of his cock is against my ass. "You can't fuck my ass," I say, trying to keep up our little act. "I've never—"

The head of his cock slides through my tight ring of muscles and I groan deeply as he sinks all the way inside of me.

"You were saying, little lamb?"

I can hardly formulate a response as he beings to move in and out of my ass.

"That looks so fucking pretty, my cock disappearing in your tight little ass." He spanks my stinging ass cheeks again, making me groan. "You love it, really? Don't you?"

"No," I say, rather unconvincingly.

"Liar's need to be punished." The flick of his switchblade makes me freeze in anticipation. "And what better way than to punish you than to brand that beautiful ass?"

I shudder as the cold tip of the knife presses into my skin. "You said you wouldn't hurt me."

His hips piston in a slow, yet forceful movement as he fucks my ass hard, pushing the tip of the knife into my skin. "I lied." And then he proceeds to cut me a little, dragging the knife in soft movements as he writes daddy on it. He loves the tattoo I got on my other ass cheek which says property of daddy. When I first got it, he couldn't stop fucking me in this position just to stare at it.

"Call me daddy," he orders.

I glance at him over my shoulder. "No."

His jaw clenches. "Call me daddy or I'll cut deeper."

I swallow hard. "Daddy," I murmur.

"Louder," he growls, as he finishes carving the word into my skin. "I want you to scream it."

He runs his fingers over the cut, making it sting more.

"Daddy," I cry, my body so hot it's like I'm setting on fire.

"Look at me," he orders.

I glance at him over my shoulder.

"You taste heavenly," he murmurs, sucking my blood off his fingers. "I want to consume you in everyway possible." His thrusts become deeper and harder as he parts my ass cheeks, eyes fixed on where our bodies meet. "Your enjoying every second of taking my cock up that ass, and do you know how I know you love it?"

His eyes meet mine, blazing with such fire.

I shake my head in response.

"Because your pussy is dripping wet and I can tell you're going to come with my cock up there, while I fuck you hard and rough and make you scream so loud they hear you back in Chicago."

I moan, shutting my eyes as the tension in my body builds. "It's too much." I can't keep pretending I don't like it. "Fuck me harder, daddy."

He spanks my ass cheeks. "Good girl, I knew you

wanted my cock really," he purrs, gripping my hips so roughly they'll be bruised by the morning. "Tell me how much you want it?"

"So much, daddy. I love your cock in my ass," I cry.

Spartak's teeth sink into my shoulder hard as he thrusts into me brutally, taking everything and giving it all at the same time. My vision blurs as the mix of pain and pleasure threatens to unravel me.

"Harder," I cry out.

He grabs a fistful of my hair and yanks my head back, forcing me to arch my back unnaturally. "Are you sure that's what you want, baby girl? I don't want you to break."

"Fuck me harder," I growl.

He uses my hair and fucks me with no mercy, both of us getting lost in the passion of the moment. The intensity of our feelings for each other coming to a head as we become one. "Come for me like a good girl. Come for me with my cock up your ass," he orders.

"Fuck, yes, daddy," I scream at the top of my lungs, the intensity of my orgasm so strong I squirt all over the sofa beneath me.

Spartak roars as he comes at the same time, filling my ass with his cum. "Your tight little ass is squeezing me so fucking hard, baby girl," he growls, as he drains every drop. "So fucking perfect."

I can hardly formulate words as my vision continues to blur, my orgasm spiking through my nerves over and over. It takes a few minutes to recover as Spartak slides his cock out of me, leaving me empty. And then he replaces it with a thick butt-plug.

"What's that for?" I ask as I stand and face him.

"To make sure my cum stays inside of you as long as possible, baby girl." He grabs my hand and drags me toward the decking outside of the cabin. "Now in you get."

He nods to the hot tub, which I climb into, sighing at the warmth of the water. He's quick to join me and wraps his arms around me, pulling me between his legs on one of the seats. "That was perfect and only a teaser of what fun we're going to have this week."

I groan, my body aching already. "I don't know how much of that I can take."

He nibbles on my ear. "You'll take everything I give you and love it, malishka."

"Or what?"

He smirks against the back of my neck. "Or I'll punish you."

I shake my head. "Don't be an ass."

He tightens his grasp on me. "You love it really, just like I love you, little lamb."

I glance at him over my shoulder. "Are you ever going to stop calling me that?"

"Perhaps when I'm dead."

"You're an idiot."

He growls softly.

"But, you're right. I love it and I love you."

"Good girl," he praises, tightening his grasp on me

as we both listen to the sounds of the surrounding woodland.

I've never been happier than I am when I'm in my husband's arms, even if he's crazy. He's my crazy and I wouldn't change a thing about him.

THANK you so much for reading Imalia's and Spartak's story, I hope you enjoyed it and are enjoying the Chicago Mafia Dons Series.

The next book is going to follow Imalia's cousin, Massimo. Here is the cover and the blurb! It's due to be released on May 31st and will be free to read with a KU subscription, or can be purchased on Amazon in ebook or paperback format from the release date.

Cruel Vows: A Dark Forced Marriage Mafia Romance

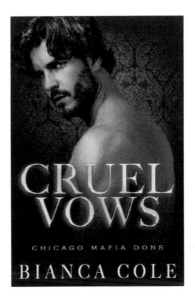

He's a cruel man, and he's taking me against my will.

Bar tending at the Devil's Alpha bar was supposed to be temporary. Until my brother got in too deep with the MC that runs it. Now I'm stuck in this dead-end job in the worst part of Chicago. Until a fated night, where things take a darker turn.

The night a tall and gorgeous stranger enters the bar. He sticks out like a sore thumb, with his designer suit and expensive watch. Axel is making a deal with the Morrone family. The man is the eldest son, Massimo Morrone, heir to the Morrone mafia throne.

They come to an agreement, but there's one problematic condition. Massimo Morrone won't supply them unless they give him me. My brother tries to fight it, but Axel is the president. What he says goes, and I'm not worth messing up a lucrative deal.

Despite not being theirs to trade, I end up the property of a filthy rich Italian mob boss. Massimo drags me kicking and swearing out of the bar. He makes it clear he wants my submission the moment we're alone. He thinks he can take me and make me his plaything as if he's God.

Before I know it, I'm marched to the end of an altar in front of people that I don't know. A gun pressed to my back while I'm forced to say my vows. He puts his ring on my finger, binding us together in the eyes of the law. If he thinks that makes me his, he'll have a shock.

I belong to no one, and by the time I'm through with Massimo Morrone, he'll wish he never married me.

ALSO BY BIANCA COLE

The Syndicate Academy

Corrupt Educator: A Dark Forbidden Mafia Academy Romance

Cruel Bully: A Dark Mafia Academy Romance

Chicago Mafia Dons

Merciless Defender: A Dark Forbidden Mafia Romance

Violent Leader: A Dark Enemies to Lovers Captive Mafia Romance

Evil Prince: A Dark Arranged Marriage Romance

Brutal Daddy: A Dark Captive Mafia Romance

Cruel Vows: A Dark Forced Marriage Mafia Romance

Boston Mafia Dons Series

Cruel Daddy: A Dark Mafia Arranged Marriage Romance

Savage Daddy: A Dark Captive Mafia Roamnce

Ruthless Daddy: A Dark Forbidden Mafia Romance

Vicious Daddy: A Dark Brother's Best Friend Mafia Romance

Wicked Daddy: A Dark Captive Mafia Romance

New York Mafia Doms Series

Her Irish Daddy: A Dark Mafia Romance

Her Russian Daddy: A Dark Mafia Romance

Her Italian Daddy: A Dark Mafia Romance

Her Cartel Daddy: A Dark Mafia Romance

Romano Mafia Brother's Series

Her Mafia Daddy: A Dark Daddy Romance

Her Mafia Boss: A Dark Romance

Her Mafia King: A Dark Romance

Bratva Brotherhood Series

Bought by the Bratva: A Dark Mafia Romance

Captured by the Bratva: A Dark Mafia Romance

Claimed by the Bratva: A Dark Mafia Romance

Bound by the Bratva: A Dark Mafia Romance

Taken by the Bratva: A Dark Mafia Romance

Wynton Series

Filthy Boss: A Forbidden Office Romance

Filthy Professor: A First Time Professor And Student Romance

Filthy Lawyer: A Forbidden Hate to Love Romance

Filthy Doctor: A Fordbidden Romance

Royally Mated Series

Her Faerie King: A Faerie Royalty Paranormal Romance

Her Alpha King: A Royal Wolf Shifter Paranormal Romance

Her Dragon King: A Dragon Shifter Paranormal Romance

Her Vampire King: A Dark Vampire Romance

ABOUT THE AUTHOR

I love to write stories about over the top alpha bad boys who have heart beneath it all, fiery heroines, and happily-ever-after endings with heart and heat. My stories have twists and turns that will keep you flipping the pages and heat to set your kindle on fire.

For as long as I can remember, I've been a sucker for a good romance story. I've always loved to read. Suddenly, I realized why not combine my love of two things, books and romance?

My love of writing has grown over the past four years and I now publish on Amazon exclusively, weaving stories about dirty mafia bad boys and the women they fall head over heels in love with.

If you enjoyed this book please follow me on Amazon, Bookbub or any of the below social media platforms for alerts when more books are released.

Printed in Great Britain
by Amazon